WHEN SORRY IS
NOT ENOUGH

WHEN SORRY IS NOT ENOUGH

MILLIE GRAY

BLACK & WHITE PUBLISHING

First published 2014
by Black & White Publishing Ltd
29 Ocean Drive, Edinburgh EH6 6JL

1 3 5 7 9 10 8 6 4 2   14 15 16 17

ISBN   978 1 84502 778 0

Typeset by RefineCatch Limited, Bungay, Suffolk
Printed and bound by Grafica Veneta S.p.A. Italy

AUTHOR'S NOTE

This story tells of one family's life in Leith in the early twentieth century. Although it echoes some of the writer's experiences and personal feelings, the characters portrayed in the book are wholly fictitious and bear no relation to any persons, living or dead. Many of the street names, localities and other details from that period in Leith's history have been preserved, however.

This book is dedicated to my sister Mary Gillon,
who has been such an important person in my life.

ACKNOWLEDGEMENTS

Special thanks to Iain Grant in Australia for sharing all his colonial police stories with me, and to the team at my publishers Black & White and, in particular, Karyn Millar for her painstaking editing and John Richardson for his ever-willing assistance.

1

The highly polished storm door of the guest house in Seaview Terrace opened and Sally stepped out. As her eyes scanned the horizon she deeply breathed in the salt-sprayed fresh air.

Since she had arrived here three years ago, at the start of the 1970s, she had never tired of this panorama. Today the sun was rising on an ebb tide and the small ripples on the blue sea danced like diamonds in its rays. Inhaling again, she was delighted that she could see the ships lying at anchor in the Forth Estuary and also straight across to the green hills of Fife. She shrugged before admitting there were also days when because of the dreich Scottish weather you couldn't even see over to the bus stop on the other side of the street, never mind over to the Fair Kingdom. *But*, she smiled as she thought, *it isn't like that today.*

Maggie, who had surreptitiously come to stand behind her, broke into her thoughts by saying, 'You're getting a lovely day for your trip.'

Sally half turned. Maggie, traitor Maggie, whom, against her better judgement, she'd hired as a cleaner three years ago for her recently acquired bed and breakfast, was in a jubilant mood. 'Aye,' was all Sally murmured in reply because she was thinking back. Thinking back to five years ago when feckless Maggie had tried to commit suicide. This desperate act had come about because Sally's cheating ex-husband Harry had dumped poor Maggie for a younger model. And if that hadn't been enough to caw the feet from her, had she not then found herself sectioned and imprisoned in a psychiatric hospital? Too soon Maggie realised that getting herself committed into the asylum was difficult but much easier than getting herself out. After weeks of begging and imploring to be set free she was eventually released but her troubles were far from over. Yes, not only did she require to be dealing with the ignominy of her earlier betrayal of Sally and her later attempted suicide, but she had also to accept how difficult it was to secure employment when employers, biased against any type of mental illness, were convinced you were some sort of lunatic. All this resulted in her begging Sally, the only true friend she had ever had, to take her on in one of the two public houses Sally had the tenancy for. Sally at first resisted Maggie's pleas to hire her but then she thought, *would it not be poetic justice for me to hire Maggie as the scrubber in my newly acquired guest house? Bonus of that would be that I could then swan about in my finery whilst passing the time of day with the guests!*

Maggie was unaware that Sally was thinking back to the time when she had stolen her husband, good-for-nothing Harry, from her. This act of treachery had left Sally financially crippled which meant she had to find a full-time job to keep herself and her three bairns. However, if Sally was being truthful, which she didn't like to be whilst dealing with Maggie, Harry deserting her and the children had been the best thing to happen to Sally in her troubled life. Some ten years on she was now financially secure, an acknowledged Leith businesswoman who had helped to clean up the Jungle pubs. She was also a valued member of the Licensed Trade Association Committee and the owner of both this guest house, to which the Scottish Tourist Board had awarded a 'Highly Commended', a luxury holiday flat in Menorca and the brand-new car sitting at her door.

Her meanderings, however, were halted when Maggie, who was not as submissive as she had been when Sally had given in and hired her, pointedly said, 'I know the car is brand new so it shouldn't break down – but with you only passing your driving test last week, do you not think it's being *a wee bit irresponsible* to be driving all the way to Peterhead and back so soon? And know something else, Sally, I'd really miss you if you got yourself killed.'

The catty backchat from Maggie put Sally's back up. She had to restrain herself from sending her packing there and then. Fortunately one of Sally's assets was common sense and when it came to her rescue yet again she reluctantly conceded that she had now become dependent on Maggie to run the bed and breakfast. This allowed her the freedom to attend to all the problems that arose in the pubs and within her family. This was all true but she also acknowledged that every day Maggie was growing stronger in her self-confidence to the point where she was now questioning Sally's judgements and in a way that became more recalcitrant as time went by.

Sally knew she should shove Maggie right back into her shell where she belonged, and she was more than capable of doing that, but not today. Today she had to get to Peterhead Prison. Her brother Luke was coming back home on leave from the Hong Kong Police Service. A letter from him had arrived three weeks ago and in it he had begged her to go and visit Joe Kelly, or Irish, as Luke had nicknamed him. Sally knew Irish was the lad Luke had befriended when he was a raw recruit police constable on the Shore beat in Leith. Poor Irish was now doing a life term in Peterhead

Prison for the murder of his prostitute wife. From the start Luke had truly believed Irish was innocent and now he was asking Sally to visit him and get him to talk about what he knew about the murder of his wife, Marie.

LUKE'S STORY

Luke always had the wanderlust. He literally wanted to see the world. However, he had come home to Leith from Australia because there were family matters he was convinced he had to get retribution for. Now, after accepting how wrong he was, the desire for revenge from Sally was laid to rest. Recently, however, he had become restless. Promotion took years and years to achieve in Edinburgh and another factor for his discontent was the fact that annual leave in Edinburgh City Police was predetermined and dictated by your collar number so that last year Luke had been awarded his summer holidays at the end of October when winter had decided to put in a ferocious early appearance.

Sally did all she could to persuade Luke not to recklessly throw away his career; nonetheless she did concede that one of the older guys, who had served thirty years as a cop and twenty of them on the Easter Road beat, could be a good enough reason for Luke to move on. Allowing herself a tongue-in-cheek chuckle she remembered Luke's exact words about Jack Green. 'Jesus, Sally,' he had expounded with blown-out cheeks, 'just imagine it – if I don't move on I could end up like old Jack with the only wonders of the world I'd ever seen being the colourful life on the Leith Shore beat and what ends up in Johansson's Junk Yard.'

'So you think Jock has wasted his life?' Sally had replied.

'No. No. That was fine for him. He's content with a full

police pension and his memories of Easter Road and the Hibs football games he's seen for nought – but I want more. And I've worked it out that the best way to get seeing the world on the cheap is to use my police experience, and the fact that I have now come first in the Scottish promotional exams gives me a shout. Okay not a loud one but at least I should get a hearing.'

Sally smiled. Her hunched shoulders dropped. *Common sense has dawned at last on my brother,* she thought.

The following Sunday Luke was scanning through the *Sunday Post* newspaper when he saw an advert from the Colonial Police Service requesting applications for trainee police inspectors on a three-year contract and all you required to rise to that rank were good passes in the police promotional exams! Passing the newspaper to Sally he said with a wink, 'That's for me. But what do you think?'

'Hmmm,' she mused before adding, 'Good passes – well – do you think coming first in the Scottish Police exams will equate to anything in England?'

'Dinnae be daft,' he sneered, pulling the paper back from her. 'When they see I'm frae Scotland they'll be begging me to join them. Everybody kens Scottish brains make English ones look like they're made o' mince.' He chuckled as he noted the other conditions of employment were that the successful applicants would be paid 25 per cent of their total salary as a gratuity at the end of the tour and four and a half months' paid leave. Laying the paper down he said to Sally, 'See they conditions, Sally, they're the clincher. I mean I would be earning one thousand five hundred a year – a year mark you. And I could be paid off with as much as a two thousand pounds gratuity that I'd stick right in my back pocket.' He breathed in deeply before adding, 'Know something, the likes of Elizabeth Taylor would fall at my feet for that kind of dough.'

Sally shook her head. She knew there was no point in arguing with him now he had divorced reality.

Luke wasn't surprised, but Sally was, when he was invited to London for an interview. Trying to create the right impression he had a shower in the King's Cross railway station lavatory when he alighted from the overnight Edinburgh to London sleeper.

Once he had brushed down his suit for the fourth time, adopting an air of nonchalance, but actually quaking inside, he headed for the Consulate. All the Colonial Police forces were supervised and run from London and the decision as to whether Luke would be accepted for any of the forces would be made there.

When he entered the grand and lavish building he became a bit downcast to see that there were numerous candidates. Taking a seat, Luke patted his chest to reassure himself he still had the written references from his Sergeant and, more importantly, his Chief Superintendent. Glancing despondently at the throng of hopefuls again he sighed. *At least*, he thought, *if I don't measure up here there is still last week's offer of a two-year secondment from Edinburgh City Police to America's Los Angeles Police Department lying on the table*. He had also been promised that if he took the assignment, on his return he would be made up to Detective Sergeant.

After what seemed like ages to Luke, but was only an hour, he was called forward for what he thought was a very cursory interview. The questions he was asked also amazed him, especially the one as to whether or not he thought he could shoot someone. Luke was past caring by now so he answered, 'That's a rather hypothetical question but I imagine if it was him or me to take a bullet, I could.'

He was then sent on to Harley Street for a medical which was even more superficial than the interview – Luke was sure that the doctor, a right Billy Bunter look-a-like whose loud bright-red braces matched his face, only counted his limbs and fingers before announcing he was medically fit.

Leaving Harley Street Luke felt his visit to London had all been a waste of time. Shrugging his shoulders he accepted that there was nothing else for it now but to head straight back to Auld Reekie on the overnight train.

Striding out for the station he philosophically thought, *I might have not managed to get myself recruited for Hong Kong or Bermuda but there is one plus in the whole sorry affair. Oh aye, with me having been dragged up in Leith, when I was given sufficient finance to be able to stay two nights in an upmarket hotel in London I just booked the overnight train backwards and forward – so I'm thirty pounds in pocket!*

A few days later it was now his turn to be surprised when a letter arrived to say he had been appointed to the Hong Kong Police. *Great*, he thought, *and won't this appointment broaden my horizons!*

He scanned the letter again, his shoulders slumped and a look of utter terror crossed his face. 'What is it?' Sally almost screeched.

'Only that the sadists are demanding that I visit a dentist before I take up my post.'

Luke now passed the letter to Sally for perusal.

Sighing, she admitted to herself that she had mixed

feelings about Luke going to Hong Kong. Of course she was pleased that Luke's dream had come true and he had been selected. After all, their childhood had been so blighted that it was only fair that their adult lives should be better. On the other hand, since things had got sorted out between Luke and herself he had slowly filled the gap left by the death of her older brother Peter – and now she must learn to live without his daily visits. Once she had sorted things out in her mind it left only one concern: Luke, her warrior brother Luke, had one big phobia – the dentist. And here, she glanced down to read the letter again, was an order that he must see one before going to Hong Kong!

Sally, against her better judgement, had accompanied Luke into the practitioner's consulting room and all she could do was shudder when the clinician announced that Luke's teeth required several fillings.

This news unnerved Luke. Strumming on the arm of the consulting-room chair he accepted he either put his hatred of dentists to bed right now or there was no Hong Kong. Without giving the problem any more consideration he announced he had decided to have *all* of his teeth extracted so could the quack immediately administer an anaesthetic and get on with the job?

Sally and the dentist tried their best to have Luke reconsider his rash decision but from past experience Sally knew once his mind was made up then that was it.

The result of the removal of his teeth meant that when he was ready to take up his post in Hong Kong he did so with a dripping blood smile and a mouthful of dentures that made him look like a cross between Red Rum and Dracula.

* * *

Luke had initially intended to do just one tour but last year he had written to Sally to say he would be signing up for another three years. He further pointed out he would be back for a long holiday which would give him time to look into what had happened to Irish. The only regret Luke had when he had left for Hong Kong was the necessity for him to go before Irish's trial. Poor Irish who continually pleaded his innocence when charged with the murder of his prostitute wife had seen Luke's departure as, at best, his abandonment of him and, at worst, him being another who had stitched him up.

It was all very well Sally reminiscing about Luke's past but she had to get to grips with what he required today so she found herself crooning, 'Now, Maggie, you will remember that you haven't to let the single room at the front of the house as that is where I intend to accommodate Luke when he comes home.'

'Are you sure he'll be coming this soon?' huffed Maggie.

'Yes, I am,' was Sally's emphatic reply.

'So you're thinking that as it's Daisy's wedding on Saturday he won't want to miss it?' snipped Maggie.

Exasperated Sally shouted, 'Maggie, he can't miss it. After all, Daisy postponed her big day until now so he could give her away.'

'Right enough,' Maggie conceded in mellowing tones but allowing a picture of a pregnant Daisy to flash before her eyes.

'Oh, look at the time. I just have to get going. You get inside, Maggie, and do what you are good at: getting squared up and disinfecting the lavatories.'

Sally stood and waited until Maggie had gone indoors

before she lightly tripped down the stairs and stood in front of her of her brand-new red Ford Escort estate car. She, however, still didn't have the confidence of a seasoned driver; hence she'd sent Maggie inside. No way did Sally wish Maggie to see that the car, perhaps, had been filled up with kangaroo petrol.

Once the car was up and running smoothly, Sally drove it towards Lochend Road, where Nancy, who ran the Royal Stuart pub for her, had been allocated an Edinburgh Corporation one-bedroomed flat. She had just drawn to a halt when Nancy appeared. Leaning over, Sally opened the passenger door of the car to allow Nancy to get in.

'Well, if this isnae luxury you cannae afford,' huffed Nancy as she struggled into the car, 'then I dinnae ken what is.'

'Aye, you're right there. And do you know, I didnae get enough change from seven hundred to buy us a cup of tea.'

'Dinnae tell me that and here's me thinking, as I'm doing you a favour, that you would be treating me to high tea,' quipped Nancy.

'Oh, you'll get that all right.' Sally sniffed before adding, 'And with a bit of luck maybe bed and breakfast thrown in.'

'Bed and breakfast?' exclaimed Nancy. 'Surely if they dinnae lock us up tae we'll hae plenty of time to get back hame.'

'Aye, if we were to go straight home,' Sally advised, 'but on our way back I intend to take a detour over country to visit Flora and Shonag at Culloden.'

'We're going to Smithton, Culloden, but why?' expounded Nancy, who couldn't keep the sense of incredulity out of her voice.

'Know something?' Sally got ready to confide to Nancy, a woman of the street whom she had rescued and now trusted to be an honest manager in the Royal Stuart for her. 'I'm no quite sure . . .' Sally hesitated, '. . . but I feel in my guts there's something far wrong there.'

'Like what?'

'Don't know. But what I do know is that Sweet William landed back there a month ago and . . .'

'Another of his dalliances gone belly up,' Nancy brusquely interrupted. 'See, Sally,' she continued, 'if he'd been a male prostitute with the number of men he's bedded, he'd be a millionaire and only the good Lord knows how many times over.'

'Millionaire?' queried Sally.

'Aye. Believe me there's no many like William is who go about touting for business on the streets.'

Sally grimaced. 'Anyway, what's different this time is he's come home and that Flora, my darling mother-in-law, who of late wouldn't have given him the time of day never mind a buckshee fiver, has gone all weepy when I ask her how things are. All she is saying is that Shonag, his mother, and herself will need to start putting themselves on Queer Street to keep him comfortable.'

Nancy didn't answer for a minute or two, and when she did she slowly drawled, 'Beggaring themselves to help him, but why?' She allowed a long pause before mumbling, 'Oh surely, good God, no.'

'What are you talking about?' Sally demanded.

Nancy shook her head and quickly changed the subject. 'Aw, here, Sally we're just about to cross the Forth Road Bridge. I'm always excited when I cross it, how about you?'

Sally didn't respond. All she could think of was that this was the first time she'd driven over the bridge and instead of being elated she was allowing sheer panic to overtake her. Glancing to her right she noticed a train crossing the rail bridge. Sighing she thought, *Oh why, oh why didn't I suggest that we go by train?* She was so engrossed looking at the racing locomotive and keeping time to its rumbles over the bridge that she was unaware, until Nancy grabbed her arm, that the traffic in front of them was stationary. She had just started to react to the situation when Nancy screamed, 'Oh, no. We're going to be killed!' Sally's car then came to an abrupt halt when it careered into the back of the car in front.

It wasn't just the insistent and impatient ringing of the door bell that annoyed Maggie, it was also the rattling of the door handle. Throwing open the heavy storm door and waving the vegetable knife she hadn't had time to put down she shrieked, 'I'm no deaf. And if you dinnae take your finger aff that bell I'll cut it aff ...' She was about to brandish the knife again when she became aware of who was standing in front of her and immediately the knife dropped submissively to her side. 'Oh, it's you, Luke. I wasn't expecting you until later,' she simpered. 'Just cutting up some carrots for putting in the broth, I was.'

Luke was taken aback. *Surely to heavens,* he thought, *that daft sister of mine heeded what I said and sent this conniving bitch packing. Only she couldn't have. But wasn't that so like Sally? Och aye*, he continued to himself, *who else but Sally would give house room to a rat like Maggie?* Maggie whom he knew would pull the rug from under Sally's feet the first chance she got.

Unaware of Luke's hostility towards her Maggie opened the door further before announcing, 'Sally said to put you in the single room at the front. I've just finished getting it ready for you.'

Luke did not respond but he did follow Maggie up the wide staircase. The door to the room Sally thought he should occupy was open but he did not venture over the threshold. 'Naw,' he drawled. 'Not quite big enough for me. Let me have a look at the palatial room that Sally is always writing to me about.'

'Fit for honeymooners that room is,' Maggie said, giving a coquettish wink before going on, 'and it costs three times as much a night as that wee single does.' Maggie then advanced into the room and immediately opened up an adjoining door to reveal the very latest in must-haves – a tasteful pastel coloured bathroom en suite. She then moved over to the king-sized double bed and bounced up and down on it. 'Never been slept in yet, it's not.'

'Then that's for me,' Luke replied, flinging his suitcase up on the bed. 'Now get me some tea.'

Maggie huffed. 'You make your own tea. All you need is on that wee table over there.'

Luke was about to tell her forcibly that she would make his tea when the doorbell shrilled. 'Anybody at home?' a loud voice hollered.

'Aye,' responded Luke, bounding down the stairs in front of Maggie.

'Well, well. If it's no the lucky bugger,' blurted the impatient police constable.

'Archie MacDonald, and are you no a sight for sore eyes?' Luke responded, holding out his hand.

Both men shook each other's hand vigorously in between

slaps on the back. 'Now, tell me this, Luke, did the tide wash you up here?'

'Naw. This is my sister's place and I've just arrived back in the country.'

'Yer sister owns this place?' Archie asked, allowing his eyes to rove about the comfortable house.

Luke nodded. Suddenly Archie was no longer smiling and he reached in his pocket for his notebook and slowly he began to read from it. 'I regret to advise you that one, Sally Mack,' he hesitated before adding, 'was travelling northwards in a vehicle that she was driving and the said vehicle was involved in a multi-car crash on the Forth Road Bridge which resulted in her and her travelling companion, one Nancy, no managed to get a surname for her, sustaining injuries that has resulted in her . . .'

'Oh my God, Sally's not dead . . . she just can't be,' Luke screeched before collapsing on the bottom stair.

Archie glanced at Luke before shaking his head and continuing, 'Being detained . . .'

'Arrested?' Maggie butted in. 'Nancy, aye, but then she should have been run in years ago but no Sally.'

'Look you, whoever you are, just gie yer tongue a rest 'til I've finished.' Archie coughed before adding, 'In the Dunfermline Infirmary.'

Luke got up and slapped Archie on the back. 'She's no dead, mate! That's marvellous. And that's one I owe you. Now I have to get going over to Fife, but tell all my other police buddies I'm back for nearly five months and we'll all meet up and get rat-arsed.'

Sally was in a receiving room in the hospital and the pain racing up and down her neck and shoulders was such that she had decided that dying would be a good idea. Especially now there was a doctor, who looked so young that he should still be in nappies, asking her to follow his finger. 'Can you remember what happened?' the young man asked as the digit wandered from left to right.

'The first bump was just a bump. I remember asking Nancy if she was all right and her saying that her having her head bounced off the windscreen might be all right to me but,' Sally sniffed, 'poor Nancy didn't finish what she was going to say because the car behind us ran into our back and everything went black.'

'Black? Do you mean it got dark or did you . . . ?'

'Oh, son,' Sally exploded, 'it's the middle of April and it doesnae get dark until about the back of eight. And before you go on, was anybody killed?' The doctor didn't respond so Sally knew there had been fatalities. 'Look son, do you know if my pal is . . . ?' stuttered Sally.

'Who would she be?'

Sally closed her eyes and immediately she was thinking back to just after the second collision. She remembered that through a haze she had looked over and Nancy's bonny face was beginning to swell and blood was spouting from her nose and mouth. 'Nancy, Nancy. Please, please say you're all right?' she had implored.

An agonising thirty seconds passed before Nancy weakly responded though gasps and pants. 'Here, Sally, are you saying you want to ken if I'm all right? And why should I no be? After all nothing happened except my heid being bounced not once but twice off your bleeding windscreen, my neck,' she hesitated to draw in breath whilst she rocked her head from side to side, 'having been stretched so far oot that I'm sure I now resemble a giraffe. And if aw that wasnae enough to gie me a headache, hasn't my national health wallies been shot oot of my mouth and are now God knows where.' She stopped again and sniffed and panted before adding, 'So, Sally, if you're asking if I'm all right? Well,' Nancy now put up her hand to try and stem the flow of blood from her nose, 'I bloody well am ... no.' Her breath which was now coming in even shorter pants had her wearily lean her head back and Sally could see that she was no longer conscious and then merciful blackness drifted over her too.

Neither Sally nor Nancy was aware of being taken to Dunfermline Infirmary in an ambulance with flashing blue lights. Nor were they conscious when the doctors first examined them. It took an hour for Sally to open her eyes and immediately a young doctor asked her where her worst pains were. The only response that Sally could give was to start weeping because, without warning, the horror of the crash flashed back to her. Again she could see that Nancy was injured and unconscious. Sally shook her head as she considered that something happening to dear Nancy that she was somehow responsible for would just be too much.

With Sally not responding verbally, the young doctor admitted defeat. He had reluctantly decided that it would be best just to leave Sally with her thoughts and she was relieved when he disappeared back through the screens.

Jumping into his car Luke acknowledged that it had been a good idea to hire a car at Heathrow Airport as he now had wheels to get over to Sally quickly. Turning on the ignition he sniggered out loud when he remembered that Maggie had offered to accompany him on the journey. He hadn't even bothered to respond to that outrageous suggestion. *Oh aye, no way would Maggie ever go anywhere with him.*

Before he knew it he was breaking the speed limit in Commercial Street and was furious when the traffic lights turned to red and he had to come to an abrupt halt at the Shore junction. Be that as it may, this enforced stop gave him time to look about. A sly smile crossed his face when he looked over towards his old police beat. Glancing to his left he could see the side of the King's Wark pub and he knew that lying adjacent to it was the Four Marys – Sally's little gold mine – where tonight his sister Josie would be pulling pints. His eyes then strayed to the chain pier and the Forth estuary behind it and he remembered how further down the Shore the body of Marie, Irish's wife, had been pulled from its watery grave. At that very moment he became more convinced than ever that he had to find out exactly what had happened to Marie and who was really responsible.

Everyone has regrets in life and knows that they let someone down. Luke knew he had put his own self interests in front of Irish's. The chance to have his dreams come true when he was offered the Hong Kong posting was just too big a temptation. *Besides*, he argued with himself, *what could he have done?* The prejudiced, lazy, blinded two Leith CID officers, as he saw them, had the case all sewn up.

A car blasting its horn to alert Luke that the lights had now turned to green had him quickly move his car forward but he was still thinking back. Thinking back to when he had hated his now beloved sister Sally.

Driving towards Dunfermline he was acting on auto-pilot. This was because he still had a need to get things about Sally straightened out in his mind. Always his thoughts had to stray back to when he believed that Sally had prematurely and unlawfully ended his beloved mother's life. He sniffed and grunted when he thought of that fateful Saturday in the Four Marys bar when he found out that Sally was innocent.

All the family was there that day; Sally and his other sister, Josie, his stepsister Daisy, Sally's children, and Angela, the niece he never knew he had until she arrived from America to face up to her mother Josie who had given her away in 1945.

Nobody had expected that old Jock Thomson was going to use Angela's farewell party to unburden his soul. They all thought he had invited himself there to do some story-telling and they were completely stunned and flabbergasted when he started confessing his lifelong affair with their mother. This continual dalliance had resulted in him not only fathering Peter, Sally's deceased but still beloved eldest brother, but also Sally, Josie and Luke! If that wasn't bad enough he had gone on to say how he had, as a Leith Police Constable, carried out the birching on poor defenceless Peter. Trying to lessen the horror of what he had done, he went on to tell them that the court had sentenced Peter to detention in the Industrial School but his and their mother, his paramour, had said, 'No – birch him!'

An uneasy silence had followed which was eventually broken by Luke when he haltingly asked Sally if the disgraceful treatment of Peter, when he was just a fourteen-year-old slip of a lad, was the reason she had hastened their mother's departure from this world.

'No. But God in heaven knows I wanted to,' was Sally's indignant reply. Then, in almost a whisper, she had told them of the suffering she and Peter had endured from their mother. When she finished with her heart-rending account, not a sound could be heard in the saloon. Luke knew for sure then that instead of putting his mother on a pedestal it should have been Sally that was hoisted up there. He then had bowed his head to hide the tears that were streaming down his face.

Reliving these memories was hard for Luke. It was an unexpected relief for him when he realised he had arrived at the Dunfermline Infirmary. Breathing in, he pushed the hateful reminiscences back into his subconscious where he hoped they would remain.

Sally had been transferred from the accident and emergency department into a general ward. The admitting nurse there assured Sally that she would probably be discharged the following day. This was because her injuries from the accident, although very painful, were not serious. Relieved, Sally had gone to ask if there had been any enquiries about her and the nurse had just said, 'No. Not yet,' when Luke strode into the ward.

'It can't be you,' Sally sobbed as she attempted to get out of bed to greet him.

'Whoa, whoa,' he exclaimed whilst pushing her back down on her pillows. Very gently he then took up her hand and kissed it. 'And as to it no being me, it cannae be onybody else but me,' Luke replied before searching in his pockets for a handkerchief to wipe Sally's dripping eyes and nose. 'Now, are you able to tell me how you got yourself in here and when we can get you out?'

Sally shook her head. 'I will get around to that but first I want you to go and make enquiries about Nancy.'

'Nancy who?'

'You know fine Nancy from the docks. And you know very well in her life before she came to work for me she had numerous aliases.' Sally hesitated and sighed before going on. 'But I think the legal one might be White.' Sally nodded her head before adding, 'So go right now and ask about a Nancy White.' Tears sprang to her eyes again. 'Oh Luke, some involved in the crash didnae make it and I am terrified one of them is Nancy. I couldn't live with that.'

'What did you say your friend's name was?' asked the hospital receptionist, who had obviously taken a liking to Luke.

'Know it's Nancy and it might be followed by . . . White or some other colour.'

'No White on my list,' the woman answered. 'And before I search further, are you sure she was involved in the accident?' Luke nodded. The young woman then donned a coquettish smile before adding, 'Know what, I'm beginning to think you're a reporter trying to take advantage of a naive young lassie.'

'Naw. Naw,' blustered Luke. 'I came in looking for my sister and I found her in Ward Four and she was driving her pal, Nancy White, and she somehow has got lost in the system or something.'

The woman was not convinced but it was evident she did fancy Luke. Tantalisingly licking her lips she simpered, 'Like to try another shade, big boy?'

Luke nodded and winked. 'What would you suggest? Hot, cold or . . .'

'Well if I was you,' she drawled, 'I would go for a cool but exotic experience.'

Luke thought, *This is ridiculous. Here am I trying to find Nancy, a one-time scarlet woman, and this naive lassie, who is young enough to be jailbait, vamping me. But aw, to hell – so I've got to humour her and think of a colour a Fifer would think exotic. Well as the only thing they've got going for them is the Forth Rail Bridge, should I suggest orange? Oh, but I forgot there are the coal mines so should I go for black or brown in the hope that this Goth-like lassie thinks one of them is exotic?*

He was thankfully saved from further contemplation when the damsel was summoned from behind her desk to take the mail from a porter. This allowed Luke, an expert at reading upside down, a quick scan of her register. Halfway down the page he noticed there was listed a person called 'Blue'.

When the receptionist returned to give him her full attention again she was delighted when he said, 'How about Blue? That's it. And like her name she's always on the cold side.'

The lassie, who was still determined to flirt with Luke, smiled broadly before pointing him in the direction of Ward Three. 'Mind you,' she called out after his retreating figure, 'if anybody asks you how you found out where she was – remember it definitely wasnae me!'

Luke only gave the young woman a cursory backwards wave. He was in a hurry. He was on his way to see this Miss Blue.

He couldn't keep a big grin growing over his face because if this Blue woman was Nancy then she was alive – and that would be the news he wished to take to Sally.

When he barged through the Ward Three doors he was whistling. Being used to flashing his warrant card and then progressing anywhere he wished to go, he was taken aback when a staff nurse put up her hand and asked, 'And where do you think you're going, my bonnie lad?'

Hesitating, he wondered whether he should turn on the charm which usually worked wonders for him. Or should he try the official 'I'm a policeman on official duty and you have no right to bar my way'? Then he remembered he had no official standing in Scotland now. 'Look,' he began with a little chuckle, 'I just wish to say hello to my sister's friend, Nancy Blue.'

The nurse shook her head. 'You would be wasting your time. She's not really with us.'

'She's not dead?'

'No,' the nurse inhaled deeply before going on, 'she's with us in body but she would appear unable, or unwilling, to interact with anyone. Difficult it is to know how to help her so we've sent for a psychiatrist.'

'A head shrinker for Nancy? You've got to be joking. Don't you realise Nancy is a street fighter?'

'That right? Well that will be past tense now because,' the nurse looked up the ward towards a woman slumped in a chair before adding, 'right now she's incapable of doing battle with a wet paper bag.'

'Look, please let me try to talk to her.'

'Okay. But I hope you're a ventriloquist.'

With an air of optimism Luke approached the Nancy Blue woman. Although the woman's face was hidden, because her head was slumped down onto her chest, a feeling of relief immediately washed over him. The distinctive mop of curly hair in front of him could belong to none other than the Nancy he was looking for.

Drawing up a chair he sat in front of her. 'Well now,' he

began, 'I've just come from Sally and she's doing well. But what she wants to know is – how about you?'

Not only did Nancy not reply but there was also no body movement – not even a blink of an eye.

Being a trained detective now, Luke felt he had the experience to get through to Nancy and have her talk, but ten minutes later he had to admit defeat.

On his departure from the ward he approached the nurse again. 'Couldn't get any response from her,' he reluctantly admitted. 'Have you any idea what's wrong?'

'Well there is the extensive bruising to her face but no broken bones there. As you can see we have strapped up her left arm because she has a broken collar bone – that will be very painful but in most people it wouldn't result in deep melancholy.' The nurse shrugged. 'Suppose in time she may respond.'

Luke knew he had to tell Sally the truth. But what was that? Nancy was alive, and she had no life-threatening or even serious injuries. Just a broken collar bone, extensive bruising to her face – all minor wounds which meant she could be released tomorrow – but there was this worrying deep, deep depression she had sunk into.

'You say she's responding to no one because a morbid gloom has descended on her?' Sally, unable to hide her scepticism, asked. Then for a while she pondered before saying, 'Right. Help me to get to her.'

Luke did as Sally bade and when Sally sat in front of Nancy she signalled for Luke to leave but to also draw the screens around them.

A short three minutes later Luke and the Staff Nurse were surprised when the screens were opened and Sally emerged to say, 'It's all right. I know what's ailing her. Get her ready to leave tomorrow then we'll get her home and sorted out.'

'You do know you'll require to take her to see a psychologist or some other psychiatric practitioner?'

Sally laughed before spluttering, 'Psychologist! And what use would he be to Nancy? Naw, naw, all she needs, once her face swelling goes down, is a visit to a dental technician to get a new set of false teeth!'

'What?' Luke guffawed loudly. 'But with the life she's led.'

Sally shot him a warning stare before pointedly saying, 'We are all proud and have levels we'll not sink beneath and in Nancy's case when she smiles she likes people to see her as being toothsome and not gummy!'

2

Sally's good friend and business confidante, Ginny, always seemed to have a solution to any problem. Today she had persuaded Pauline, one of the beauticians from the exclusive Jenners department store, to come down to Sally's with the view of making Sally presentable for her younger sister Daisy's wedding.

As soon as Pauline entered Sally's home and witnessed her bruised and battered face her enthusiasm for an urgent but well paid make-up job visibly waned. Nonetheless, her professionalism surfaced and without uttering a word she started to unload her case of tricks onto the table someone called Maggie had provided.

'Okay,' Pauline muttered as she turned to size up the damage to Sally's face again, 'and . . . just how long is it since you were . . . ?'

'Dragged out of the ring after having lost ten bouts to Cassius Clay?'

Pauline, infected by Sally's sense of humour, laughed. Sally also giggled before informing, 'Three days and the bruises are much worse now. But look, dear, just do your best. I just have to be able to go into the church, you know St Philip's along the way there, and see my wee sister married. What I mean is I want everybody to be looking at the beautiful bride and not me, the side freak show'

'Okay, sit down here and I'll see what I can do.' Pauline then turned Sally's face this way and that way and after what seemed a long time she sighed and said, 'Don't suppose you'd consider hiding behind a thick veil?' Sally shook her head. Pauline sniffed and began to twitter nervously before saying, 'Fine. I'll do my best but just you remember I am a make-up artist and not a bleeding magician.'

'After all your worries, you did enjoy yesterday,' Luke said as he buttered himself another piece of toast.

Sally nodded and a sly smile crept up her face. She didn't need to try hard to remember yesterday. It would be a day she would always remember especially as Daisy would be immigrating to Canada today and memories would be all Sally would now have of her.

Daisy was twenty years younger than Sally and since the day she was born Sally had always had a special place in her heart for her stepsister. She had also been jealous of her. Unlike herself, Daisy had always known who her father was and okay Paddy Doyle was a rough diamond who had hailed out of the Australian Outback, but Daisy always knew he was there for her.

The confessions of Jock Thomson must have shaken Daisy. After all, by the time he had finished confessing she realised her beloved brother Luke whom she followed everywhere – even over half the world – was in fact only her half brother. Sally twittered as she thought, if ever Luke was only half of anything. Yesterday, she remembered with joy how he had been like a peacock with two tails when he had escorted Daisy up the aisle. It must have been difficult for him to hand Daisy into the safe keeping of Dr Ian Falconer especially when he had been going to castrate the man when he had found out that Daisy was five months pregnant and would therefore be getting married in any colour but virgin white.

Unaware that she was reminiscing, Luke suddenly burst into her meanderings. 'But,' he began through a mouthful of toast, 'now the wedding is over and Daisy will be leaving for Canada this morning, do you not think you could wash your make-up off?'

Sally, who was still a bit soporific, had to blink herself fully awake before she said, 'Know something, Luke, I think a second-day make-up job is preferable to the mess my face is in right now.'

Luke nodded. 'Oh by the way, I still have to get to Peterhead. When do you think Nancy will be able to go with me?'

'Just as soon as she has had new teeth fitted. But know something, that could be at least two weeks away.'

Before Luke could respond the door bell rang. Sally had half risen to answer the summons but then she sank down again and rubbed her hands over her cheeks. 'I know,' she began with a twitter, 'as quite a number of the family are camped in here that we have no vacancies, but there is no need for us to frighten future customers away.'

Luke was already on his feet and walking towards the door when it opened and in walked Maggie. 'Nothing to worry you, Sally. It's just Chief Inspector, David Stock,' Maggie informed, 'and he's no come to arrest you, just wondering he is how you are.'

'That's fine, Maggie. Now could you brew another pot of tea and toast some more bread?' Sally now turned her attention to David and her eyes danced with pleasure. 'Nice to see you, David,' she enthused. 'It's such a long time since we had time to just jaw and sort the world out.'

David pulled out a chair. Sitting down he turned his attention to Luke. 'Heard you were back.' Luke nodded.

Chief Inspector Stock was not a person that Luke would ever consider as a friend. There was something about the man that always made Luke's scalp tingle. He had said so to his sister Josie who had just laughed before saying, 'It's because Sally's sweet on him and if ever he is free he will marry her.'

Sally and David were unaware of what Luke was thinking and they couldn't understand him shaking his head and mumbling, 'It's more than that.'

Maggie came in with the refreshments. Sally then busied herself being mother whilst David turned his attention to Luke. 'Now if you're thinking of rejoining the police here in Edinburgh, and I hope that you are, I could put in a good word for you. Of course that would be dependent . . .'

Sally was about to advise David that Luke had signed up for another tour in Hong Kong when Luke put up his hand to silence her. 'Now, Chief Inspector,' Luke sneered, 'would this be subject to my agreeing to drop down to constable level . . . ?'

David shook his head before mumbling, 'Eh, eh . . . well . . . not constable for long. I would expect . . . yes I suppose . . . that in no time at all you being made up to uniform sergeant.'

'Uniform! But what about my three years experience firstly as a trainee and then at the promoted rank of detective inspector in Hong Kong?'

David began to bluster. 'Come on now, Luke, you know the colonial service don't take on anything like the responsibility of the forces here on mainland Britain.'

'Could have fooled me,' Luke butted in.

'And,' David continued, ignoring Luke's comment, 'as you know our force detectives are specially selected.'

'Aye, but not for their brains and impartiality,' Luke jibed.

David, who was still refusing to respond to Luke putting his oar in, took a sip from his tea before saying, 'And another condition . . . eh . . . the most important one would be . . .'

'I think you mean ultimatum and that is the real reason you're here today.'

'What ultimatum?' Sally asked, looking from David to Luke.

David stayed silent so Luke said, 'That I make no contact with Joe Kelly in Peterhead because there are two lazy Leith detectives who might end up with egg on their faces.'

Sally looked directly at David who was now pulling on his lower lip. 'David,' she asked when the silence had gone on long enough, 'is this true?'

Blowing out his cheeks David said, 'That's rubbish. All we would ask is that he toes the line. In our job we all cover each other's backs.'

Luke's hysterical laughter rang around the room and he went over and slapped David on the back. 'If by that,' he hissed into David's ear, 'you mean I let Irish stew in prison, then I have to tell you . . . *no*. And what's more I've just signed up for another tour in Hong Kong and within months I will be matching your rank. And when it's awarded I will have earned it by honesty and hard work. So I don't need your invitation to rejoin you lot and could I suggest you go and tell them who sent you, to stick their offer up where the sun don't shine.'

David sniffed, his eyes glinted, he lifted his hat up from the table and without any further conversation with Luke he made for the door. Sally followed. 'David,' was all she said.

He turned, held out his hands to register the hopelessness he felt and whispered, 'This makes no difference to you and I, Sally. Believe me this was not the top brasses' idea that I came here today . . .' He head shook desolately from side to side. 'I was just trying to help out a couple of mates – save them from having to endure an enquiry. But most importantly, I'm here because of what I feel for you. Attempting, I was, to keep your brother from falling on his arrogant face. Joe Kelly's was a fair trial. He is guilty but if Luke goes on, like I think he will, he will never ever be accepted back in the Edinburgh force. Try and get him to see sense, Sally.'

Sally looked back to Luke but he was just staring out of the window and his stance was such that Sally knew that two of the most important men in her life would now be forever at loggerheads.

The midday London train was about to leave. Any ill feelings Luke and Sally may be having about this morning's altercation due to David Stocks were well hidden. They were determined that Daisy and her doctor husband would board the train knowing that all of the family was assembled in harmony to see them off.

Sally did feel tears spring to her eyes. Daisy had been such a delightful part of her life for such a long time now. Wasn't it true she had mothered her? And like a mother Sally was concerned that pregnant Daisy would face motherhood without her by her side. The pregnancy was no mistake – it had been planned because Daisy was thirty-seven years of age and she was afraid that she may take after Sally's daughter, Margo, who was the same age and was having such difficulties in conceiving. *Besides,* thought Sally*, getting yourself pregnant while unwed doesn't carry the same stigma and condemnation that it used to. And*, she agreed, *rightly so.*

All too soon the guard blew his whistle. The train slowly began to depart from the station. Sally let go of Luke's arm and she raced up the platform calling to Daisy, 'Don't forget me. Please, please, don't forget me, Daisy.'

'Mum, for heaven's sake. The way you're carrying on you would think Daisy was your daughter instead of me,' Margo spluttered through her tears. 'She's got it all. She won't need to go out and work because her husband will always be a big earner. And . . .' Margo, who couldn't conceal her abject misery any longer, stopped to wipe her tears before hollering, 'and in four months, just four months, that you didn't even seem to think was obscene because it was her, she will have a b,b,b,baby.'

Sally turned to face Margo. Margo was her beloved first born who had broken her heart more times than she wished to remember. She firstly recalled how she had sided with Harry when he had callously left her to set up home with Maggie, her supposedly best friend. Margo hadn't even tried to comfort her but she did manage to point out that her father's going was all Sally's fault. Evidently she thought Sally had spent too much time on other people. These people were her children, one of whom was Margo, and Harry's mother who Sally always made sure had a home with her even when Harry left. Sally sniffed and brushed her fingers under her nose when she thought back to the time all those years ago when Margo hadn't even told her she was pregnant. In her hour of need when the little lad was stillborn she hadn't even called out to her, her mother, to comfort her. Sally was now gnawing on her thumb when the picture that forever haunted her flashed into her consciousness.

The picture was of Maggie, traitor Maggie whom Margo had given Sally's place to in her life. There she was sitting by distraught Margo's hospital bed consoling her. Sally was nobody's fool and her mind now started to wonder just why Margo was crying out to her today – crying out for Sally to be her mother. She nodded before silently acknowledging that there was a reason, there most certainly was, and Margo would reveal just exactly what that reason was in the very near future.

3

Sally, who was giving Maggie a hand to clear up the breakfast tables, looked up expectantly when Nancy came into the room.

'You know I'm so excited,' Nancy announced.

'About what?'

'Sally, you know fine that Luke's taking me today to that denture technician in Musselburgh to get a new set of gnashers fitted.'

'And you know fine well how I feel about it. Another week of letting your face heal up before subjecting it to breaking in new teeth would make all the difference.'

'Luke says he's going to have the man make up the teeth exactly like his.' Nancy sighed. 'Imagine it. Me with a smile as bonny as his.'

'Nancy, the teeth Luke is sporting now are not the false teeth he left here with when he went to Hong Kong.' Sally stopped. Her eyes flashed to the ceiling. 'Sure the dentures he left with were so big they made him look like the ass that he is.'

'Are you saying the ones he has now were made in Hong Kong?'

'Yes, Nancy, I am. You see the original set got kicked out and lost in a brawl. So Luke being Luke demanded that the Colonial Police Service stump up for the new ones – and of course nothing but the very latest in technology was good enough for him.'

'So what are you trying to say?'

'Just don't expect your ones to be as natural looking as his.'

'Know something, Sally; I think you're jealous that he's willing to shell out for private ones for me.'

'Jealous! Me! Certainly not and could I point out he's only meeting the expense so you and he can get over to Peterhead next week.'

Nancy pouted her lips. 'Know what?'

'Not until you tell me.'

'It's just that I'm wondering why he needs me to go with him so badly that he's stumping up for my teeth.'

'Nancy, you're his insurance policy. He knows Irish will not agree to see him but he will allow you to visit because you were a pal of Marie's.'

'I don't think that's his motive and neither do you,' Nancy muttered, making a slow shake of her head.

'That right?'

'Aye. Because the real reason he needs me to be lead visitor is David Stock and co. will have asked the prison authorities not to allow him in.'

Sally shook her head before replying, 'That right? Well, Nancy dear, all I've got to suggest is why don't you stop reading Agatha Christie and putting yourself in the role of Miss Marple?'

Moving her head from side to side Nancy was delighted with what she saw in the mirror. 'Here, Sally,' she began as she grinned at her reflection, 'there's a plus in everything. Sure these pearlies are just so much better than the ones I lost. Look like my own teeth they do.' Nancy turned to look directly at Sally. 'Now come on, admit it, they do make me look ten years younger.' Nancy turned back to gaze in the mirror again. 'With a little bit of luck I could get signed up for the telly ad. You know the one,' she now began to sing, 'You'll wonder where the yellow went when you brush your teeth with Pepsodent!'

Sally was about to respond when the door opened and in came Luke. 'Here, Sally, what do you think of Nancy's teeth?' He went over to Nancy and began waltzing her around the room. 'Sure she looks that good everybody will be thinking she could be mistaken for Scarlett O'Hara . . .'

'Is that because you think your new dentures make you look like Rhett Butler?'

'He was dark. I'm fair. More like Alan Ladd.'

Sally shook her head. 'When are we leaving?'

'So you're coming too.'

Lifting up her coat, Sally nodded. 'Only,' she drawled, 'because you need some extra insurance and you have promised me you will take me to Smithton on the way back.'

One thing for certain was that Luke was a first-class driver and the trio were over the bridge before the two women had a chance to realise they had passed the spot of their crash ordeal.

Journeying on with his foot hard down on the accelerator he made even better time than he had done in the city.

'Any chance of a stop . . . ?' Nancy asked.

'For a cup of tea?' was Luke's disgruntled reply.

'That and a call of nature,' hissed Nancy.

He did stop but that was the only break he allowed. Reaching Peterhead was his priority and even Aberdeen had to be bypassed at speed.

* * *

Sally felt quite spellbound as they approached Peterhead. She knew that the town itself lay on the north-east coast of Scotland and was in the main a prosperous and busy fishing port, but what she hadn't expected was that the scenery surrounding the town would be so beautiful and spectacular. However, the panoramic scene changed when they were confronted with the prison itself. To Sally it looked like a soulless place that had been deliberately erected on the edge of the unbridled waters of the North Sea to ensure the inmates were always aware that there was no means of escape.

A creeping chill overtook Sally as she realised that Peterhead was a tough prison, a very tough one. She knew, because she had made enquiries about the place, that half of the prisoners held there were the most violent and uncontrollable inmates who had been transferred from other Scottish prisons. These unfortunate jailbirds had been judged to be uncontrollable and unredeemable, and they now found themselves housed alongside the other clientele – violent sex convicts and child molestors. Sally gave a derisive snigger when she recalled that the disillusioned inmates at Peterhead had labelled the monstrous institution the 'Hate Factory'.

Sally had made contact with the prison authoritites three days before their visit and explained that she and Nancy would like to call to see one of their prisoners – one Joseph Kelly. This request was granted and here they were waiting, along with other visitors, to be allowed into the prison.

When the doors opened the anxious relatives surged forward but Sally had a desire to turn and run. Somehow she just knew that if she was to be deprived of her liberty it would be too much for her to bear. She knew that Irish had been a sailor who liked nothing better than to be out in the open air with the wind whistling through his hair. How, she wondered, had he coped in here? The day was uncommonly warm but she shivered as the chill of the hopelessness the prison exuded penetrated every bone in her body.

Sally and Nancy were shown to a small table and seated down at it to await Joe. When he entered the hall Sally wanted to run up to him and grab him into an embrace. The pathetic, stooped and wild-looking creature advancing towards them just couldn't be the Irish she had known. Sally's hand flew to her lips when she tried to connect with his wary eyes that were sunken into their sockets. His pallor reminded her of all those who spent time in prison. In Irish's case it was more emphasised because in the past his complexion was always that of a weather-beaten sailor's.

Irish had just reluctantly seated himself down opposite Sally and Nancy when Luke walked forward. 'Who let this bastard in here?' Irish hissed and he began to spring at Luke.

'No. No, Irish,' Sally pleaded, 'please hear us out. You know me and that I would only ever want to help you.'

Slumping back down Irish looked defeated. Sally tried to figure out how establishments that were supposed to support and rehabilitate people could breed such awful despair.

'Irish,' Nancy, who had winced when she first saw Irish, began before Luke or Sally could continue, 'you know me and ye ken fine I worked with your Marie. Now we are only here today to see if we can do anything for you.'

'Like put in some more stitches?' Irish shouted as his head twitched.

'No,' responded Luke, 'we just need to figure out how

you, the pussy cat that you were, got yourself transferred out of Saughton Prison to here?'

'Oh, is that all you want to know? Well it might be because I was convicted of killing my Marie. Sure I was going to leave her because she wouldn't come off the game, but kill her . . . ?' He now stared down at his work-worn hands and his head shook from side to side. 'No. I could never have used these hands of mine to choke the life out of her.' Irish's voice then dropped to a near whisper before he added, 'Told the court that when they found me guilty but they didn't believe me.' He hunched his shoulders. 'Didn't believe my mother either, they didn't, when she screamed from the gallery that they were making a big mistake.'

'We understand that,' Sally softly said, leaning over to tap the table in front of Irish. 'But why were you transferred to here?'

'Simple. I went crazy. Berserk. I couldn't stand not being able to go back to sea – to be free – to be able to go and have a piss without permission. And then the psychos thought I was some kind of wife mutilator and . . .' He stopped and looked Sally straight in the eye before whispering, 'Can you imagine what it feels like to be knocked out cold against the shower room wall and all you were doing was washing the filth from your body? Shit scared I am to even take a shite in here.'

Sally leaned back. Her head shook from side to side. Tears welled up and spilled from her eyes. She was still very delicate from her recent car crash and was therefore emotionally frail. However, she knew she had to look straight into Irish's eyes because she wanted him to know she believed him. *No way*, she argued with herself, *could the gentle Irish whom she had served in her bar have brutally ended his sweet Marie's life.*

Luke sighed. 'Irish, are you saying you became violent to protect yourself and in doing so you landed up in here?'

Banging the table with a clenched fist, Irish began to cackle. 'Do you really think,' he sneered, 'that they sent me here for the good of my health?' Irish then raised his hand in despair. 'Can't you see this is a place of no hope, no redemption. It's filled with the criminally insane – paedophiles, sexual deviants, and all I can do to survive is keep my head down and my back always to the wall.'

Luke nodded and leaned over towards Irish. 'Look, son,' he began, 'what I want you to do is *not* retaliate no matter how much you are goaded. Do all that is asked of you. And I will see if I can get you a transfer back to Saughton.' Luke paused. He could see Irish was not convinced, so reaching out to pat Irish's hand he gently added, 'Your mother could come over from Ireland and visit you there. You don't want her coming to this place, do you?'

Irish nodded in unison with Nancy and Sally.

'Now why I am here today is . . . I want you to try and remember everything about the day, everything you did that day, the day Marie was . . .'

The clock on the wall ticked the long seconds while Luke, Sally and Nancy waited for Irish to respond. Nancy shifted uneasily in her chair as she silently willed him to tell them anything he could.

As if talking in a dream Irish began, 'My ship was supposed to come in on the late tide but we had had a fair wind from Spain and we arrived on the early one. I was so madly in love with her that as soon as the gang plank was down I was running down it. Couldn't wait to surprise her,

I couldn't.' Pulling at his nose with one hand then with the other he pulled at his hair before going on, 'But it was me that got the surprise. Shock really. You see, there standing at the door of the wee flat I had rented for her were two men. One of them had the bloody cheek to say to me that Marie was with his mate and he and his other pal were next in the queue. Suggested he did that I go to the pub and get a drink and then come back. The bastard even said he would keep my place so I could have her after him. Me, her legal, stupid husband, was to wait in line to get a service from her!'

Irish began to sob.

Luke waited until Irish began to get some control back. 'Now, can you remember what these men were like?'

'Sailors like me. Just docked I think.' Irish gnawed on his thumb. 'I remember lashing out at the two of them and telling them to get the hell out of it. They just laughed and lunged at me and I fell backwards down the stairs. Kind of stunned I was, but I remember picking up my kit bag and then going over to the foot of Leith Walk and staggering up it doing a pub crawl 'til nearly at Balfour Street – you know where the Chinese takeaway is.'

'And,' Luke leaned forward and with hand gestures he tried to egg Irish on.

'Nothing. I thought I ordered fried rice and something else then all went black. I came to in their back shop and they said I'd been out cold for a couple of hours.'

'And?' Luke repeated, who was now shaking with anticipation.

'Nice folk they are. They let me wash myself down and sponged my suit – I'd been sick you see. Then I went down to the Carriers Pub and I got quietly drunk again. That was,' Irish was now glaring at Luke, 'when I met you and you said to give myself up to the two bastards in Leith Police Station.'

Sally looked hopefully at Luke before asking, 'Has anything he has said made you feel any different as to whether he is guilty or not?'

'Hmmm,' Luke began, 'I'll think about it. I gave him the wrong advice before so I want to be sure before I raise his hopes. One thing for sure though is that I'm going to immediately try and get him transferred back to Edinburgh's Saughton Prison.' He now turned to Irish. 'Now it is important that you stop causing mayhem because you feel all the world is agin you. Keep your nose clean and we may not get this unsafe verdict overturned but we can get life made a lot easier for you. And remember I only have four months so the change in you starts this very minute.'

'And why should I listen to you? Listening to you got me in here.'

Luke shook his head. 'I know that. But I believed then it was the right thing to do. I didn't know that there was a lot of corroborating evidence against you.'

'What evidence? Surely you're not suggesting Stan Roper's mouthpiece Jessie Scott should have been believed?'

'No she shouldn't. And I know, and the whole of the seedy vice side of Leith knew, she was furious that Stan had taken Marie into his stable of whores on better terms than he was giving her.'

Irish rose and it looked as if he was going to punch Luke when Nancy hissed, 'Sit down, Irish. Your temper gets out of hand when someone says anything . . . well you know . . . not complimentary about Marie.'

Luke held out his hand to Irish. 'Look, son,' he said, 'I'm truly sorry about what happened to you. Believe me I am.'

Ignoring the hand of friendship offered to him Irish hunched his shoulders before spitting, 'So you think saying sorry should be enough for me?'

Shaking his head Luke answered with a quiver in his voice, 'You're bloody right, sorry is not enough. And when it's not enough you have to try and find another way of squaring things up. Please, Irish, give me the chance to do just that.' He stopped and inhaled deeply before whispering, 'Let me try. You see I have to do something to help you or I'll never be able to live with myself.'

Sally was choking back her tears. She could see that as Luke had been wrong about her and had been very sorry when it was too late to matter, he was now in the same position with Irish. Irish's life and that of his mother back in Donegal had been ruined. But could things ever be put right? She knew that Luke desperately wanted to do right by Irish – but were Luke's endeavours going to be enough? She doubted it and if Luke failed again to get those in authority to listen, Irish's despondency could end up killing him.

Nancy, who had sat silently, got up and leaning over towards Irish she whispered, 'I know you don't want to trust Luke again. But you know me and I knew Marie so what I am saying is, you have no other choice but to let him try and I will be at his back every inch of the way to make sure he doesn't waver. So what do you say?'

'I suppose you're right, but tell me, Nancy, why does a woman go on the game? Why was the better life I was slaving to give her not enough for Marie?'

'Can't talk for Marie. All I know is there was a time in

my life that punting on the streets was the only thing I thought I was any good at. Pity Sally never got her hands on Marie because I know, like me, Marie would eventually have made the break. And she had an even better incentive . . . a good husband like you.'

The prison doors had just clanged shut behind them when Luke looked up and down the road. 'It will take us a few hours to get to Smithton so we need to eat. You two fancy some fish and chips? At least here we know the fish will be fresh.'

Sally and Nancy looked from one to the other. 'Don't know if I have much stomach for eating right now,' Sally mumbled.

Nancy looked at Luke. She judged he needed some normality in his life and it just might be that another trauma awaited them at Smithton. So thinking it would be better to be prepared for what was to come on a full stomach she said, 'Fish and chips you said, Luke? Now that's just what we need – especially as you'll be paying.'

It was seven thirty when they arrived at Smithton. Luke banged the knocker and then he opened the door and walked in.

Flora, drying her hands on her apron, came out of the kitchen and squinted at the three intruders. 'Oh my, is that you, Luke, and my, Sally? Praise be to God for this lovely surprise. Have you eaten?'

'Aye,' replied Nancy, 'we feasted on fish and chips in Peterhead. Real guid they were tae.'

'Och, but you will be ready for a cuppa. Just wait there until I run next door and fetch Shonag. Sure she'll be as pleased as me to be seeing you. Then you can get me up to date about what's been happening down in Leith. Leith, sunny Leith, how I remember it well.'

Flora had just left when Luke turned to Sally. 'Everything seems normal. She's just like her old self.' Luke now looked at the table that had been set for three. 'And look, she's been baking and not only some nice scones but also some gingerbread. Here, do you think she remembered that I just love her gingerbread and that somehow she knew I was coming?'

'Mmmmm,' was all Sally replied before suggesting to Nancy that she go into the kitchen and switch the kettle on.

The kettle had just started to boil when Flora returned with Shonag and Shonag's son William. Most people referred to William as Sweet William, because he was effeminate but Sally always said him being inoffensively camp just seemed to add to his charm.

Sally and Luke tried not to look at each other in case they registered their disbelief at the state of William. Nancy, however, started to grin. She was delighted that he did not appear to have been ravished with the, as yet unnamed, disease that she thought he had contracted. This was the condition that nobody really spoke out about. It was a justifiable affliction, according to some misguided religious fanatics, visited on those who had disobeyed God and had decided to be gay or indulge themselves with narcotics. The poor victims were too often ostracised and shunned as lepers had been back in biblical times. *But*, she thought as she smiled again, *here was William and yes, he was hobbling about and required the assistance of crutches to do just that but his bones were still covered amply by healthy flesh.*

'What's she grinning at?' William sullenly asked of Sally. 'Has she never seen a bloke crippled by a sadist before?'

Ever astute Sally knew that Nancy had feared the worst for William and to be truthful she had too but had kept her suspicions to herself. Knowing she had to defuse the situation she went over and pecked William on the cheek while she whispered in his ear, 'Look at her teeth, William. They're new and the very latest in design. She's desperate for people to notice them, she is.'

William sniggered. 'Here, Nancy,' he began, 'there's something different about you. I know what it is now,' he winked before adding, 'old Sam Steele left you his falsies when he died. Mind you I think they look better in your mouth.'

Everybody, even Nancy, laughed. This was the ever-jocular William that they knew.

Flora had been busying herself with the tea and she called them all forward to the table. 'Great to see the lot of you,' she began, as she lifted the teapot. 'Och, Sally,' she went on, looking directly at Sally and nearly pouring the tea on the table instead of into the cups, 'see when I don't see or hear from you I'm fair down in the dumps. And there's something you and I have to discuss . . . privately . . . before you leave.' Sally nodded.

'Now, William, what happened to you? I mean, did you have an accident?'

William licked some jam from his index finger before he sighed and drawled, 'Accident? Suppose it could be classed as that. You see I got friendly, real friendly, with Roy McGregor's wee brother, Stuart. Then Roy blamed me for Stuart turning gay. The laugh is he didn't turn gay, he was born gay.' William stopped to sneer. 'The only folk that hadn't worked that out were his bible-punching, prejudiced family.'

'But what has that to do with you being on crutches?'

'Oh, just that Roy vowed to deal with me and, to be truthful, I didn't want any trouble so, even although it broke his heart, I sent wee Stuart packing.' William sighed again. 'But that wasn't good enough for Roy so two months ago he saw me in the woods there, just by the clootie well, and he started to chase me. Caught up with me on the battlefield . . . aye well . . . there wasn't much I could do to defend myself. You see it wasn't a fair fight – he had another three of his relatives with him.'

'So they broke your legs.'

'No. I managed to get away from them and I was out-running them when I tripped and fell into that damned stinking clootie well.' William stopped to lift a piece of cake before finishing with, 'Know something, that well stinks so much I'm sure the corpses of Bonnie Prince Charlie's forty-five rebels are still decomposing in there. Didn't even give me a hand to get out of the filth, the bleeding pigs didn't. Even chucked in some stinking leaf mould to make it even more difficult for me.'

'Anyway,' interrupted Shonag who had listened long enough to William's tale of woe, 'his accident means that Flora and I have to take on *all* of the work on the croft.' She sighed and those looking at her could see tears were not far away. 'And we're just too old. I mean have you ever seen two octogenarians trying to learn to drive a tractor?'

Sally quickly rushed her hand to cover her mouth to stop herself from laughing out loud. Her merriment was due to the picture that had just popped into her head of Flora and

Shonag, suitably dressed in balaclavas and Wellington boots, trying to steer a tractor over the hilly, boulder-strewn terrain.

'Never mind the hysterics, Shonag,' Flora hissed before banging the table with her fist. 'I've told you – I think I have the answer.'

'And what would that be?' enquired Luke.

'Och, it's just that we need . . .' Flora stopped abruptly and dismissed Luke with a disdainful wave of her hand. 'None of your business, sir,' she emphatically blurted before turning her full attention on to Sally. 'Before you leave, lass, you and I have to have a private chat.' She now lifted the teapot. 'Anyone for another cuppa?'

Everyone except Flora and Sally had vacated the living room to allow the women the privacy for their urgent tête-à-tête.

Sally sat with her elbows on the table and her chin cupped in her hands. Flora seemed apprehensive but tentatively she said, 'Sally, I need money.'

'Are you saying you need a loan?' Flora bristled but Sally continued. 'Because that wouldn't be a problem. You know I could refuse you nothing. After all I owe you.'

'Sally, Sally, you won't want to help me.' Flora hesitated before adding, 'You see, my dear, the money is for Harry.'

Sally flung her head back and then banged her forehead with the palms of her hands. 'You're right, Flora. I couldn't even say yes to you begging me if I knew it was for him.'

An uneasy silence followed before Sally asked, 'And what has he done now?'

'The lassie he was living with has put him out. And before you ask, yes he was cheating on her too.'

'So, could he not move in with his present plaything?'

'Be a bit crowded that would be,' Flora replied with a long sniff. 'You see . . . not only has she a husband and four bairns biding with her, she also has her two brothers and their four greyhound dogs.'

Sally had yet again to stifle her desire to laugh out loud.

Oblivious to Sally's reaction, Flora was absently nodding and as she sucked in her lips she mumbled, 'And I just have to get a roof over his head – a roof of his own. So you see, Sally, I'm not asking you, or even begging you, because the amount of money I need to sort him out is too much for even you to find. So . . .' Flora started to pull at her hair. 'Try and understand. I know he's a wrong one but he's my flesh and blood and somehow I must have steered him wrong . . . I just can't see him on the streets.'

Rising, Sally went over to Flora and she began rubbing her shoulder. 'Sure, Flora, when things go very wrong all us mothers think we must be to blame. You are in no way responsible for Harry being a womaniser. Maybe if I'd taken him back when he pleaded with me to give him another chance, it might have worked for him. But, Flora, even although I owe you – I just couldn't – no I just couldn't have tied him around my neck.'

'I wouldn't have expected you to. And, Sally, there's not only Harry that has to be provided for, there's William too.'

'William too,' Sally blurted. 'But Flora, surely you realise that you and Shonag are not the welfare state.'

'I know that. But we do have all this land here that we can no longer farm.'

'Don't tell me you think you can make enough to sort out your problems by renting it out?'

Vigorously shaking her head, Flora went on. 'Things are

progressing here. They need land to create a road – a proper road to link us with the south not a dirt track that gets bogged down in the winter – and,' she added very quickly, 'there's also housing needed. Inverness is bursting at the seams and if they laid on some decent public transport, this place would be very attractive. It's only a ten minute drive to the town.'

As was usual with Sally when she was thinking through a problem she began to gnaw on her right thumb and stare into space. Flora on the other hand just looked out of the window until she could stand the silence no longer. 'Sally,' she said, leaning over to pat Sally's arm, 'you do understand. He has nowhere to stay. He's out of work. I'm too old to take him on. What I was thinking was if Flora and I sold up we could sort out our boys – I know this will mean me selling up hundreds of years of our family history. Nothing will be left for my grandchildren . . . these two bonny lassies you gave me and our darling boy, Bobby, but they have you so they are truly blessed.'

'Just a minute though. Selling up will leave you and Shonag homeless.'

'We'll get somewhere to rent Inverness way. We're too old to come back to live in a city, especially Shonag, she has always lived here.'

'No . . . Look . . . Bobby,' Sally sighed before relief seeped into her. 'Oh, Flora,' she gasped, 'that's who we'll ask to get you out of this mess. I just knew,' she almost sang, 'that there had to be another way. And it will be through my clever, clever Bobby, who knows and is qualified in the law that we will find out what way you should take.' Sally hesitated and blew out her lips before she conceded, 'And okay, he's now a defence solicitor, and a very able one at that, but Lois, his uppity wife, she has specialised in house and land sales so she can keep him right. ' Sally was visibly relaxed. She was just so pleased to think that somehow there might be better answers to the problems facing Flora and Shonag that she began to do a jig around the room.

On the return journey from Smithton to Edinburgh the chit-chat in the car was light. Everyone seemed to be walking on chipped eggs and afraid to broach Sally on the subject that she had discussed with Flora.

They had just left the lights of Aviemore behind when Sally said, 'What do you think of this, Luke?'

'Of what?'

'Flora and Shonag proposing to sell up and use the money they get from the sale to make life easier for,' Sally abruptly stopped to 'huh' twice before continuing, 'for Flora's darling albatross, Harry, and, would you believe, feckless William. Evidently Flora and Shonag have been approached by a road and housing developer.'

'Are you sure?'

'I am but why do you ask?'

'Just that I thought they would need the crofting association's permission first . . . and they would be unlikely to grant it.' Luke hesitated to ponder before uttering, 'Besides, a developer will take those two dearies to the cleaners.'

'Ah, but I know we all call it croft estate but it's not . . . the land is theirs.' Sally began tutting until she added, 'Has been in their family since the early seventeen hundreds.'

'That's good. But developers are sharks.'

'I know that, and that is why I have said Bobby will come up and advise them.'

'Bobby and not Lois,' Luke almost shrieked.

'Well if necessary she can keep Bobby right on anything he's not quite sure of . . . but I'm sure there won't be anything.'

'That right?' Luke replied. 'Look, for what it's worth, I think you should forget Bobby. He'll be too busy defending in the court and getting Irish's appeal started.'

Sally gasped. 'You're going to ask Bobby to get an appeal going for Irish when I need him to be concentrating on getting things sorted out at Smithon?'

Luke nodded. 'Aye and he is best suited to that. Clever laddie he is. Not only did he set up his business in a wee shop in Leith where most of clients are housed but he also goes and purchases himself a house in Craighall Road.'

'What's clever about that?' Nancy, who had made up her mind not to get involved in any dispute between Luke and Sally, asked.

'Simple,' replied Luke. 'There are more solicitors looking for work in Leith than there is work. Therefore Bobby presenting himself as a Leither, and as Leithers like to keep their own in employment, our Bobby gets the lion's share.'

'Oh, so there's nae limit to the amount of Legal Aid you can earn?'

'No, Nancy, there's not,' Sally responded before asking Luke, 'So what am I going to do about Flora?'

'Simple that is, my dear sister, do what you should have done when your Bobby married Lois – get on her good side. She's clever and she excels in her speciality – housing and estate matters.'

Sally huffed. She knew that all she could do now was change the subject. 'Nancy, I know you said that you wanted to go back to your own house now but I think you should still stay at my place for another day or two.'

'No. No. Take me home tonight. I have a friend coming to visit me so I will be okay.'

'A friend?' Sally enquired before doing a half turn in her seat. 'What sex?'

'Oh,' spluttered Nancy, 'we haven't got around to sex yet. You see, Sally,' Nancy paused, 'look I think it would be better if I talked it over with you first before I say any more. Could I come and see you tomorrow?'

'And why not? After all, quite suddenly everybody seems to require an agony aunt called Sally.'

When Luke and Sally arrived back at the guest house in Seaview Terrace, Sally was pleased to note the 'No Vacancies' sign was propped up in the front window. 'Well, at least something seems to have gone right today,' she remarked as the door was opened by Maggie.

'Thought you would be back ages ago,' Maggie huffed. 'Had to let the single room at the front to myself because as sure as hell I'm not going home at this time in the morning.' Neither Sally nor Luke responded so Maggie continued, 'I mean a single woman like me walking the streets in these early hours could end up attacked.'

Luke wanted to respond that it would take a brave man indeed to assault Maggie. However, it had been a long day and he was tired, and a comfy bed was beckoning so he just nodded and started to ascend the stairs.

'Oh, Sally, before we all turn in. Your Margo came along this afternoon. Looking for you she was and she said to tell you it was a matter of life or death as far as she's concerned. Evidently she just has to see you as you're the only person who can sort things out.'

Sally sighed and dropped down on the bottom step.

Weariness was engulfing her and all she could manage to mumble was, 'Helen or Josie havenae been in touch too, have they?'

Bewildered Maggie could only utter, 'No. Were you expecting them to?'

'No. It was just that as disasters all seem to happen in three I thought that perhaps one of them had decided to land me with a hat-trick!'

Luke who was now halfway up the stairs stopped and called back, 'And remember, Sally, I'm only here for four months and I'm beginning to wonder if that will be long enough to sort out all your problems!'

4

Normally Sally would toss and turn the whole night long as she tried to sort all her problems but not tonight. Early on she realised she had to be up bright and early with her wits about her. Nothing else for it then, she counselled herself, other than to go through a relaxing routine. She was only halfway through it when she was fast asleep.

Arriving in the dining room the next morning she was pleased to see that Maggie was already serving breakfast to the customers who wished to be up and away early.

'Fancy a cooked breakfast?' Maggie asked Sally.

Grimacing, Sally shook her head. 'No. Just tea and toast. I have to get to Bobby's office before he goes up to the court.'

'Oh,' was all Maggie, whose curiosity was now roused, said before going on very slowly, 'someone suing you?'

Sally shook her head. 'No. We just have to go over some confidential family business that he will be taking care of for me.'

'Con...fi...den...tial?' Maggie drawled. 'And whit does that mean?'

'That it's none of your bleeding business,' was Sally's quick rejoinder.

The contract taxi had just put Sally down in Great Junction Street, which meant she only had a few yards to walk up King Street to the entrance of her son Bobby's office.

The office had originally been the victual dealer's shop that had sold a variety of foodstuffs to all manner of people. Bobby's change of use of the shop had only changed the product being on offer to the customers. Now only his professional expertise was for sale but the variety of clientele buying on the premises was still as varied.

Pushing open the door she was greeted with a cool smile from the receptionist who said, 'Can I assist you?'

'Yes,' was Sally's emphatic reply, 'I wish to see Mr Stuart, and right now.'

The young woman laughed. 'I'm sorry but that's just not possible. Mr Stuart is about to leave for the sheriff court so he would not be able to see you until late on this afternoon.'

'I beg your pardon,' Sally expounded before proceeding over to the door marked private. 'Do you know who I am?'

'No,' the assistant replied, quickly rising to bar Sally from barging into Bobby's office.

Luckily Bobby had heard Sally and Ursula's raised voices so he immediately opened the door and, giving his assistant a knowing wink, he then quickly said, 'Come away in, Mother. But I can only give you five minutes. A taxi will be arriving then to take me to court.'

Sally was a bit put out at that. Bobby had been her favourite child because she had felt he needed her more. He'd been born with a short leg and she had always encouraged him to study because she felt he was not robust enough for manual work. She had been delighted when all her cajoling had paid off and he had been accepted for Edinburgh University. She was even more elated when he told her he would be studying law. It was at the university that he had met Lois. Sally remembered how she had felt when Lois had come on the scene and she was somehow less important in Bobby's life. This feeling of rejection became even stronger when Lois told her that her ambition was for Bobby and herself to start up a legal practice together. Like today, all Sally could do then was to accept that she was no longer top priority in Bobby's life. Difficult it had been to also realise that she did not have first call on his time either. However, it turned out that even though Lois thought she would map out their career path, Bobby, who had been taught to think for himself, thought differently. Sally had wished she'd been a fly on the wall when he announced to Lois that he was going to pursue a career on his own. That career path would take him into defending, mostly the indefensible in Sally's eyes, those who were charged with being in breach of the law.

'Okay, I accept that you are busy but then so am I. Nonetheless, your Granny Flora, who always put herself out for you, is in need of your expert assistance.'

Bobby rubbed his hand over his chin. 'In what way?'

The next three precious minutes were spent with Sally giving a detailed report on the problems that were facing Flora and Shonag.

Bobby nodded, inhaled, then blew out his lips. 'Yes, I can see this could all be tricky. But what do you think I could do about it?'

'Look into the legality of this sale. Try and find a way of salvaging something for the two of them. Make sure they are not going to be fleeced.' Sally was now quite agitated. She began waving her hands about aimlessly and her words were accompanied with sprays of saliva. 'Look,' she shouted, 'I beggared myself to put you through law school and all I'm asking is for a wee pay back.'

'And, Mum,' Bobby quietly replied, 'I will willingly

freely represent you when you eventually murder Maggie or Margo but I cannot advise you on a matter that relates to property or inheritance – that is Lois's field of expertise.'

'But surely she could keep you right.'

'Mum,' Bobby emphasised, 'what you require being advised on . . . is for Lois to do. And could I suggest that you ask her to assist you?' He paused before softly saying, 'She's not the ogre you like to think she is. She was just brought up differently to me but she is a warm, loving human being . . .'

'Who comes across as being distant,' butted in Sally.

'To you and only you,' Bobby emphasised while glancing at his watch. 'And that is because you have always kept her at arm's length.' He sighed before looking at his watch again. 'Look, Mum, time's moving on and so must I. So it's make up your mind time. The problem is you need someone to help you sort things out for granny. Lois is more than capable of doing that but *you* have to ask her.'

'Bobby, please,' Sally wheedled.

'No, Mum. I have advised you on what to do. Tell you what though, to make it easier for you, tomorrow is Friday. Why don't you and Uncle Luke come over to Craighall for a meal?' He consulted his watch again. 'Let's say about seven o'clock.'

Before there could be any further verbal intercourse between mother and son, a wild-looking woman about thirty years of age burst into the office. 'Bobby,' she screeched, 'you've got to get them to drop the wife-beating charges against my Jimmy or he's gonnae dae me in.'

Bobby turned to his mother. 'See you tomorrow, Mum. Lois and I will so enjoy having you and Uncle Luke over at our place.'

The receptionist came forward to say, 'Bobby, your taxi has arrived.'

'Fine. Just give me a minute with Fran.'

Sally was making for the door when the assistant came forward. 'Fran is forever having these dramatic scenes but Bobby will have her calmed down in next to no time. You know he does so understand her and that is surprising because she had such a deprived childhood and he tells me that he on the other hand . . .' she paused before adding, 'was always provided with a new Burberry coat and Start-rite shoes and every year at that.'

Sally felt the woman was waiting for a comment from her but she was struck dumb.

On leaving King Street Sally decided to stroll down to the Four Marys pub on the Shore. She was the licensee but she now trusted the management of the lucrative establishment to Josie. Some people thought that this was a reckless action on Sally's part as Josie was . . . . well, as Sally conceded, Josie was as Josie was.

As she ambled over Cables Wynd and looked up at the high-rise building, she shuddered. Never would she consider that the soulless-looking place should be classed as suitable housing for mothers and bairns. Nothing she could do about that so she strolled on and then passed the Model Lodging House in Parliament Street. Her thoughts now turned again to Josie. But then when in her life had she not thought about her? She smiled when she thought how Josie had changed in the last three years. The change had come about when Angela, the child Josie had abandoned at birth, had turned up on the doorstep of the Four Marys bar. Sally could still remember the night she had come face to face with the very attractive young woman. That was the night Sally had ended up assaulted – not only by her niece, Angela, who mistakenly thought she was the mother who had callously abandoned her, but also her brother, Luke, who wrongly assumed she had assisted their mother, Peggy Mack, out of this world.

Since Angela had come on the scene Josie seemed to have grown up. It was true she still flirted with the men that came into the bar, but the squandering of her money had stopped. Every penny was a prisoner now. All Josie could think about was how she could speedily amass another aeroplane fare to California.

Sally was nearly on top of the Four Marys when she stopped to remember Angela's wedding. The invitation had come to her and for a partner of her choice. Sally had not hesitated to return it to Angela with the suggestion that she should redirect it to her mother, Josie. She had gone on to say that it was right that Angela was angry with Josie for leaving her in the unmarried mothers' home but could she not accept that Josie was only fifteen years of age at the time. All alone in the world, okay by her choice she was, so naturally she had panicked and done the only thing she thought she could do – leave her baby because she was incapable of providing for her. This mistake, Sally went on to point out, had blighted the whole of Josie's life. Never a day went by that she didn't think and long for Angela. The letter had done the trick and Angela had then sent on an invitation to Josie who of course had asked Sally to accompany her to California for her daughter's big day.

Sally recalled with gladness how Joy Yorkston, Angela's grandmother, had welcomed both Josie and herself into her home. Indeed Sally was very grateful to Joy for going out of her way to willingly accept Josie as her daughter-in-law. The wedding day itself was all that Josie could have wished it to be. Everybody, including Angela and Joy, toasted the mother of the bride, Josie, who had made a big effort to charm everybody. Sally chuckled when she accepted that the wedding had been Josie's passport to America and every year since then, come rain or shine, Josie was at least once on a transatlantic flight.

The front doors of the Four Marys were open wide and Sally's meanderings were brought to a halt by Rita's rendering of 'Galway Bay' assaulting her ears. Rita did so like to sing. The only problem with that was Rita was so tuneless that if the rat catcher hadn't got rid of all the rats, then her singing would certainly have had them throwing themselves into the water that lapped the Shore.

'Morning,' Sally shouted. But Rita had decided to ignore everyone until the last line of the song was belted out and all in hearing distance knew that she hoped in her closing seconds of life she would see the sun going down on 'Galway Bay'.

'Rita, before you launch into "When Irish Eyes Are Smiling",' Sally hollered in the kitchen door, 'could you stop and have a cup of tea and a chat with me?'

'Och, it's yourself, Sally,' Rita responded while flicking the switch on the kettle down. 'Now would you like a wee bit of toast to go with your cuppa?'

Sally nodded. 'What time are you expecting Josie?'

'Oh, you've just missed her. But she'll be back shortly. Just went over to the Post Office to mail a letter to . . . to . . .'

'America?'

'Naw. That would be far too sensible.'

'What do you mean?'

'Just that she's got in with that halfwit Senga . . . you ken her that drinks a double malt through a straw and can only smoke her fags if they're in a long holder . . . anyway the two of them have been writing to a lonely hearts column.'

'A what?'

'Ye ken. They newspaper folk that charge you for putting in an advert like . . . well in Josie's case it read . . . "Sophisticated intelligent born again virgin who runs her own lucrative business seeks mature gentleman for companionship. Likes travel, including American and Continental holidays, music and drama."'

'What? And as to drama I hope she said it wasn't that she liked watching them but that she bleeding well creates them.'

'Oh, Sally, if you think Josie went over the top with her advert you should have read Senga's.'

'No thanks. I just have to allow the picture of the last time I saw fifty-year-old Senga in her hot pants to flash into my conscious mind and I get the general idea – and also the boak.'

Before Rita could respond, Josie rushed into the bar with a large bag of morning rolls. 'Thought I would save you a journey, Rita, so here are the lunchtime rolls.'

Josie then became aware of Sally. 'Oh, Sally, how's your face? David Stock was just telling me that he had seen you since I had and that it was so much better.' Josie laid the rolls on the bar, then lowering her voice and cocking her head to the side she confided, 'And here, do you ken his wife is really poorly? Taken her into the infirmary, they have.' She sucked in her breath before continuing, 'Seems there's no much they can do for her.' She exhaled and clucked before adding, 'Mind you she has lasted longer than anybody thought she would. I mean Sally, how long have you been hanging on for David?'

Sally gasped. 'Josie,' she exclaimed, 'I have not been twiddling my thumbs waiting for David. I have got on with my life.'

'Aye, but you've always been waiting in the wings for Elspeth to fall off her perch.'

'Oh!' shrieked Sally, who was appalled that people may have seen the relationship between her and David that way. 'We have only ever been very good friends who have occasionally gone out to the theatre or had a bite of supper together.'

'Bite of supper you call it,' mocked Josie. 'Here Rita, go on and be brave and tell her what you think a bite of supper is in her case.'

Rita started for the kitchen. 'Leave me out of this. I ken nothing. And I'm pleased to ken nothing.'

Once Rita was safely in the kitchen Sally turned her full attention onto Josie. 'What on earth has got into you? You've never spoken to me like you have just done. I have supported you all through your life. Made excuses for you. Sorted out so many messes for you I've lost count. So out with it – what's going on?'

Josie pulled herself up as far as she could. But before replying to Sally she took a long look at herself in the large mirror above the bar and running her fingers through her hair she said, 'Better get used to the new me, Sally. Gone are the days when you can use me to run your businesses for a pittance. From here on in . . .'

Sally guffawed and spluttered. 'Have you lost your marbles or something, Josie?' she asked through her mirth.

'I pay you more than I pay anyone . . . and more than you're blooming worth.'

'You think so?' jeered Josie.

'I do. And have you ever thought how much gallivanting over to America you would do if I wasn't subsidising you?'

Josie looked in the mirror again. 'Sally, I'm sorry but I have been put wise to you and how you use everyone, especially me, to your own ends.'

Sally quite suddenly stopped chortling because she just couldn't believe what she was hearing. Reluctantly she had to consider, *what or who had got into Josie?* 'Look,' she managed to eventually stutter, 'who has been putting all this rubbish into your head?'

'Victor. And it's not rubbish. He has spent hours getting me to see my true value and how I am being taken a loan of.'

Rita, who had been listening behind the kitchen door and missing some of the important bits of the conversation, quietly opened the door and slunk into the far end of the saloon.

'And who the hell is Victor and where did you meet him?' Sally demanded as she grabbed Josie by the arm and birled her around so they were facing each other.

This action caused Josie to become aware that she was upsetting Sally so she backed away a little before croaking, 'Victor Castello is the son of an Italian nobleman who has studied economics at university.' This statement to Sally seemed to boost Josie's confidence and she then added with a sneer, 'And he, thankfully, was the one who answered my lonely hearts advert. And he has become my advocate and mentor. Oh yes, on my time off we nip into the Caledonian

Hotel on Princes Street and sip cocktails. That's when he counsels and advises me.'

The plaintive uttering of 'Oh, my gawd' that rang around the bar did not come from Sally but from Rita who had decided to rush over and close the outside doors. Sally's reaction was to sink down on a chair before she began trying to tear her hair out.

'So you see, Sally,' Josie continued, unaware of Sally's consternation, 'I'm not like you waiting patiently for a few crumbs that might fall off the table. I know I am my own woman now and I'm grabbing all the chances life puts my way.'

Sally took her fingers out of her hair and started to shake her head before uttering, 'Are you saying this Victor, who has just come into your life, is now your advocate and mentor?' Josie nodded with an air of alluring disdain.

'But, Josie,' Sally went on contemptuously, 'when I last saw you, a few days ago, you couldn't even spell advocate or mentor . . . never mind know the meaning of such words.'

Josie bristled. 'Funny you should try to bring me down like that. That's exactly what Victor says you have done to me all of my life. But he's now educating me to think for myself and to think big. So, Sally, get used to it because he will be coming in here from tonight to be my assistant manager.'

'Oh. Naw. Naw. Naw,' exclaimed Rita. 'Somebody get the Leith polis quick . . . there's gonnae be a murder.'

'You're wrong there, Rita. No a murder. Because she's no worth doing time for. All that is going to happen is . . .' Sally now moved over to the outside door which she forcibly flung open wide. With a cock of her head she then hollered, 'Right, Josie. You're out there on your arse. And I hope your advocate and mentor will be able to tell you what to do about that.'

'You can't do this to me!' Josie protested.

Advancing towards Josie, Sally grabbed her by the shoulder and pushed her out into the street. 'That right?' Sally asked as Josie fell on to the pavement. 'Well it seems I just have.'

The door had just banged shut when Rita asked, 'Do you think you've done the right thing? Josie is so very good at running this bar for you.'

Sally's head furiously bobbed up and down. 'Maybe so,' she agreed, 'but I'm not having some money-grabbing gigolo turning her head. The one way for her to see sense is to have her go out and find a job that'll keep her and Victor in the manner they seem to have become accustomed to . . . cocktails in the Caledonian Hotel at my expense.'

'But, Sally, who's going to run the Four Marys? Just remember that right now you're so busy with your family problems and guest house that you have very little time left for the licence business these days – and – ' Rita hesitated. She was apprehensive then she decided to throw caution to the wind and forcibly uttered, 'Your two bars are where all the money that you need to keep everyone afloat is made.'

Josie had been standing on the pavement outside the Four Marys wondering what she should do when she discovered she had not lifted up her handbag. She had just decided to go back in and not only demand her handbag be returned to her but also her job when the door opened and her bag landed at her feet.

'That's it,' she screamed at the banging door. 'I was willing to give you the chance to say sorry but, Sally, you will have to come crawling now. I'm away to Victor and he and I will decide on what to do next.'

There are times in life when everything appears to go belly up and the more you try to keep them from getting worse the more they do. Sally had just decided that she would have to run the Four Marys herself until she could find a suitable, honest replacement for Josie when Margo, her first born and the most difficult child to deal with, slunk in. Without asking why Sally was serving behind the bar, Margo immediately announced that she was in a predicament and only Sally could get her out of it. In fact she had gone on to say that it was Sally's duty as her mother to do just that.

'And, Margo, just what is it I will be doing or being responsible for?' Sally enquired when the lunch time buzz began to abate.

'As you know, Mum, I am in my mid-thirties and I am childless.'

'Surely that is a problem for you and your husband. Have you spoken to Johnny about it?'

'Of course we have spoken about it. And before you ask, yes I have taken my temperature and sent for Johnny the minute it was at the right degree. And do you know that boss of his just laughed when I phoned last week and asked for Johnny to be sent home straight away. And as my Johnny ran across the showroom floor the chief mechanic not only opened the factory gate so he could dash through it . . .' Margo was now weeping sorely but she continued on bravely, '. . . he also handed him a bottle of Mackeson's Stout and said that everybody knew that there was a bonny baby in every bottle.' Margo stopped to dry her eyes and catch her breath before her verbal tirade continued. 'Honestly,' she went on, 'as if life wasn't hard enough. And half of the times I summoned Johnny he came home so stressed and nervous he couldn't even raise . . . well he couldn't. And when he did manage to do what he required to do, I then had to endure the embarrassment of lying in bed with my legs in the air. And see the day when I forgot the window cleaners were due, my blood pressure leapt through the roof when his ladders banged against my bedroom window.'

The images of all that Margo had been relating to Sally were now floating before her eyes. Try as she might she could not repress her giggles. *Sally*, she thought to herself, *this is no laughing matter. It is obviously so distressing to Margo not to mention onerous for poor Johnny who spends all of his life trying to please dominating Margo.*

'Margo, my dear,' she managed at last to splutter, 'I accept all that you say but how can I help? Surely it's a fertility expert you should consult.'

'And haven't I done just that? And his solution is for you to get involved.'

The laughter had now died in Sally's throat. 'Oh no, Margo,' she stuttered, 'I know some mothers have children for their bairns nowadays but I'm just about to say hello to the other side of fifty and I'm no longer . . . Surely you don't think I'm fertile and could carry a child for you? No. No. No way . . .'

'Mum, don't be ridiculous. I know you're over the hill. It's not your body I need, it's your wallet.'

'My wallet! But how could that help?'

'You know, Mum, you should try and broaden your horizons.'

'What do you mean?'

'Just that you think the whole world, no universe, is within this pub.'

'No I don't. Have I not moved out to Portobello?'

'Portobello! That's the posh refugee camp for everyone who wants to emigrate from Leith.'

'Oh,' was all Sally commented as she began to wipe over the bar.

'Anyway, what I'm saying is I don't suppose you've heard of these exclusive clinics in Switzerland. These are places where people like Johnny and I are treated.'

Sally's mouth gaped.

'You see at the correct time of my monthly cycle Johnny and I would go to the clinic and stay for a whole week. It is situated up in the hills far, far away from pollution, noise and there is nothing but peace and a feeling of well-being and contentment to affect and surround you.'

Sally noted that Margo was now sitting quietly with her hands outstretched on her lap and it was as if she was already in residence at the clinic. Not really wishing to break into Margo's spell but realising she had to get on, Sally whispered, 'And how do they help you to get . . . well you know?'

Inhaling deeply Margo slowly began to respond. 'My Johnny and I would be housed in luxurious accommodation, fed on food fit for the gods before being counselled, given hypnotherapy and taught deep relaxation techniques. All this positive intervention would then enable us to approach our sexual union from different emotional and more positive planes.'

Sally was dumfounded. Had Margo, she wondered, lost the plot? Nonetheless she managed to stammer, 'Margo, believe me, I accept you are desperate and you must try any way you can to become pregnant but really again I ask what has it to do with me?'

'Oh, Mum, don't you realise that if ever I am to become a mother I will have to go down the Switzerland route. It's the only chance left.'

'So if you've made up your mind to do that – then just get on with it.'

'I would but it costs a lot of money that I don't have but you do. So as I know you are desperate to become a granny, it's only right that you fund our treatment.'

A long silence followed that was only broken by the ticking of the clock.

Eventually Sally, who had been recalling the thrill that she'd felt when her three children were born and laid in her arms, asked, 'How much does the Swiss treatment cost?'

'There is a problem. It may be that we would have to have more than one session there for it to be successful.' Margo halted before quietly pleading, 'Mum, please understand I would just have to know that the additional funds for at least two extra treatments would be available.'

'Margo, my head doesn't button up the back so out with it – how much are you looking for?'

'Well to finance three stays at the exclusive clinic it would only be . . . let's say . . . four or five . . .'

'Hundred!' shrieked Sally.

'Eh . . . Eh . . . No.' Margo lowered her voice to a whisper before blurting, 'Thousand,' and then hurriedly adding, 'but that would be it. I promise you . . . I wouldn't come back for more.'

'You sure as hell couldn't because if I give you that then there is no more.'

Margo visibly relaxed. 'Oh, Mum, are you saying you'll agree to us leaving for Switzerland next week?'

Sally hesitated. She was wondering if she was being foolhardy. But then was it not every woman's right to have the joy of being a mother? Thinking back to all the happiness she had known through her children she conceded that money, although important if you were hungry, was only money – and parents had a duty to smooth their children's paths when necessary. Eventually she slowly nodded. 'But, Margo,' she cautioned, 'five thousand is a lot of money so it will have to come out of what I would be leaving you when I depart this life.'

Margo began to cry. 'Thank you, Mum,' she sobbed. 'I knew you wouldn't let me down and if there is ever anything I can do for you . . . just ask.'

'Well,' simpered Sally, 'there is something.' Alarm sprung into Margo's eyes but Sally continued, 'Tomorrow night, could you come down here and run the bar?'

'Why?'

'Because it is something I would like you to do and you said I only had to ask.'

'I know I said that, Mum. But where is Josie and if she's not available tomorrow how about yourself?'

'Josie, my dear deluded sister, will be up at the Caledonian Hotel sipping Manhattans whilst she tells the new love in her life that I have just sacked her.'

'Sacked her!' exclaimed Margo. 'But you need her . . . so was that not a bit stupid?'

'No. You see she met this man through a lonely hearts column and he started to fill her head with nonsense. Even was going to have himself coming in here and running my bar.'

Margo began to chuckle. 'You're joking?'

'No I'm not. And I've been invited to Bobby's for a meal tomorrow night and I have to go because . . .' Sally screwed up her face and grimaced, '. . . I have to eat humble pie and beg Lois to get a problem of Flora and Shonag's sorted out.'

'Oh,' said Margo, who had now become quite animated with curiosity. 'Do tell. The mind boggles. I mean why would two old biddies like them require a solicitor?'

'Because your Uncle William and your father have got themselves further into the mire.'

'Yes, I know about Dad. I tried biting his ear for the Swiss treatment before I came to you.'

Sally's facial expression changed and she struggled not to let Margo see how much she had been hurt. Yes, yet again Margo was telling her that she preferred her father, undependable Harry, to herself. Sally knew she should withdraw the financial support she had just promised Margo but she knew she wouldn't do that. After all, Margo was her first born and no matter what the callous little bitch dished up, Sally was incapable of cutting her out of her life. Sally allowed an involuntary chuckle to escape her as she thought, *Then there is poor Johnny, Margo's husband. So if she needed an excuse for allowing Margo to trample all over her again then it was him. After all, the poor soul must be exhausted rushing for home every time the thermometer told Margo her egg was on the boil and a week getting pampered and hypnotised before having to perform would probably be just what he needed.*

'Here, take these spare keys with you as that will save me dropping them off at your house later on,' Sally said, picking up the keys and handing them to Margo. 'And there is no use saying you can't oblige me because if you can't then I can't come up with the money you are asking for.'

Josie wasn't quite sure what to do when she found herself thrown out of the Four Marys. She was experiencing feelings of doubt. Unconsciously she thought back to the discussions she and Victor had had about their future together. He had been unsure as to whether the Four Marys was a big enough organisation to give them the rewards they were both seeking. He had suggested that before they did anything he would come and work in the Four Marys to see if there was any way that his business expertise could see a way to extend or even change the business. Thinking how clever and confident Victor was made Josie smile. He had then gone on to say that his restaurant in the heart of the New Town just off Queensferry Street could be left in the capable hands of his Uncle Fredo whom he had personally trained. After all, if Uncle couldn't manage, Victor could always jump in and save the day. Victor had also said that if he couldn't work a miracle with the Four Marys then they would just accept that and cut their losses. The two of them would then go up town, where Josie really belonged, and run the William Street restaurant. Josie bristled. She just couldn't believe her luck. Here she was at the age of forty-five about to become the wife of the owner of the famous bar and restaurant Alfredo's. Sighing with satisfaction, Josie nearly tripped over the pavement when she began to chase the bus that would take her to Edinburgh's West End.

Whilst travelling up town to acquaint the new love in her life, Victor Castello, about the happenings of the morning, Josie began to wonder if severing her ties with Sally had been a good thing for Sally and was it necessary? After all Sally had trusted her to run the Four Marys for over three years now. Under her forward-thinking leadership, as she saw it, it was now flourishing as it had never done before. More money was coming over the bar. The evening restaurant was what the well-heeled clientele called 'a gourmet heaven'. It was just a pity that Sally never gave her the credit she thought she deserved.

As the bus whisked her along she told herself that the time had come for her to forget Sally. The opportunity that was now presenting itself to her only came along once in a lifetime. She had now to consider what was best for herself – without a doubt that was being with Victor and assisting him with running his uptown business. She sighed with contentment when she remembered how thrilled she was that Victor, who was just too busy to go a-courting, had answered her lonely hearts advert. She was still wallowing in the wonder of the luck and romance she was now experiencing that she nearly passed the Atholl Crescent bus stop that she should alight from.

Before crossing the road to William Street she sat down on a garden bench and tidied herself up. She just had to create the right first impression on the people Victor employed. So just a little bit of lipstick, a quick brush of her hair and then a fine skoosh behind the ears of exotic Chanel No. 5 and she felt quite ready to meet her future relatives and staff.

The first thing that she noticed when she started to meander along William Street was the 'Alfredo's Italian Restaurant' sign that was jutting out from the wall. She just couldn't help but gulp as the feeling of elation engulfed her. The thought that she should pinch herself awake because she was sure she was in a wonderful dream also overtook her.

She was still experiencing the delicious pain of her nails digging into her palms when she arrived at the entrance to the premises. Breathing in deeply she hesitated before opening the door. Through the adjacent window she took note that the tables were dressed in red and white gingham checked table cloths and napkins. This pleased her because wasn't Sally always saying that the mark of an upper-class eatery was whether they had cloth napkins and not the paper ones that were now being widely used in more common establishments.

Two customers wishing entry to the restaurant meant she had to open the door and step inside. Immediately an Italian-looking older woman, whom she judged was an employee, walked towards her and asked if she wished a table for one or was she being joined by others? Josie shook her head. She wasn't quite sure what to do as there was no sign of Victor. This was causing her a problem. Would it be right, she wondered, to tell the hired help that she was here because she would soon be their boss? Maybe not. Surely that was information that Victor should give them. So, smiling, she said, 'Table for one, please.'

She had been consulting the menu for over five minutes when her attention was drawn to the assistant who had shown her to her table and was now hovering in the background.

Josie thought that this woman, whom she was convinced was an employee of the business, was the epitome of an Italian female – bonny face and voluptuous figure that in this lady's case had gone to seed due to several pregnancies, but her smiling countenance still exuded a zest for living.

Realising that Josie was gazing intently at her, the assistant thought this attention was because Josie was ready to order. 'Have you made up your mind what you would like for your lunch?' the woman asked in an unmistakable continental accent.

'Yes. Yes,' Josie stuttered, 'I'll have the minestrone soup and some garlic bread. And that will do me just fine.'

The woman was about to walk away when Josie asked, 'How long have you worked in this establishment?'

'Longer than I wish to remember,' the woman chuckled. 'Oh yes, I was but a child when we came over from Italy and my father started up this business. Father says he's too old now to live in the cold winters here so he's taken himself back to Italy where he can sun himself every day.' The assistant stopped and sighed before adding, 'My darling husband and I run the business now.' The woman began to giggle. 'With the help of our sons – our two wonderful boys.'

Josie gasped. *Good grief*, she thought, *this lady is Victor's mother. I'm going to have another mother-in-law.* She had never considered that Victor would have a family. Of course that was the Italian way. It was a family set up . . . a family business that Victor, who was so infatuated with her, was inviting her into.

Josie had finished her lunch and still she was marvelling at having discovered that Victor wanted her to be part of his family. How brave he was. Normally he would have been expected to select a bride from within the Edinburgh Italian community but he was his own man and he had picked his partner himself.

The lunchtime trade was coming to a close so Josie decided she would just go now and try to contact Victor later in the evening. She smiled warmly to the woman who had served her. Again she scrutinised the lady. Obviously she was like herself and had given birth to her boys when she was in her early teens and that was the reason, also like herself, she had worn well.

Josie was now clear of the restaurant but she squinted back through the window to assess the woman again. *Yes,* she thought, *you're wearing so well you could have been mistaken for Victor's much older sister . . . but then not only were you possibly married young, I bet you never required to scrimp and save like I have.* Josie let out a short cackle as she looked down at her work-worn hands. Rubbing her palms over each other she conceded that probably the woman had never been expected to assist in the business other than to help out with the lunchtime trade.

Having left William Street far behind Josie decided that she would go into the Caledonian Hotel – her and Victor's special place. When she arrived there she would sit herself down on their special settee and order a cocktail. To be truthful she really didn't require any alcoholic stimulant as she was still intoxicated with all she had discovered at Alfredo's.

On her arrival at the Caledonian Hotel the doorman not only smiled at her but he also saluted. *And so he should,* she thought, while stepping lightly through the revolving doors. *After all, I am a regular, valued customer here now.*

To her dismay the special couch was occupied. She observed that one of the trespassers was an older lady whose face had obviously been subjected to being plastered in excessive, heavy make-up which only served to have her look pathetic. Her companion's face, on the other hand, was hidden from view because of the subtle lighting.

Poor Josie had no other alternative than to find herself another seat which she did in the far dark corner.

Her cocktail had just been delivered to her when in through the revolving doors came Victor's mother. Immediately Josie thought the woman had found out who she was and that she wished to join her and make her welcome to the family. Jumping up, Josie waved to the woman but she ignored Josie and leapt over the floor to the settee that Josie had wanted to sit on. Once there she swung her handbag up in the air before she brought it down on the head of the older woman who screamed out in protest.

Josie, who was used to sorting out squabbles in the Four Marys, immediately sprung towards the fracas. However, she drew up abruptly when the gentleman companion of the recently assaulted woman stood up. It was none other than Victor – her Victor – this poor woman's son.

'Victor,' Josie gasped, 'what's going on? Why has your mother assaulted this woman?' Josie's hand flew to her mouth. 'Oh no, your mum is trying to keep you solely for me.'

Immediately Victor's mother spun around to face Josie and she slapped her hard across the face before yelling, 'His mother! Listen, darling, I am Anna, his long-suffering wife, and he must be getting desperate if all he can now attract are old has-beens like you two.'

Josie looked pleadingly at Victor. He shrugged. She began to cry. 'Don't you realise, Victor, I have given up everything for you,' she sniffed before tears cascaded down. 'Even said goodbye to Sally and that means I have no job now.' Josie was becoming hysterical and could only blubber, 'Why did you lead me on, dear?'

Victor shrugged again. 'Suppose I thought I might get

lucky this time and escape from Anna,' he said, pointing to his wife. 'Josie, I know you won't believe me but I'm sorry it didn't work out between us.' He paused before cruelly adding, 'And to be truthful it was so good for my confidence when you swallowed all my chat-up lines.'

The management had now arrived in force. All four of the people involved in the rumpus were asked to leave and not return to the prestigious hotel ever again.

'I'd drink to that,' screamed Anna. 'I'm fed up coming in here to prise a long line of dried-up bimbos off his arm.' She stopped, and looking directly at Victor and indicating to him with a jerk of her thumb to get moving, she spat, 'And if he ever does darken your doors again be sure to ring me and I'll then arrange for him to sing soprano for ever more – believe me I will.'

Once the party were out of the hotel Victor and the other woman he had duped made a hasty getaway. Josie was left looking at Anna whose face had now become a picture of misery. 'Look, Anna, I may call you Anna, can I?' Anna nodded. 'I'm so sorry. I never knew he had a wife. If I had I would never have got involved with him – never hurt you.'

Anna sniffed. 'Oh. You're sorry, are you? Well the number of times I've been told that not only by the stupid women he hoodwinked but also by him.' Brushing tears from her eyes Anna hesitated before saying, 'And know something? Everyone being sorry for me is no longer *bloody* good enough.'

Josie nodded. 'I can see that. Look,' she now held out her hand to Anna, 'would you let me be your friend so I can make amends with you?' Anna nodded. Josie then added, 'Good. Now how about we stroll along Princes Street and then go into Jenners for afternoon tea.' Anna seemed reluctant so Josie quickly added, 'I could also let you enjoy watching me eat a large portion of humble pie there.'

Anna nodded before linking arms with Josie and laughing raucously.

Leith has always been a town of two faces. There are the areas where the manual and working classes are housed. In these schemes mothers strive to give their children a good life and encourage them to do well at school as that will be their passport to the more prosperous areas where the higher in the pecking order – the professional and successful business people – reside.

Sally had never said to Bobby how proud she was when he bought his first house in upper-class Craighall. She felt that somehow this move proved that she had been a good mother and had provided and educated her children better than most. No one could ever have dreamt that Harry dumping her for traitor Maggie had been such a blow to Sally's self esteem. From that unhappy day, when the feet had been so ruthlessly cawed from her, she had spent her every living minute in trying to redress the balance. Bobby becoming a solicitor and then going on to reside in a large semi-detached villa in Craighall made Sally feel that everyone could now see the family was respectable and was going up in the world. Indeed she could now walk with her head held high.

Any credit that should have been given to Bobby's wife Lois for his advancement into the prestige property market where she was earning a good living, Sally chose not to acknowledge.

It was true to say there was not open war between Sally

and Lois but there was always an undercurrent between them. Sally would tell you it was all due to Lois being a cold upper-class snob but in truth Sally had never given the lassie a chance.

From their first meeting Sally had put up barriers. Truth was Sally did not wish to lose Bobby. She had always thought that because he was, as she thought, physically weak he would always be with her – always need her. Never did she imagine that at university he would meet someone like Lois who would only see what Bobby was capable of and would turn a blind eye to his disability. In fact Lois could become quite annoyed if you even suggested that there was any physical weakness in Bobby.

Right now Sally was sitting in a car being driven by her brother Luke and they were going to Craighall for dinner at Bobby and Lois' home.

This meeting had been arranged because Bobby had refused to get involved in helping his grandmother, Flora, with a complicated property matter. His utter selfishness, according to Sally, had put her in the awkward position of her having now to beg her daughter-in-law, Lois, an expert on property matters, for her assistance.

When they arrived in Duke Street Sally jumped out so she could collect a bouquet she had ordered from the florist there. On returning to the car she placed the flowers on the back seat. Luke turned to look at the creation. 'My, my,' he observed, 'must be Christmas. That lot,' he continued, pointing to the flowers, 'must have cost you a fortune and all for a lassie you really want to buy a wreath for.'

'Don't talk rubbish, Luke,' Sally countered vehemently. 'I'm only trying to build bridges.'

Luke turned back and started up the car. 'Good, because

that makes a change from you burning them where Lois is concerned.'

Bobby had been hovering in the bay window of the drawing room and the moment the car drew up in his driveway he came out to greet them. 'Nice to see you, Mum, and you too, Uncle Luke,' he enthused. 'Come away inside. Lois is in the kitchen just finishing a sauce or something.'

Sally handed the bouquet over to Bobby who had ushered them into a spacious drawing room. 'Thank you, Mum, I'll take them to Lois in the kitchen.'

Seating himself in a large armchair that was so comfortable it felt like being wrapped in an old dressing gown, Luke allowed his eyes to take in the ambience of the room. Even from his first glance he could see that Lois, in addition to being a very intelligent woman, also had breeding and taste. The decor of the room had that old world charm about it. It was a comfortable place to be in. The soft furnishings were obviously the very best of chintz and had been made to measure in Jenners world famous department store. Like old money, which Lois obviously was, the room was not ultra tidy. Luke noted that Sally too was taking in the surroundings and he wondered how she was feeling as there was nothing at all about Bobby's home she could find fault with.

Both Sally and Luke had to stop their inspection of the room when Lois came in and going over to Sally she kissed her lightly on each cheek before saying, 'The flowers are just lovely. Now how did you know that carnations and sweet peas were my favourite?'

'I didn't,' Sally replied. 'But as I also like them I thought you would too.'

Lois had now seated herself on a settee beside Bobby. 'Dinner will be ready in ten minutes. I do so hope venison is to your liking.'

'Oh no,' Sally screeched inwardly, 'I've never tasted it so I don't know if I will like it. Probably hate it. After all, as I swallow every mouthful I'll be thinking I'm devouring Bambi's mother!'

When dinner was finished Lois started to clear the table and Sally offered to assist her to take things into the kitchen. 'I could wash up for you,' Sally offered.

'No need,' Lois replied.

'Oh, I suppose you'll be having a home help coming in to do it in the morning?'

'No. I have invested in a dishwasher. And what a great gadget this is,' Lois replied, opening up the machine and starting to load it.

Once the kitchen was reasonably tidy Lois made for the door. 'Suppose we had better join the menfolk,' she said.

'Lois,' Sally stammered, 'I was wondering if I could have a quiet word with you. Confidential that is.'

'So you've guessed. I'm pregnant.' Lois chuckled before patting her stomach.

This statement caught Sally off guard. 'Pregnant,' she squealed.

Lois nodded. 'I knew you would be pleased. Bobby and I are just thrilled.'

'Of course I'm delighted,' Sally enthused, before confiding, 'and do you know Lois, becoming a granny is something I yearn for.' Sally hesitated as she didn't wish to break the magic of the moment but she knew she had to say, 'But there is something I was going to ask you to do for me but because of your condition you might not feel able.'

Lois did try to suppress her laughter but she couldn't. 'Sally,' she began, 'I am going to have a baby in seven months' time but I shall continue to work, possibly up to and including the next five months. So what is it I can do for you?'

Sally spent the next fifteen minutes outlining the problems that Flora and Shonag were facing. Lois did not interrupt and when Sally was finished she pondered awhile. Eventually whilst weighing every word before it was uttered she began. 'Sally,' she said in a tone that left Sally in no doubt that this was a business conversation, 'I am more than happy to act for Flora and Shonag. I have some spare capacity next week so I will travel up to Smithton and take their instructions. I will also liaise with our Inverness branch and if I think it necessary I will go on to interview the company who have made the offer to Shonag and Flora. However, I must stress that after tonight I will not, because I cannot, discuss any of the details of my interactions with your mother-in-law or her sister. Any information as to what I may manage to achieve on their behalf or suggestions I might lay before them are for discussion with them and them alone.' In a softer tone she added, 'You do understand I have no other alternative. I have only outlined to you the restrictions on my professional conduct that are laid down by the Law Society here in Scotland. Now, and I am sure they will, if they wish to share any information about their situation with you then that is acceptable.'

Sally sighed. 'I do understand all that but do you realise that they are old and not worldly-wise? I only want what is best for them – especially Flora. You see I owe her, and so does Bobby.'

Lois nodded but stayed silent.

With no other option other than to continue, Sally added, 'Your professional fees I will meet. Please don't worry them about them.'

This time Lois's nod was accompanied with a smile.

Two hours later Sally and Luke were driving towards the Four Marys pub. Sally had asked Luke to stop there as she wished to make sure that Margo had locked up properly. They were just crossing over from Ferry Road on to Coburg Street which would lead them towards the Shore when Sally said, 'Did you ask Bobby about Irish?'

Luke nodded. 'Aye. Clever laddie we've got there.'

We've, Sally thought disdainfully. *He's mine not ours.* Unaware of how Sally was seeing things Luke blundered on, 'Mind you, as a boy I gave him every encouragement.' Sally in no uncertain terms was about to put Luke right about who was responsible for Bobby's success when Luke continued, 'Bobby thinks it might be too difficult to have Irish proved innocent. On the other hand he did say he would take up an appeal if I could get some evidence that Irish's conviction might be unsafe. But Sally, where would I find any such proof?'

The car had now drawn up at the front door of the Four Marys and Sally was dismayed to see the lights were still on. 'Right,' she said to Luke. 'You and I had better get ourselves in there and see what's happening.'

Hammering on the stout wooden door brought a dishevelled Margo with a worried looking Johnny in tow to the door.

'Why are you not locked up?' Sally asked, pushing herself into the bar. She stood back and gasped. Normally when Margo was left in charge she left all the dirty glasses on the tables and she made no effort to tidy up. Mice hovering in the vicinity could have a good feed on the dinner scraps which were left lying about. Tonight it was as if she had had a cleaning squad in. Everything was sparkling, except Margo who was obviously worn out. Sally grinned as she acknowledged to herself that she and Rita would have an easy morning because everything was in its place.

'Oh, Mum,' Margo puffed before dropping down on a seat, 'please don't tell me you're not pleased.' Margo began to cry and through her sobs she continued, 'Johnny and I are so grateful to you for helping us that we've done all we can to make life a bit easier for you until Aunty Josie comes back.'

'Josie's away gallivanting again?' Luke shrieked, his eyes darting between Sally and Margo while awaiting an answer.

Margo and Sally looked at each other and shrugged. 'How do I get the feeling that you two are sidestepping me?' Luke continued.

Sally flicked her hair out of her eyes that were now on Luke. 'She was doing so well. Honestly, since you left for Hong Kong she has been such a great support to me. Seemed to have settled down.' Sally stopped and she bit on her lip before she blurted, 'But yesterday, oh dear . . .'

'See the word but . . . when it's said by you, Sally, it usually means things have gone belly up.'

Sally leaned forward to pat Luke on the arm. 'I'm sorry but Josie has got herself mixed up with a man again.'

'What's wrong with that, Sally?'

'Just that she found him through a lonely hearts column and I think he's taking her for a hurl.'

'Not necessarily. He could be genuine, and what would be wrong with her getting married and finding happiness?'

'Luke, she told me she was going to move him in here to run my bar. She also had the nerve to say that she's her own woman now and no longer can I exploit her.'

'Oh,' was Luke's reluctant response.

'Aye, oh. And I wouldn't care but she says he owns and runs a restaurant up town so if that's right why would he wish to come down here?'

Luke pondered awhile. Then rubbing his hand under his nose he said, 'Let me look into things tomorrow. Right now it's time we were all heading homewards.'

Unable to sleep, Sally was in the kitchen when Luke joined her. 'You not able to shut your eyes either?' she asked, rising to make him some cocoa.

'No, I just got into bed when Irish's problems put all thoughts of sleep out of my mind.' Sally did not respond. Time passed and he was sipping the hot chocolate drink when he slowly drawled, 'Sally, what did you make of the other day?'

'In the prison?' Luke nodded. 'Sure the laddie's suffering and like you I've never thought that he did murder Marie. So what we have to do is find some evidence that will lead to a successful appeal.'

'Aye. But I don't know where to start looking for that kind of evidence. I know you won't believe me Sally, but I haven't a clue where to begin. Do you?'

Sally slowly shook her head before suggesting, 'The trial records. You never know, they just might hold the answer.'

'Wish I'd been at the trial. If I had been perhaps I could have seen where there was some dubiety or misdirection.'

'Don't know about that,' Sally mumbled. 'I attended and the prosecution seemed to have dotted all the i's and crossed all the t's.'

Luke banged his cocoa mug down on the table and he reached over and grabbed Sally's hand and vigorously shook it. 'Of course you were there. Now take your time but think back. Think about what was said. What was Irish's alibi? What was disallowed and why? Who do you think was lying? Who benefited by Irish being sent down?'

Sally began to laugh quietly then dragging her hand from Luke's she responded, 'Luke, you are the detective. I'm just a wee Leith businesswoman who left school at fourteen . . . so how on blinking earth do you expect me to read a trial like a lawyer?'

'A wee insignificant businesswoman is what you want me to believe you are? Naw, when it comes to it there's nobody as sharp as you or can read it how it really is.' Sally huffed and shook her head. 'Now, Sal,' he went on, 'not right now but in your quiet times go over the trial. Picture the scenes. Think about what did not quite ring true.'

'And while I'm doing that could I suggest you go and try to straighten out our wayward sister Josie.'

'Aye I will. And talking of relatives, how's your Helen faring?'

A warm smile came to Sally's face. 'Oh, my darling baby daughter Helen, well she flew away, as you know, to teach English in a school in Menorca.'

'Still there is she?'

'Aye. Lives in my apartment.'

'By herself?'

'Yeah. Mind you there is a Filipino illegal immigrant who sings and plays a guitar who she mentions from time to time. Seems she teaches him English and they both go to Spanish classes together.'

'Illegal immigrant? Why is he allowed to stay?'

'The tourist trade is booming and during the day he works as a waiter in Dirty Dick's shack, which doubles as a restaurant, and at night he plays his guitar and sings in a band that goes around the hotels entertaining.'

Luke laughed. 'Is he any good at the singing?'

'Well, after a few sangrias Jose's rendering of "You and Your Spanish Eyes" has the half-cut holidaymakers thinking they are enjoying a night at La Scala.'

'But Sally, the La Scala's in Italy, is it no?'

'Aye. But just you wait until you hear his warbling in broken English and you too will subconsciously transport yourself to Sorrento.'

Luke was about to point out that La Scala was in Milan but he refrained. With what Sally had said he realised what she thought about Jose. This led him on to wonder if Sally's contemptuous estimate of the young man was because her Helen was perhaps transported in a different way by 'You and Your Spanish Eyes'!

'Anyway,' Sally said, bringing an end to Luke's speculations, 'you and I will get ourselves over to Santa Tomas for a wee holiday.'

'And when will that be?'

'Just as soon as we can get things sorted out here.'

Luke stared out of the window. He could see no pigs flying. 'Well,' he began so slowly she thought he was ailing, 'at the rate we're going that will be on my next trip home.'

5

Even though Sally was the licensee of the Royal Stuart pub on the Leith side of Easter Road, it was not a hostelry that Luke had often frequented. Today as he sauntered in he pretended that his visit was to say hello to Nancy now she was well enough to be back in charge.

Nancy of course was delighted to see Luke. Having no brother of her own and having been treated by Sally as a sister, she felt it only natural to look on Luke as a younger sibling.

'What's your pleasure?' Nancy asked Luke whose eyes were roving all around the salon.

'I'm driving sooo . . . just a shandy.'

While Nancy was making up his concoction Luke scrutinised the customers. A smirk of satisfaction came to his face when he noticed that the two men in the corner were none other than his long-time adversaries, Drew Washington and Phil Watson. These two detectives, better known in Leith 'D' Division as Holmes and Watson, were the people he wished to meet up with today.

Uplifting his drink he began to walk towards the men's table. Smiling broadly he asked, 'Mind if I join you?'

'Please yourself,' Drew answered, lifting his hand to indicate the vacant seat. 'Heard you were back. Since last week or was it the week before?'

'Been home three, nearly four weeks already, I have,' was Luke's jovial reply. 'See time,' he winked to the men, 'it just races in when you're enjoying yourself.'

Drew nodded. Phil, who was only allowed to talk if given permission to by Drew, just slurped his beer. 'They tell me,' Drew began as he weighed Luke up, 'you've signed up for another tour.' Luke nodded before sipping from his drink. 'Suppose it makes sense.' He paused and blew out his lips before adding, 'Because there's no way you would make detective here.'

Phil cackled and playfully jabbed Drew in the ribs.

Luke just smiled. 'You're right there. See in Hong Kong they have parameters that you have to stay within.'

Sneering, Drew asked, 'Like what?'

Luke leaned over towards Drew as if he was taking him into his confidence. 'You have to have looked into every scenario and be absolutely sure you've got it right before you accuse and charge anyone.'

Drew sniggered. 'And that must take up the whole working week for the likes of you. Here in Leith we have apprehended the culprit,' he was now helpless with laughter, 'usually before the crime is fully committed.'

'You're right there,' Luke enthused. 'See the last case I saw you work on before I left, it was a humdinger. Now what was the hapless guy's name?'

'Did you mean the gormless Irish guy?' Luke nodded and sipped from his glass again. 'That really didn't show how brilliant I am,' Drew scoffed. 'Open and shut case it was. I didnae even bother to write it up as a good capture.' Drew lifted his pint and gave a mock toast to Phil before adding, 'Gave my pal here all the credit.'

'Did you? That was good of you,' Luke answered, but he was thinking the only reason that Drew, an apology for a detective, pinned the brownie points on to Phil was because there were things that didn't quite add up! Obviously, corners had been cut. Correct procedures were not followed to the letter. This meant that if all that came to light and a miscarriage of justice was found in Irish's favour, it wouldn't be Drew's career that would come to an abrupt end but Phil's. Luke also accepted that it was amazing the lengths some officers would go to when their pensions were just about to come to fruition.

Nancy calling to Luke to come over to the bar was just what Luke required. He had discovered more in the meeting with Holmes and Watson than he had hoped. Luke hoped they still considered he was wet behind the ears. He smiled when he accepted how often his being underestimated had worked to his advantage.

'Another drink calling,' Luke said, rising to leave.

'Aye, run along, son,' Drew said slowly before quickly adding, 'but before you go, do you know that Phil here, his sister, gorgeous Barbara, is on the force now?' For some reason Luke didn't catch the meaning Drew was implying even when he added, 'The star of 'B' Division at Gayfield she is.'

He was still trying to figure out why Drew had to tell him about Phil's sister when he arrived back at the bar. Another surprise awaited him. Nancy had her coat on.

'This is Duncan, Luke,' Nancy announced, grinning. 'He's my right-hand man here. Going to hold the fort, aren't you Duncan while you, Luke, drive me over to Sally's.'

Nancy was about to get into Luke's car when she huffed, 'Ridiculous this is. Would you believe I have been trying for a week now to get Sally to have a chat with me? Has the cheek to say she's always too busy.'

'Aye, it's time she got some help in at the Four Marys now it appears Josie is not coming back.'

'She's not?'

Luke shook his head. He didn't want to discuss Josie with anyone right now. Here was another problem that was not quite adding up. Starting up the car he recalled how last week he had got the shock of his life.

Getting things sorted out between his two sisters had become Luke's priority. So without telling anybody he had taken himself up to Alfredo's restaurant last Friday at lunchtime.

He had just entered the bistro when Josie, dressed in a knee-length dress protected by a gingham red and white Dutch apron, came forward. 'Luke,' she squealed, throwing her arms around his neck. 'Oh, it's just great to see you. Want a table?'

'Aye, and a chat with you.'

'Chat with me? You see it all. So what is there to talk about?' Josie gestured with her hands for Luke to look about the room. 'Don't suppose you believe that I'm one of the family here, but I am. This is my life now, Luke. Can you believe it? I have to keep pinching myself because I'm sure I'm going to wake up and find it has all just been a lovely dream.' Josie looked about the salon and hunching her shoulders she sighed. 'I know Sally has sent you here to beg me to come back but don't waste your time, Luke.' Taking out her order pad she smiled broadly before saying, 'Now could I recommend the lasagne?'

Luke's car had just drawn up in front of Sally's guest house when Nancy jumped out and raced up the stairs. After ringing the bell, she hopped from one foot to the other waiting for Sally to open the door to her. To her disgust when her summons was answered it was Maggie and not Sally who ushered her in.

'Where's Sally?' Nancy demanded rudely, pushing past Maggie.

'As she is just about to leave for the Four Marys she's getting her coat on,' retorted Maggie.

Advancing into the hall, Nancy called out, 'Sally, it's me. I just have to speak to you.'

When Sally emerged from her downstairs bedroom she already had her coat on and her handbag was slung over her left wrist. 'Oh, Nancy,' she gasped. 'How bad this has been of me. I knew you wanted to talk and I just kept putting it off. Tell you what, let's you and I jump in the back of Luke's car and we can natter all the way along to the Shore.'

Nancy looked a bit reticent and eyed Luke suspiciously.

'Oh, you don't need to worry about my brother here, he's the soul of discretion. Believe me, he is so involved in his own worries just now he won't hear a word of what we discuss.'

Nancy was still looking somewhat nervous but Sally grabbed her by the right elbow and steered her out of the door.

The car had just left Seaview Terrace when Sally turned to face Nancy. 'Now what is it that's worrying you?'

Nancy bowed her head and sniffed. 'Sally, I've met someone,' she blurted.

'Good. Nobody should spend all their time on their own if there's an alternative.'

Hesitating and blowing out through her mouth, Nancy began to resemble a fish out of water.

Sally started to laugh. 'Nancy,' she chuckled, 'with the life you've led surely you can tell me what's bugging you.'

'It's. It's. It's . . . Oh, Sally, it's just that he wants to marry me.'

'Well that's not a problem,' Sally chortled.

'But it is. You see,' Nancy continued in a whisper, 'I don't know where he got the idea but he thinks I don't want to say *yes* because I'm afraid.'

'Of what exactly?'

'Sleeping with a man,' was Nancy's quick retort.

Luke who had not wished to eavesdrop was so astounded by Nancy's revelation that he lost control of the car. Quickly it swerved and crossed over the road and just managed to miss colliding with the Seafield Sewage Works wall.

'For goodness sake,' Sally roared. 'Have a care, Luke! I mean if you want to kill us would it not be better to steer on to the other side of the road and land us in the crematorium?'

Without uttering a word, Luke straightened the car up, crossed back over the road and brought it to an abrupt halt just outside the cemetery gates.

Sally let out a long sigh and waited until everybody had recovered from the fright before she spoke. 'Now, Luke, just get out and have a wee walk. See on the corner,' she said, pointing back to the road leading up to the Eastern General Hospital, 'there's a wee café. So away and get yourself a tea or coffee . . . or anything you like but get lost for fifteen minutes.'

Luke had just left the car when Sally turned again to face Nancy. 'Now what exactly are you trying to tell me? What did you tell this man?'

'I didn't say anything about my past to him. That pig of a Detective Inspector, Drew Washington, egged Benny on when he knew that he fancied me. Told him I was a virgin and at one time I'd taken holy orders.'

'He what?'

'Aye, laughed he did and spluttered, "Oh aye, she likes none of this and none of that."'

Sally was angry. She looked at Nancy and she could see she was distressed. Taking Nancy's hand in hers she quietly whispered, 'Nancy, how do you feel about this man?'

Tears were now cascading down Nancy's cheeks. 'Sure, since he came into the pub a year ago,' she sobbed through her tears, 'life has just been so wonderful. Sally, he's such a nice guy – a real gent. Even brings me roses and pats my cheeks.'

Sally allowed time to pass while Nancy composed herself. 'He really wants to marry me, Sally. Set me up in a wee house. Just him and I together but . . .'

Glancing through the back window of the car Sally could see Luke was returning. 'That blasted café just had to be shut, didn't it?' she mumbled as she indicated to Luke to take another stroll. Facing Nancy again she softly said, 'You have to tell him, Nancy. If you don't, all your life you will be wondering who is going to tell him that you . . . made your living . . . to hell . . . tell him the truth of how your bastard of a father put you and your sister out to sell . . . yourselves to keep him . . .' Sally gulped and gasped before uttering, 'in booze and fags.'

Nancy shook her head, mopped her brow and continued to weep. Luke returning to the car broke the unbearable silence between the two women. 'Look,' he began gently, 'it's time we were on our way to open up the Four Marys. You two can continue your conversation there while I serve the drouthie punters.'

It was as if Sally and Nancy were unaware that Luke had got back in the car. 'Sally,' Nancy began, 'how could any decent man like Benny want to set up home with an old bun like me?'

'You're belittling yourself. You are not an old bun,' Sally protested vehemently. 'Putting your past behind you is what you have to do. The only way of doing that is to tell this Benny what you were but add what you are now.'

The car had drawn up in front of the pub. All alighted and Nancy's cynical laughter echoed down the Shore.

'You can cackle all you like Nancy but I haven't put in all the work I have into making you respectable to let you throw it away. There has to be a way for it to work out for you and I promise you I will find that way.'

'Good, Sally,' remarked Luke, 'but in the meantime do you think you could get back to making a living?'

It was nearly midnight when Sally got home and she was surprised that Luke's car was parked on the front street. Earlier in the evening he had elected to drive Nancy from the Four Marys back up to the Royal Stuart. From there, he said, he was going up town to attend to some of his own business.

He did go up town but he decided to park the car in Seaview Terrace first then jump on a Princes-Street-bound bus.

Striding over the east end of Princes Street towards Wellington Statue, Luke was surprised when he heard someone call his name. Glancing towards the Register Clock House he was pleased to acknowledge his half-brother, John Thomson.

Both men slapped each other's backs. 'Good to see you,

mate,' Luke exclaimed. 'Meant to get down to visit you but it has been like a merry-go-round since I set foot in Sally's door.'

'Aye, and since the powers that be decided that I was too friendly with the pub staff in Leith . . .'

Luke laughed before butting in with, 'Did you no tell them Sally was your sister?'

John shrugged. 'Think they knew that and that was another reason for putting me up to Box Seventeen in Rose Street to finish my thirty.'

'Rose Street. So what are you doing here?'

'Just strolled along because the young guys here at Box Twelve just need a wee bit of support when they have a capture.' John shook his head. 'You see, Luke, the recruits the day are mair academic than we were. Believe me, they nearly shit themselves when they have to lock up an angry man.'

Luke laughed. 'So they wouldn't make the grade in Leith?'

'Nae chance. But come on, I have to get back to my beat so why don't you walk with me?'

They were just passing Marks & Spencer's when Luke blurted, 'Sorry about your old man.'

'Your old man too if we believe his story that your mother and him had an affair that lasted a lifetime.'

Luke squinted over to John. He would never be able to explain the fact that from his first day as a raw recruit in Leith, he had taken to John – the two of them had bonded. It was uncanny the way they always looked out for each other. It was as if they had known before Sally, Josie and himself that they were related by blood. That day in the Four Marys when old Jock had confessed he had fathered them all, Luke, although stunned, felt a warm glow grow inside him – he was delighted that John who was eighteen years his senior and whom he had always looked on as a much older brother really was related to him by blood. Right then Luke took a vow to get more involved in John's life. Give him what he longed for: a younger brother.

Both men had now stopped and were facing each other. 'Makes no difference now,' Luke said with a sigh. 'We're all his bairns. He was a good cop. Bloody rotten father but then you cannae win them all. And at least the girls, Sally and Josie, were able to say they at last knew who their father was.'

'Talking of the girls,' John blurted. 'What's the story with Josie?'

'Have you come across her up this way?'

'Aye. Somebody told me she wasn't in the Four Marys now and know what, I was surprised when I saw her dishing out ice cream in . . .' Before John could go on, his radio sounded and he answered it. 'Aye. Aye. Aye. Okay. Going back there right now but would it not make mair sense to put someone with experience with thae young lads?' He signalled with a hunch of his shoulders to Luke before saying into his mouthpiece, 'Aye, well we aw ken our inspector couldnae organise a piss up in a brewery.' John switched off his radio, grimaced, then immediately began to run back along Princes Street while he hollered back to Luke, 'Sorry, mate. Seems Box Twelve is under siege and the only cavalry man in the area is me.' Luckily Luke was not quite out of earshot when John shouted, 'Catch up with you tomorrow. Have something to tell you about Josie that I think you should do something about.'

* * *

Luke watched John's retreating figure until it was lost in the crowds meandering in Princes Street. It had been his intention to do a pub crawl in the hope he would bump into one or two of the mates he had socialised with before he had left for Hong Kong.

He had just entered Robertsons Bar, a popular pub on Rose Street that he had enjoyed frequenting, when John's parting words rang in his ears again.

The barmaid, Lorna, who remembered Luke, smiled. 'Well are you not a sight for sore eyes?' she enthused. 'And what's your pleasure tonight?'

Luke didn't respond. He had not heard a word Lorna had uttered. The only sound he was aware of was the echo of John saying, 'Have to tell you something about Josie that I think you should do something about.' *What on earth was John going on about*, he wondered, before about-turning and exiting from the bar.

Once outside he knew he had to revisit Alfredo's restaurant. He just had to confront Josie again. Okay, she had said she had made her decision and now she wanted to be left in peace to enjoy her new life and bond with her new family. Again Luke's mind was racing ahead.

Before he had left for Hong Kong he had been a good, very good, cop – a community man who had seen the best in everybody and tried to help out wherever he could. Three years experience in the CID in Hong Kong had changed his outlook. No longer could he just accept anything at face value. He was always looking for other reasons, other solutions, wondering if people's relationships were really as secure and as wonderful as was being presented to the outside world. Yes, he still loved his fellow man and wanted to see the best in him but he was now aware, especially since what had happened to Irish, those things and relationships were not always what they appeared to be.

Accepting that he had now become a detective, he knew there would be no rest for him tonight if he did not confront Josie again.

The lights in Alfredo's restaurant were lit, and it was evident from the condensation on the windows that the restaurant was busy and this might not be the best time to confront Josie. Nonetheless, Luke, who was used to having the right to barge in anywhere, decided to enter quietly.

Glancing around the salon Luke could only see three male waiters. The older man that he assumed was Victor the owner, the man Josie had told him she was about to marry, and two young student types who were possibly working to finance themselves through university.

After handing one of the young lads an order chitty to take to the kitchen, the older man turned his attention to Luke. 'Table for one, sir?' he asked with a half bow. Luke nodded. The waiter sniffed and looked about the room. 'As you see, we are very busy so there is just that little table in the corner. Bit of a squeeze but I will shift you if a better table becomes available.'

Luke nodded his acceptance. 'Yes, you are busy tonight. Just you and the boys on duty?'

Victor nodded. 'Yes, the women do lunches.' He sniggered, 'Well they usually do but Anna has taken herself over to Italy so I've had to get in a temp.'

'A temp?' Luke queried.

'Aye, an older woman,' Victor replied, his pencil poised to take Luke's order. 'Bit past it the old dear is but . . . she was needing a job . . .' Victor gestured towards the tables that were all occupied, 'and the lunchtime trade is a quick turn about . . . business lunches so nobody is expecting any refinement.' He sniffed before adding, 'Just as well 'cause they sure wouldn't be getting any.'

An hour had gone by before Luke left the restaurant. He was even more confused than ever about Josie. Hailing a passing taxi he asked the driver to take him to Josie's house at Ryehill.

The evening trade in the Royal Stuart had been brisk at the start of the evening but as the night wore on it got slower and slower. The result was that when ten o'clock came, Nancy had most of the tidying up done.

She had just safely installed the day's takings into her handbag and was donning her coat when a timid knock sounded on the front door.

Lifting her faithful rammy deterrent, an old hockey stick, she went over and cautiously opened the door and her spirits rose when she was confronted with Benny.

'Oh,' she sighed, 'I'm pleased to see you. Come away in. But what's bringing you here at this time of night?'

Benny removed his flat tweed cap from his head and began twisting it in his hand before stuttering, 'Cannae bear the waiting. Sure by now you must,' he stopped briefly before adding tersely, 'well you must know whether or not . . . that is . . . or at least considered if you want to . . . marry me.'

Nancy thought back to what Sally's advice had been. Indicating to Benny to take a seat she then sat down opposite him. He was a simple man, not in intelligence, just in his outlook in life. She knew he just wanted to have a home with a wife in it and for the two of them just to be content and happy. She admitted that she too longed for someone to care for her. For someone to want to share his life with her and she could think of no one better than Benny. Drumming her fingers on the table she felt like screaming, *Benny, Benny why could you not have come into my life when I was a teenager?* From posing that question, albeit to herself, she went on to imagine what life could have been like for her. Pictures of Benny and herself getting married, having a nice wee house and a couple of children shouting, 'Mammy, mammy, daddy, daddy look at me.' Imagining the children brought a lump to her throat, causing her to swallow hard. In her past she had always vowed children were not for her. After the childhood she had had she would never bring children into this world. Sniffing, she tried to compose herself but memories of children she could have had but had decided to . . . was it because of what she had done to those unborn children that she had been plagued with bad luck? Hunching her shoulders she then had to admit that this was probably not the case because how then would Sally have come into her life? Sally had been the catalyst in her life. Nancy happily conceded that from the day they met life had just got better and better for herself.

All the foregoing was true but what was she going to do about Benny? Sally's advice, when she had followed it to the letter, had always proved to be sound. So should she try sticking her courage to the sticking place and tell Benny the truth about herself? She wanted to. She needed to but she was afraid that he would, in disgust and loathing, run out of her life.

Benny took her hand in his and brought an end to her speculations. 'Nancy,' he wheedled, 'how about we go up to Michael's Fish Shop and I'll treat us to a fish supper, just the one between the two of us. And we could then go on to your house and have a midnight feast?'

Nancy felt warm tears spring to her eyes. This was what she meant when she said he saw life as being just so simple. To him a fish supper being shared between the two of them was his idea of heaven. Okay, they would have the fish and chips and after they'd washed them down with his must-have beverage at room temperature, some Vimto, she would tell him the truth.

The cab driver who dropped Luke off at Josie's door had enquired if he should wait but Luke had waved him away. He was convinced that his meeting with Josie would last a while and he could always phone for a taxi when they were finished.

Pulling the bell, he stood further back in the driveway so that she could see through her security peephole that it was him. Seeing the light in the hall go on brought a smile to his face. The door was then opened up not by Josie but by a scantily clad young lassie, a teenager Luke guessed, who was asking what he wanted.

'I'm Josie's brother,' he managed to stammer. 'Is she at home?'

The lassie shook her head. 'I'm just her lodger . . . well me and Susie are.'

'What?' exclaimed Luke.

The young lassie looked perplexed and quickly added, 'All I know is she works up the town in a restaurant and she doesn't get in until . . . I don't know . . . wait 'til I ask Susie. Here Susie,' the young woman hollered back into the house, 'what time does Josie usually get in?'

'After midnight,' was the disgruntled retort.

This information completely confused Luke. He had to accept Josie wasn't at home. She'd taken in two lodgers. He remembered vividly when she had bought the house her saying how pleased she was that she wouldn't need to share with anyone as she could more than meet the mortgage. Running his fingers through his hair he accepted that he knew for sure she was not on duty at Alfredo's where she was supposed to be working. What was even more alarming was he had known she was working at lunchtime in the restaurant because he had met her there dressed in a red checked apron! So where was she? What was going on?

By the time he had pondered all the probabilities and possibilities the young woman had closed the door on him. He was tempted to knock on the door again and ask the young lassie to telephone for a taxi for him but he decided the long walk home to Sally's would give him time to think.

Waverley station is always busy, very busy, in the early morning – people commuting all over the country and beyond to England and Wales are dashing about buying tickets and boarding trains.

Lois would normally have driven herself to Inverness but she was suffering from severe morning sickness that was exacerbated by car travel. Bobby had dropped her off on the Waverley Bridge and she was rushing down the brae when she noticed that quite far in front of her was the familiar figure of her mother-in-law, Sally. 'Blast,' she hissed inwardly. 'Bet she's going to Smithton. The old dears must have told her I was coming today but I really need to be talking to them without anyone else being present. Especially Sally who I just know from past experience will comment on everything I have to say to them.' Lois stopped to consider if it would not be better to go back home and reschedule her visit to Culloden but then she thought, *What good would that do?* Flora obviously would not take any advice from herself that had not been approved by Sally. So the best she could do today was to make sure she did not travel north in the same carriage as Sally. This meant she required to purchase a first-class ticket. With her mind now made up Lois lurked behind a kiosk until Sally had purchased her ticket and had begun to make her way across the concourse towards the waiting trains before she approached the booking clerk.

By the time Lois was about to get on the train the guard had his whistle in his mouth so she had no other alternative but to jump aboard the first carriage. Realising that she was standing in a third-class carriage had her screw up her eyes and inhale deeply. Opening her eyes she was delighted to note that Sally was not in the carriage. *Good*, she thought, *and as soon as this train stops at Haymarket to allow other travellers to board I'll get myself into a first-class carriage where I will be able to work in peace and quiet.*

On reaching Inverness Lois decided, because she knew there would be no way she could escape meeting up with Sally now, that she would go to her firm's offices in town. This would mean she could honestly say to Sally that she should travel on to Smithton and she would meet up with her there.

Allowing her eyes to scan the platform, she was perplexed. There was no sign of Sally. But she had seen her in Waverley station. She saw her buy a ticket. So where was she?

Emerging from the station she was dismayed to find that

the rain was relentlessly falling down. Immediately, she summoned a taxi from the outside rank. However, when the driver asked her where her destination was she scanned the horizon before emphasising with a sigh of relief, 'Smithton village.'

The taxi drew to a halt at the bottom of the brae. 'Sorry, miss,' the driver said, turning to address Lois, 'but see they farm roads – dirt tracks really – don't do your motor any good. Could you manage on your own from here?'

'Well,' exclaimed Lois, who had just taken a pound note from her purse to pay the man and was now opening the door so she could alight. 'I suppose I must.' Handing over the pound note to the driver through his open window she forcefully stated, 'Take your fare and just your fare. I only tip for good service and that is what you haven't afforded me.'

She didn't care that the driver, who had immediately turned the cab around and was now racing back to town, was disgruntled. She wasn't too happy herself about *his* behaviour.

Her demeanour took a further downward spiral when she looked at the rock strewn and sodden track she was required to navigate in her high-heeled shoes in order to get herself up to Flora and Shonag's homes.

A disembodied voice was saying, 'I just said to Shonag that you wouldn't know to be wearing suitable footwear. So aren't you lucky that I've come down with a pair of my old Wellingtons that I think will fit you.'

Common sense was something that Lois had plenty of, so without a word of protest she leant against Flora to exchange her Saxone shoes for a pair of over-sized, rather grubby and distinctively smelly boots. Then arm in arm, Flora and Lois started to climb the brae.

Even though it was summer there was a chill in the air and when they arrived in the house, Lois was pleased to see that a cheery fire was crackling in the hearth and that the table was set for lunch.

Lunch had just been cleared away and the three women, Flora, Shonag and Lois, were again sitting around the table. The two older women were very apprehensive. Lois on the other hand was very relaxed, especially as her stocking clad toes were facing the fire.

'Now ladies, I have already done quite a bit of work on your case. Our office up here has done a wonderful job in getting me all the information I require.'

'So there could, or might, be something you can do for us?' Flora babbled before taking Shonag's hand into hers.

'Yes. But there's a lot of preliminary work to be done. Firstly, I will employ a land surveyor to isolate the houses on the land deeds. Draw up new boundaries and . . .'

'What does that mean exactly?' Shonag blustered as her eyes began to pop.

'Nothing for you to worry about,' Lois reassured. 'All that is going to happen, if you and Flora are in agreement of course, is that your homes will always be yours. You will both have a small garden and room for a couple of outhouses which will leave you free to sell off the rest, the majority of the land, which will in turn raise the capital you require.'

Shonag, who was thinking deeply but was unable to grasp all of the implications, could only respond, 'Mmmm.'

Whereas Flora who was as usual on the ball asked, 'Are

you saying, Lois, that we can stay here and have a wee bit of land to grow some vegetables for our own use and perhaps enough for a few hens to scratch about?'

Lois nodded. Flora nodded sniffed and sucked in her cheeks.

'But,' Shonag twittered, 'we can't agree to that just now. Surely Flora you're not forgetting that our four ladies are in a delicate condition.' She leaned over and patted Lois' hand before adding, 'Just like yourself my dear and we must see them through before we agree to anything.'

Lois quickly withdrew her hand from Shonag's grasp and leaned back. She was confused. She reasoned the expectant girls could not be their daughters. Both ladies were in their eighties. Surely, she went on to think, these two old dears weren't running a maternity clinic for unmarried mothers. Finally she mumbled, 'But surely these ladies have families who should be taking care of them?'

Shonag huffed. 'But we are their family. We have had them since they were calves. Bought them at the Perth sales, so we did.'

Flora nodded. 'And Lois we just have to be on hand for Nellie.' She lowered her voice to a whisper. 'You see as soon as she gives birth she tries to murder the calf.' She discreetly looked about the room before adding, 'We just have to get it away from her. Infanticide . . . well it's just despicable.'

'Aye,' butted in Shonag, 'but be fair to her, after she's got over the trauma of giving birth she changes and becomes a doting mother.'

Lois decided not to get involved with the cows' birthing arrangements but to steer the conversation back on to the drawing up of the new boundaries. 'Right,' she said rolling the 'r' to indicate it was time to be back to the business in hand, 'in addition to enquiring into the drawing up of the isolation of your homes I have also tried to estimate what the sale of the rest of your land would fetch.'

'I'm praying that there will still be enough to fix things for the boys. Our boys are problems but they are our boys and are important to us,' Flora confided.

Lois smiled. 'Believe me, you will have more than enough money to sort out your problems.'

Shonag and Flora exchange excited glances before Flora stuttered, 'More than enough!'

Nodding again, Lois allowed her smile to become a wide grin. Seeing the old ladies' growing anticipation, their eyes widening, their cheeks flushing, Lois was tempted to tease them by allowing a long pause but she couldn't be that cruel so quickly she added, 'Yes indeed. In fact once you take out the houses and small gardens the rest will probably, and I stress probably, bring you,' she hesitated as she had no desire to over-estimate what the old women could expect, 'at least twice as much as the developer had offered you for the whole estate.'

Flora and Shonag grabbed for each other's hands again. 'See, Shonag,' Flora gulped, through her tears, 'this lassie *is* as clever as our Sally said she was.'

'She said that?' Lois chuckled. 'And what else did she say?'

Flora mused before replying, 'Just that you were a lucky lassie to have snared her Bobby.' And thinking she was imparting good news she added with a chuckle and a patronising nod, 'And that you're doing so well now because his common sense has rubbed off on you.'

Although burning indignation was now beginning to boil

up inside her, Lois decided that retaliation was not a good idea – especially as gentle Flora and Shonag would never knowingly insult her. It was just that they belonged to a simple culture where malice and intrigue were alien to them so they would not have been aware of the slights in Sally's comments. So with a disarming smile she sweetly asked, 'Talking of my *dear* mother-in-law, are you expecting her here today?'

'No. No,' replied Flora. 'She said she wouldn't be able to come up this month.' Flora became pensive before mumbling, 'Aye, said something about her priority was to get herself up to Peterhead. Do you think she's considering buying her fish for the pubs there?'

Lois could only shake her head. Knowing Sally she knew full well that fishing would be her reason for going to Peterhead but not to purchase boxes of it – no, she would be visiting Joseph Kelly, the young lad Bobby was working on an appeal for. Shaking her head and sighing, Lois conceded that Bobby would have a hard job convincing his mother that he was capable of carrying out his remit without any assistance from her.

Reluctantly Luke opened his eyes and fished over to the table to lift his watch. Eleven thirty it registered. Time he was up and acquainting Sally with his worries about Josie. He would have done that last night but by the time he arrived at Seaview Terrace it was gone one thirty and the household had bedded down for the night.

Maggie was still in the process of clearing away all the breakfast dishes when he entered the dining room. 'See, Luke,' she began as she brushed some crumbs from the middle table, 'if you're giving your mind a treat and think

I'll be serving you up some breakfast or early lunch – think again. I've five rooms still needing changing.'

'Sally hasn't given you a hand?'

'Nope,' was Maggie's terse reply as she began to leave the room dragging a vacuum behind her.

Racing after her, Luke called out, 'What time did she leave for the Four Marys?'

Maggie banged the vacuum against the wall before turning to hiss, 'She left at seven this morning. And she may well be in the Four Marys now but she told the taxi driver to take her to the Waverley train station.'

'The Waverley? The train station?' Luke shrieked. 'Where the hell was she going?'

Maggie offered a shrug before stating, 'I don't know. But she said she wouldn't be back until late . . . very late . . . and once more the skivvy of the year that I am – I am left with this entire place to square up.' She lifted up the vacuum again before sniping, 'So if you don't mind I have to get on. And please don't tell me you don't know how to switch the toaster on because I'm not blooming interested.'

Luke decided there and then not to bother with breakfast. As to Sally, he would have to wait until she returned to speak to her. But what he could do now was go and find out where Josie was and what was going on with her.

He arrived at Alfredo's in time for a late lunch. To his surprise Josie was on duty and she smiled as she showed him to the cramped table for one in the corner.

It was quite disconcerting for him that before he could speak to Josie on private matters customers required her service. 'Speak to you later,' was all Josie said before taking up her waitress duties.

An hour passed before Josie came over to Luke's table and sat down. 'Oh,' she exclaimed, 'see this family business of ours, you just have to muck in and do anything that requires doing.'

'Family of yours?' Luke questioned in a derisory tone.

'Yes,' Josie, who was well aware that Luke was mocking her, rejoined quickly, 'and when Victor and I marry then I will take over here while he is opening up another restaurant down on Leith Walk.'

Luke's contemptuous laughter rang around the salon. 'Josie,' he spluttered, 'Victor is married to Anna and as far as I am aware this is still a monogamous country.'

Now it was Josie's turn to cackle. 'Oh, Luke, you are so old fashioned. Victor still being married to Anna is just a small inconvenience.'

'That right?'

'Yes, Anna has decided to live permanently in Italy. She finds the climate here a bit on the chilly side.'

Luke had to stop to close his gawping mouth before being able to say, 'Are you saying she is divorcing Victor because she doesn't like the cold?'

Josie nodded. 'Yes, the three of us sat down last Monday and we worked it all out to our mutual satisfaction.'

'Oh Josie, don't tell me you've been on the happy pills again?'

'No. It's all true. So if you're here on Sally's behalf again to beg me to come back, the answer,' Josie now flicked a napkin over Luke's table, 'is no. Josie, doormat Josie, is getting married and soon.' Josie now pointed to the owner's name above the front door. 'Her name will be up there.' Luke was nodding and then shaking his head in turns. His eyes bulged and his mouth gaped. Josie, amused at the effect she had on him, mischievously added, 'Imagine it, dear brother, up there it will not read Anna Castello but Josephina Castello!'

It was after eleven when Sally's taxi drew to a halt at her guest house. After paying off the driver she ran lightly up the steps. She had hoped that Maggie would have gone to bed but she thought it was a forlorn hope as the bottom floor lounge light was burning brightly.

'Sorry I'm late,' Sally called out as she opened the door to face Maggie's wrath.

'And so you should be,' replied Luke.

Sally allowed her travelling bag to slip from her hand as she sank against the wall. 'Oh, Luke,' she exclaimed, 'you'll never know how wonderful it is that you are here.'

Luke winked and laughed. 'Oh I see, you thought you were going to be faced with the wicked witch of the north.'

Sally nodded before kicking off her shoes. 'I had to go to Peterheard to try and make sense of something that just dawned on me.' She halted before adding, 'Look I'm just dying for a cup of tea. C'mon through to the kitchen and we can have a good natter about it all.'

The tea was brewed, the kitchen was filled with the wonderful aroma of freshly toasted bread and Sally and Luke sat facing each other. 'Fancy telling me why you went to the prison?' Luke asked as he lazily stirred his tea.

Sally placed her cup back in its saucer and she dragged her hands down over her face and blew out her cheeks. 'Remember,' she said slowly, 'you asked me to remember what I could about Irish's trial. Anything that didn't seem right then and seems even now to be,' she hesitated, 'to be

. . . oh well, Luke, I just know it couldn't have been like they said. But . . . but I was afraid to say anything in case I'm wrong. You see I would be so upset if I built up Irish's hopes and then saw them dashed.' She hesitated and began biting her bottom lip as she wrung her hands. 'You see I couldn't do that. It would be better if I just kept quiet.'

Luke nodded in agreement. 'So he had no idea why you were visiting?'

Sally shook her head vigorously. 'No, I told him I was just passing and I thought I would pop in and see him.'

'He would believe that right enough,' was Luke's scornful reply. 'And how did you get him around to telling you about . . . well him being stitched up?'

Sally offered a shrug. 'Just asked him if he could tell me exactly what had happened on the night Marie was killed as I had heard so many conflicting stories.'

Luke seemed amazed at Sally's simple attempt to get Irish's confidence but he had to admit she probably would get some sort of story out of him. Perhaps, he mused, there was going to be a breakthrough. The necessary breakthrough that was required if Bobby and himself were ever going to get anywhere with Irish's appeal. After drumming his fingers on the table he stood up, picked up his chair, took it over and placed it closer to Sally. 'Look,' he said placing his hands over hers to stop her wringing them, 'just take it easy and tell me what you think is wrong. You've no need to worry. I will carefully analyse what you say and you're right, we will not go forward with anything unless we know positively that we have questions that need answers.' Luke leaned back and placed his entwined fingers behind his head. 'Now,' he drawled, 'take your time but let me be hearing from you.'

Sally looked up at the ceiling as if there was someone there who could help her remember exactly what had happened at the prison. 'It is just that Irish said part of the case against him was that he had gone up Leith Walk to the Chinese takeaway the night *before* Marie was killed and not *on* the night of the tragedy. He is clear that the Leith CID interviewed the Chinese owners several times because they were unsure which night Irish had gone to their place. In the end they confirmed to the police that it was not the night Marie was killed but the night before.'

'So?'

'Well his ship only docked the day Marie was murdered and he was taken into custody that night.'

Luke jumped up. 'That's right. He was at sea the day before and had been arrested the same night as he docked.'

Sally nodded. 'But if he was still aboard his ship, how was it that the police got Mr and Mrs Lee to say he was in their shop the night before Marie was murdered and that he had dropped down dead drunk?'

Luke was growing agitated. 'I remember clearly that the Lees said they let him sleep it off in their back shop.'

Luke began to dance around the room. 'Sally,' he exclaimed, 'you are a genius.'

Trying to keep her emotions in check, Sally mumbled, 'Are you saying there might be something we can do for Irish?'

'I'm sure we can. But first I will lay all these facts before our bonny lad and ask him to take them and use them for an appeal.'

Pretending to be bashful, Sally twittered before saying, 'Of course my Bobby will know what to do.' Stifling a long yawn she announced, 'Don't know about you, Luke, but now I am so tired I'm turning in. Wish I didn't have to do the whole day in the Four Marys tomorrow.'

Luke's euphoria suddenly vanished. 'Ah,' he said, 'I was waiting up for you because . . . Oh, Sally there is something that is just not adding up with Josie – can't lay my finger on it though.'

'Like what?' Sally moaned as she gaped again.

'She says this Victor is going to marry her. But he's already married to Anna and they have two grown sons. It's true that Anna has run off to Italy. And it's also true that our Josie is working and running the restaurant at lunchtimes but she's not there in the evening. She says she does the books then.'

'That's a lie,' Sally scornfully butted in, 'Josie doing the books? Huh. Don't you know she's innumerate?'

Luke nodded. 'I do know that and that's why I have doubts about her stories. And to add to my confusion, when I spoke to Victor the other night he didn't seem to think he and Anna were heading for the divorce courts.' Sally shook her head. Luke went on, 'But, Sally, why is Josie installed in Alfredo's and why has she taken in lodgers at her house in Ryehill?'

Glancing up at the clock and noticing it was now well past three o'clock, Sally stood up. 'Know something, Luke?' she said ruffling his hair, 'You and I are both too tired to wrestle with any of our problems right now. So how about we go to bed and sleep on it all and in the morning we can talk about what we think we should do.'

6

Clumsy Johnny Souter wanted to stretch himself before getting out of bed but . . . what if he disturbed Margo?

Life had so changed for him in the last two weeks since Margo had had it confirmed that she was pregnant – definitely pregnant. He *had* to agree with her that it was probably because she was so keen to become a mother that she had only required one visit to the Swiss Clinic before she had a positive reaction.

After slipping out of bed Johnny grabbed his work clothes. Without switching on the bedside light he began tiptoeing as quietly as he could towards the bedroom door but unfortunately he tripped over Margo's slippers.

'What on earth is going on?' asked a plaintive cry from the bed.

'Sorry, Margo,' Johnny mumbled, 'I just fell over. Nothing to worry about. I think I just split my head open when I fell against the corner of the dressing table.'

Half sitting up in bed Margo fumbled before stretching out to turn on the bedside light. 'Good heavens,' she exclaimed when she saw the blood spurting from Johnny's forehead. 'Here is poor me in the early stages of pregnancy being put in a state of fear and alarm. Honestly, Johnny, why can't you pick a more convenient time to kill yourself? I mean surely you don't want our baby to be born fatherless.'

The blood was now seeping into Johnny's eyes so he grabbed the first piece of cloth he could to stem the bleeding. Unfortunately it just happened to be the nightdress Margo had purchased only yesterday, the one she intended to be wearing when her visitors came to see her in the Maternity.

There are pluses in everything and the utter despair that was now registering on Margo's face as she saw her precious nightie smeared in blood had Johnny forget just how painful his head wound was.

'I'll get you another one if the blood doesn't wash out,' he mumbled, screwing the garment into a ball.

'And I suppose threatening to buy another one is your way of reminding me how dishonest it is of me to hold on to the money my mother gave me for three visits to the Swiss Clinic.'

'No. No. No, Margo,' he stuttered. 'You have explained to me that now it has worked you will be taking things easy and getting the nursery all fitted out. And believe me I think your mum will understand that when you get around to telling her.'

Margo had now swung her legs over the bed to sit on the side and she was pleased when she realised she could admire herself in the dressing table mirror. Lovingly patting her stomach she said, 'But Mum won't be upset about her money right now because I don't intend to tell her until it becomes,' she stroked her tummy again before simpering, 'evident.'

'But you've told your dad,' Johnny exclaimed.

'So?'

'Is that fair? Your mum does more for you.'

'Yes, for me. But she's never been good to or understood my poor old dad.'

* * *

At seven o'clock precisely the telephone shrilled and Sally dashed to answer it as she thought some of her paying guests might still be asleep. 'Mack's Guest House,' she announced into the mouthpiece. 'And good morning to you too, Nancy,' she continued when she realised who the caller was. Looking up at the wall clock she checked the time again. 'I hope this early call doesn't mean there's a problem?'

'Sally,' spluttered Nancy, 'do you know that David Stock's wife died last night?'

Shaking her head, Sally whimpered, 'Oh no. Poor, poor Elspeth. What a long, painful journey she has had.'

'Will you be contacting him?'

'Contacting him?' was Sally's pensive reply. 'I would love to but I can't really. This is a time for his girls and himself to be united as a family. They won't want any outsiders.'

'Suppose you're right.'

'By the way, Nancy,' Sally enquired hopefully, 'any word from Benny?'

Nancy allowed a long silence before replying, 'Funny you should ask that. Yesterday, out of the blue, I received a letter from him asking if I'll meet him down by the bandstand on Leith Links this coming Sunday afternoon.'

'Oh,' was all Sally replied as her thoughts raced back to two weeks ago when Nancy had told her what had happened when she had picked up the courage to confess to Benny about the sordid life she had once led.

NANCY'S STORY
They hadn't bothered with plates for the fish supper. They just spread it out on the wrapping paper. Then with relish they attacked the delicacy with fingers and forks. Benny

could not hide his amusement when Nancy poured the Vimto into two Edinburgh Crystal glasses.

Lifting the sparkling goblet he started to toast Nancy. 'Here's to my beautiful lassie,' he huskily said before asking, 'Have you an answer for me, Nancy?'

Cupping her face in her hands and slightly bending her head she then breathed in deeply. Time silently ticked by until she eventually raised her head and looked straight into Benny's eyes. 'Benny,' she falteringly began, 'nothing would suit me better than to become your wife. Honestly I think you and I could make a go of it but . . .' Nancy had to stop talking because Benny had jumped up and was now running and whooping around the room.

'Thank you, thank you,' he cackled. 'You have made me so happy.'

'Benny,' Nancy forcibly shouted, 'hear me out first before you start to be so happy.'

'Huh,' chirped Benny, 'and what would you have to say now that would change how I feel?'

Indicating to the chair he had just vacated, Nancy signalled that Benny should sit back down on it. Once he was in position she reluctantly began. 'Benny, I have not always been the woman I am today. The woman you know who honestly earns her daily crust.'

'Look,' spluttered Benny, 'if you're trying to tell me that you've you been a tea leaf in your day, so what?'

'No I was never a thief. But . . .' Nancy had to leave off for a minute as the sheer panic rising in her breast began to choke her. '. . . Oh, Benny, try and understand I had an awful father . . . my sister and I were just about to become teenagers . . .' Tears welled in her eyes and she was finding difficulty in going on. These memories, her haunting demons, she had buried deep into her subconscious were now being brought to the surface again. She must, there was no other way other than to confess them to Benny if they were ever to have any future together. Buoyed up with courage, she was unaware that she had suddenly blurted, 'The swine sold us to the highest bidder.' These tragic words had an awesome effect on Benny. Nancy could see something in his eyes – was it anger or disgust? *Too late now to spare him the truth*, she thought and *I might as well tell him it all now. What have I to lose?* 'And from then on, Benny, up until I met Sally Mack, I made my living selling myself for the best price I could get. My poor sister was not as hard as me and instead of continuing with that sort of living . . . she ended her life.'

A frightening silence, only broken by their laboured breathing, overtook the room. Nancy was still looking into Benny's eyes and she cringed because in his hypnotic stare there appeared to be a smouldering hatred.

Without a word to her he got up and left the house. She knew he had been shocked at what she had imparted to him. His attitude had left her feeling small and dirty. All she could do now was put life with Benny to bed with all the other dreams she had had in her life that had never come to fruition.

Slowly she made her way into the bathroom and filled the bath so she could immerse herself. She didn't seem to notice that the water was scalding . . . all she wished to do was sit there for at least an hour and scrub and scrub at herself in a futile effort to cleanse away all the filth and shame she felt was still clinging to her.

Two weeks is not a long time in the legal world. On the other hand, to Luke who was on a tight time schedule it was an eternity. He was so anxious to find out what progress Bobby had made on Irish's appeal that without an invitation or an advanced courtesy telephone call he pitched up at Bobby's Leith office.

He had just opened the door and stepped inside when Ursula, Bobby's receptionist, greeted him with a broad smile. 'Can I help you, sir?' she coyly asked.

'I'm Mr Stuart's uncle, is he in?'

'Maybe yes,' she teased, 'but then maybe not.'

'And what will be the deciding factor?' Luke replied with a wink.

'Quite simply it will be if Bobby recognises you as his uncle.' Ursula lifted the phone and switched on the intercom. 'Mr Stuart, sorry to bother you, sir, but there's a man, who looks young enough,' she drawled, 'to be your slightly older brother, in the outer office here demanding to see you. Claims he's your uncle.'

Luke bent over and putting his cheek close to Ursula's he then hollered in the mouthpiece, 'Chinese Whispers wants a word.'

Immediately the door of Bobby's private office opened and giving an over-exaggerated bow Luke was invited to enter the inner sanctum.

'I was just passing,' Luke lied, 'wondering if you'd got anywhere with Irish's . . .' Luke hesitated before adding, 'Bobby, we just have to put up a good fight for him. He's innocent. And before you say anything, I have always had this gut feeling that he is.'

'That's an interesting theory you have there,' Bobby agreed before slowly adding, 'you see there is just one problem with that.'

'And what's that?'

'Nothing other than an unbiased jury considering the facts of the prosecution's case found him guilty.'

'But you know very well Holmes and Watson twisted the evidence to suit,' Luke emphasised. 'Surely I've not been the only one to interview Mr Lee and his wife,' Luke now beseeched, 'and have them admit they were confused about which day it exactly was.'

'Proving that Mr and Mrs Lee were deliberately bamboozled is just scratching the surface. We need more evidence than that. And before you offer, I have an ex-police officer, who I have engaged as my precognition officer, working on the case.'

'But I could assist . . .'

'No. I have taken instructions from one Joseph Kelly to lodge an appeal and when I present my procedural hearing dossier I wish the members of the Appeal Board to note that everything I have done on the case is in line with the laid down procedures. That means, Uncle, that they must be able to see that all of our enquiries were carried out by upstanding impartial investigators. What I am saying is, I may lose on the first round but I would not wish it to happen because the board was advised that the investigations were carried out by . . . persons like you with an axe to grind. Please try and understand that what I'm trying to achieve is agreement to go forward to a full hearing.'

Luke became animated. 'You've already played them the overture?'

Bobby nodded. 'And they have agreed with the prison authorities that Joseph Kelly be transferred back to Saughton Prison today.'

'That is just tickety-boo,' chorused Luke. 'So he'll get off.'

Bobby shook his head and stressed, 'It is too early to think that but what we do have is a chance to have a full hearing to *consider* the original verdict.' Waggling his finger in Luke's direction he continued, 'Now, Uncle, I can't tell you much more right now. So *please* just keep your powder dry.'

'I will. I will. But just remember to question the evidence of Jessie Scott, corroborated by Jenny Geddes, that they saw Irish arguing with Marie. And don't forget there is also Stan Roper to be looked at, after all he was pimping all three of them.'

Bobby was becoming exasperated. He knew his job and strongly objected to well-meaning amateurs telling him how he should proceed. But Luke was his uncle whom he did not wish to offend, so all he replied was, 'Stan Roper is a pimp with his fingers in all sorts of illegal pies, extortion, drugs, you name it but he's not stupid.'

'What do you mean?'

'Marie was a high earner for him. No way would that wily boy kill the goose that was laying the golden eggs. Anyway what you're saying is only supposition – fortunately I deal in concrete evidence because I don't like getting laughed out of court.'

'Okay, I'll grant you Stan Roper but what about Jessie?'

'What about her, Uncle?' Bobby's temper was reaching boiling point with Luke. Then in a softer tone he added, 'Please try and accept that I am a solicitor and I am only interested in winning this appeal that I have agreed to undertake.'

'I know that. But if we can prove Jessie Scott wasn't exactly chuffed that Marie was now the favourite in Stan's stable and she . . .'

Bobby held up his hand to silence Luke. 'Don't you listen?' he expounded so sharply that Luke sat up straight in his chair. 'I am only concerned with Joseph Kelly. Should we be successful, which I intend to be, it will result in all the evidence being scrutinised again. It will also be of concern to senior officers in the police force if, and here I stress *if,* it looks as if any of their detectives involved in the case should be investigated, perhaps disciplined or moved back to uniform – all that has nothing to do with me. I repeat, I am a solicitor who looks after his client's interests and thank goodness I'm not like you – a vigilante detective dreaming up scenarios. And think about it, Uncle Luke, this mess just may have been the result of detectives not ensuring they had built up a watertight case on proven *undisputable* facts and not on sheer speculation and personal dislike of a person!'

Luke sprang up to his feet and offered Bobby his hand. 'Point taken, son,' was all he had to say.

On leaving Bobby's office Luke headed for Taylor Gardens where he sat down on a bench. Staring unseeing ahead and sucking on both his thumbs he began to think.

He considered it was true that when the case against Irish was proved to be a stitch-up of the making of Holmes and Watson then the two of them could find themselves suspended. An enquiry by senior officers from another police force in Scotland would then be undertaken. *Bobby,* he found himself saying inwardly, *you are wrong, I certainly don't want to see the two of them in the shit – especially Drew Washington who is nearing his thirty.* After all that was what all police officers looked forward to: retirement on a nice lump sum and two thirds final salary pension after thirty years' exemplary service.

Still pensive, his thoughts now turned to the interview he had had with Mr and Mrs Lee. When he had entered the shop he had prayed that the Lees would understand the Cantonese dialect as spoken by him and they were not solely fluent in the Mandarin dialect. If they were then they would not understand a word he said. He was naturally very proud of being able to speak Cantonese. With a sly smile he remembered that when he had first arrived in Hong Kong he had undertaken an eight-week crash course in the language. He grinned again when he remembered that to get a better grounding in the tongue he would go down to the bars to 'practise' with the local maidens! He had to do that because the language was quite difficult. He hadn't of course studied the Chinese characters and had only learnt conversational Cantonese using Romanized English sounds for words. He did so pray that his scant knowledge of the language would stand him in good stead today.

Mrs Lee was waiting to take his order and he fortuitously remembered that the word 'Face' in Cantonese is very important. He thought that in their culture it probably translated to meaning 'giving due respect and not unduly embarrassing someone'. He also recalled it was not good manners to openly or harshly criticise someone in front of others – even if it was justified. So elders like Mr and Mrs Lee he should give 'face' to if he hoped to get any assistance from them.

Starting to order from the menu in Cantonese, he grew excited when Mrs Lee indicated to her husband that here was someone in Leith ordering from their menu in their mother tongue.

After taking possession of his Lemon Chicken dish he

casually asked if the Lees remembered the Irish lad who had been found guilty of his wife's murder. Mr Lee shook his head and waved his hands about. In his native tongue he managed to convey to Luke that he never wished to have the bad men, Luke took this to mean Holmes and Watson, in his shop again. Luke, remembering to be giving 'Face' to the Lees, assured them that he was not like them and had no desire to bully them or mistrust them.

By the time Luke had left the takeaway he and the Lees were firm friends. He had also managed to establish that Irish had indeed been looked after by them and at the time of the assault on Marie he had been in a drunken stupor in their back shop.

Luke congratulated himself when he remembered he had taken that information to Bobby. Up 'til then, Bobby wasn't sure if he would go to appeal for Irish. He had considered it could turn out to be an embarrassing rebuttal. But now with the Lees and the ship's log saying that Irish could not have been in the takeaway the night before his ship docked, Bobby was more than happy to take on the case that would become high profile. Still gnawing on his thumbs, Luke conceded further that Bobby's precognition officer had only got the best out of the Lees because he had advised Bobby that the Lees must be given 'Face' and when they were given due respect and not embarrassed in any way they then would give their full cooperation.

Luke, deep in contemplation, was still sitting on the bench when his half-brother, John, called out to him. Slowly coming back from musing, Luke looked up and beckoned to John to come and join him.

'Can only stay a minute,' John informed. 'See here,

Ellen,' he said to the little girl who was holding him tightly by the hand. 'This here is your very own Uncle Luke and he's home on leave from Hong Kong.'

Luke appraised the little girl. He was trying to see if there was any family resemblance he could identify. That was a vain hope. Ellen had natural blonde hair that was matched with large soulful blue eyes and unlike his undersized sisters, Sally and Josie, she was tall and willowy. Even though he could see no family likeness, he was hypnotised by the child. John smiled when he became aware that between Luke and Ellen there was obviously love at first sight.

'What's your name and how old are you?' Luke asked with a wink.

'Ellen, and I'm six years old today but if you ask me again next week I'll be seven.'

John and Luke exchanged a knowing glance before they both laughed.

'What a lucky guy you are, John, to have an angel like this for a grandchild.'

John was chortling. 'My lassie Nell's wee lassie she is. Our dad was just besotted with her before he passed over. Here Luke, seeing you like bairns, have you never thought of getting married and getting a wee brood of your own? Best thing you could do, mate.'

Sucking on his lips, Luke sniffed before replying, 'I do think about marrying from time to time but I'm a bit too old and set in my ways. But . . .'

'I know you, Luke, and without telling me I know there is now someone that has taken more than your fancy.'

'Maybe, but she's not from around here and she's much too young I'm afraid.'

'Too young?' John shrieked. 'Rubbish. You're a catch for any age now – so go for it boy.'

Ellen who was tired of listening to Luke and John sparring with each other, unceremoniously butted in with, 'I know you're an uncle of mine and I was just wondering if you knew an aunty of mine called Josie.'

'You've met my sister Josie,' Luke replied in mock disbelief.

'Yes and she gave me extra ice cream for nothing.' Ellen stopped abruptly and her left hand flew up over her mouth. 'Oh, that was to be a secret so please don't tell anyone.'

Crossing his heart Luke replied to Ellen, 'Your secret is safe with me.' Turning to John he said, 'You took a six-year-old out to an Italian restaurant?'

While vigorously shaking his head John spluttered, 'No.'

'Then where did Ellen bump into Josie?'

'In the Odeon Picture House on South Clerk Street.'

'What was showing?'

'It was the bairns' late-afternoon cartoon matinee.'

The conversation was causing Luke to become confused and he drawled, 'But why would Josie be going to a children's matinee?'

'She wasn't. You do remember I told you she was doing something that seemed odd and you should do something about it?'

'And what exactly is she doing that needs fixing?'

'Selling ice creams and drinks on a stick in the interval.'

Eyes now bulging, Luke expounded, 'Are you saying she's doing an usherette's job?'

John nodded. 'She is and with poor Sally run off her feet trying to keep the Four Marys and everything else afloat, do you not think Josie should be called back to her old job?

I mean she's a wizard at it and I'm sure Sally pays her more handsomely than the Odeon management.'

Luke nodded. He looked again at Ellen and fishing in his pocket he brought out a fistful of change which, without counting, he then pressed into her hand.

'Granddad, Granddad,' she exclaimed while starting to count the money, 'You said he was my very own uncle but you never said he was a millionaire!'

Both John and Luke laughed uproariously before Luke said, 'Look, John, I would give you a lift to wherever you're going but I just have to get up to South Clerk Street.'

'That's okay, mate,' John replied. 'Besides, we're going in the other direction and look, here comes the number sixteen bus.'

'You're a good bit late for the first house and much too early for the second,' the nippy cashier told Luke when he had asked for a ticket.

'That's okay,' he replied quickly, 'I really don't wish to see the film, I just want to buy an ice cream from the sales girl at the interval.'

Thinking that she had a right one here the assistant began ever so loudly drumming her fingers on the counter. 'If you only want an ice cream,' she repeated so loudly she alerted the male under manager, 'could I suggest you try the shop round the corner or you could get one in the café on the other side of the road.'

'Aye, you're right there,' Luke responded, slapping down a ten-shilling note, 'but it'll no be served up by the lassie. I just have to have a word with in her shell-like ear.'

'Here,' the woman expounded loudly, 'you're no this guy that's so madly in love with her that he stalks her?'

'Me?' exclaimed Luke.

The woman now scrutinised Luke before drawling, 'Right enough. You're a bit on the young side to have earned enough to be going to retire to the south of France.'

This statement from the cashier did not shake Luke. He had more than enough experience to know that Josie had taken the poor deluded woman for a trip up the yellow brick road. However he was more than a bit put out when the woman added, 'By the way, Josie was a bit under the weather so she left for home half an hour ago.'

Sheer frustration caused Luke to lift up his money and turning on his heel he fled the foyer.

Luke had just turned down into Restalrig Road and had to slow down as a thirty-five bus drew out in front of him. He was just about to signal his annoyance to the driver when he noticed that Josie was now standing at the front of the bus waiting to alight at the next stop which was around the corner in Lochend Avenue.

Drawing to a halt further down Restalrig Road, Luke waited until Josie started the final leg of her journey home to Ryehill.

When she drew level with Luke's car he leaned over and opened the passenger door. 'Right, Josie,' he cried, 'in you get.'

Josie appeared to freeze with fear. Eyes bulging she stuttered, 'Oh, it's you, Luke. You fair scared me. Thought you were . . . well never mind who I thought you were.' Hesitating for a minute, her demeanour very quickly changed from that of presenting herself as an alarmed rabbit to one of a flighty, naughty bird. 'Oh, Luke,' she teased, 'you've caught me out. Just sneaking down to Ryehill, I am, to make sure everything is all right and then I'll be in a hurry to get back to my love nest in William Street. Oh, I do so hope Victor isn't worried about where I am.'

Luke was now out of the car, and seizing Josie by the arm he bundled her into the passenger seat of his car. 'Just give it a rest, Josie,' he exploded. 'I rumbled what you were doing from the start. Now just hold your wheesht until I get you down to your house. And my lady, when we get there you and I are going to sit down and draw up a plan to get you out of the mess you've gotten yourself into.'

'You are wrong. Victor . . .'

'Victor has a long-suffering wife. He has no intention of marrying you or any of his other playthings.' Luke started up the car but before he released the brake he spat, 'And get real because Victor, although he won't admit it, is nearly over the hill so he will never *ever* leave Anna.'

'He will,' she protested vehemently.

'No he won't! And that's because, besides them being staunch Catholic, she's a good meal ticket for him.'

'What do you mean?'

'Just that any paramour can be replaced but Anna and her family's money is his insurance policy for a comfortable old age. And Anna, God bless the fool that she is, will never divorce him. Bet when she vowed to stay with him for better or for worse she always knew it would be for worse.'

The rain was falling steadily when Bobby arrived home and he raised his briefcase over his head so he could shelter from the worst of it as he raced to get indoors.

He didn't require his keys to gain entry to his home as Lois was standing in the open doorway to welcome him.

Throwing down his briefcase he exclaimed, 'You saw me coming?'

She beamed. 'I've been standing in the drawing-room window for half an hour just willing you to put in an appearance.'

'Oh,' he replied, removing his sodden raincoat, 'from that remark I take it your two-day trip to Inverness has been eventful.'

She nodded. By now they were seated facing each other at the large kitchen table. Bobby grimaced. 'I know how you feel. I haven't had an easy time either with this Joseph Kelly's appeal.'

Lois got up and poured herself and Bobby a cup of freshly brewed coffee. 'Right,' she began, 'as the meal will take another half hour to cook itself how about you and I go through to the drawing room and sit down and you tell me what your worries are?'

Bobby was sitting beside Lois on the sofa when he started to speak. 'You see, the more I go into Irish's, as Luke calls him, case the more I get sucked into the mire.' Bobby was now unconsciously twisting a lock of Lois' hair through his fingers. 'There's just so much that is wrong. So much that has been botched and in trying to be fair to Joseph Kelly, and he is my client so I have to be, I may have to see a brother solicitor brought before the Law Society.'

Lois remained silent while she considered what Bobby had just imparted to her. Pensively she said, 'No names. I don't wish you to identify the person, just acquaint me with the problem.'

'Alcohol!'

Nodding steadily she allowed a solitary 'Ah' to escape her mouth before she became just a listener again.

'He was qualified. Very much so, and more experienced than I am to take on the defence of someone accused of murder, but,' Bobby sighed, 'why had it to be that when he most needed to be on his toes he was completely befuddled by booze?' Blowing out his lips Bobby allowed a long pause before he continued, 'You see he should have known and pointed out to the jury that Joseph Kelly was still aboard his seagoing ship on the night that the Leith detectives, Washington and Watson, managed to bully the Lees into saying he had been in the takeaway.' Still toying with Lois' hair Bobby stopped deliberating while he thought again.

Lois knew that the best way she could assist him with his dilemma was to remain sitting silently beside him. Eventually, in a faltering voice Bobby went on, 'You see, the opening up again of this case could result in the destruction of at least three people's careers – but I have a duty to ensure that any miscarriages of justice are put right – so I do not intend to warn anybody of the grounds I am preparing the appeal on. They know what they have done and what the consequences will probably be. And if they were in my shoes they would also follow procedure.'

Bobby turned then to Lois and smiled. 'How selfish of me, now my darling, you have my full attention so what was it you wished to discuss with me?'

'Just that I need your full attention in the kitchen. Our evening meal should be well and truly cooked.' Leading the way out of the room she allowed her laughter to ripple as she advanced into the kitchen. 'Well done, did I say?' she continued as she rescued the dish from the oven. 'Some might even say well fired.'

*   *   *

Luke and Josie were sitting at the kitchen table refreshing themselves with coffee. Without warning Josie spluttered, 'It is not what you think, Luke. Okay, I was led up the garden path by Victor and he's now a closed book. Taking that into consideration I am managing very well.'

Luke gave out a long sarcastic cackle. 'So you are! And how many jobs do you have and how much do you make from selling choc ices?'

There was no immediate verbal reply from Josie but she did signal by raising three fingers on her left hand to indicate the number of different work places she was servicing.

'And where and what are they?'

'Alfredo's at lunchtime but,' she squirmed, 'that will only be for another two days as I am only filling in for Anna. I promised her I'd stay until she gets back.' She grimaced. 'Two more days is all that I have.'

'And?'

'The usherette's job and, okay, the pay is basic but Luke,' Josie garbled while becoming animated, 'it has its perks.'

'Such as?'

'I don't have to pay to watch the pictures, and if an ice cream is melting . . .'

'For heaven's sake, Josie, you are how old?'

'Mid-forties . . . but I pass for late-thirties, don't you think?'

Rolling his eyes to look at the ceiling, Luke despaired. 'To be truthful, the way you are carrying on you could pass for ten. And the other job?'

Drawing lazy circles on the tablecloth with her index finger, Josie confided, 'I'm a bingo caller . . . just in the Bowling Club . . . but they say I'm so good at it I should apply to the Capitol in Manderson Street.'

'That is just bloody capital,' shrieked Luke.

'So what do you want me to do? I have to pay my mortgage. I have to eat.'

'You do and tomorrow you are going to have a great big feed of . . .'

He was looking directly at her and she could see he meant business so she mumbled, 'Humble pie.'

He nodded.

Lois and Bobby were lying comfortably in bed when Lois said, 'I managed to sort everything out at Smithton.'

'You did?' Bobby chuckled. 'But then I always knew you would.'

Lois was now twittering too. 'I knew I had the skill but it was keeping your mother out of my hair that I thought would be the problem.'

Bobby was now laughing uncontrollably and through his shrieks he stuttered, 'Aye, but you didn't know I had arranged for her to be kept busy down here.'

'Like how?'

'Like having Aunt Josie going off on another love affair which left Mum having to run the Four Marys.'

'Right enough. And with Margo requiring her copulation visit to a Swiss clinic financed she could hardly shut up shop.'

Bobby pretended to become slowly serious and, taking Lois in his arms, he mischievously murmured in her ear, 'And, my dear, aren't we lucky that we didn't need to yodel up a Swiss mountain before you . . . ?'

Lois was now shaking with laughter as she mumbled in Bobby's ear, 'And isn't it wonderful for us, and us alone, to know what a randy, persistent never-satisfied stud you are?'

'That reminds me, how about you relieve my stress the way you usually do?'

'Bobby, I'm an expectant mother now so try and behave,' Lois replied as she snuggled closer into him.

Saturday morning's weather was perfect for a funeral. The dark eerie clouds appeared to be so heavy that they merged into the sea. Sally, looking out of the window and across to the shoreline, was in two minds as to whether she would go to Elspeth Stock's funeral or not.

To be truthful she had never met the woman but she did know about her through her husband, David. It was also true that David and she had an understanding and a good relationship had developed between them. She knew he would be requiring support and she felt, as she was to be the future Mrs Stock, it was her place to be his tower of strength. However, in addition to David's need there were also his two young adult daughters to be considered. With all this in mind she decided she would go to the funeral but she would be the soul of discretion and stay unobtrusively in the background.

When she arrived by taxi at the Seafield Road entrance to Leith's crematorium she was so pleased to see Nancy waiting at the gates for her. She sighed before thinking, *It's true I have done a lot for Nancy but she has always more than paid me back. Who else would have thought that today it would be good for me to have a friend beside me?*

Typical of Sally she ushered Nancy into the waiting room. From there they would be able to go unobtrusively into the back of the chapel.

Neither Nancy nor Sally tried to make idle conversation while they awaited the arrival of the hearse and official cars which would be carrying the principal mourners.

The entourage had just come into view when Sally grabbed Nancy's arm and steered her towards the flight of steps at the back entrance.

As funeral turnouts go Elspeth's was moderate so there were not many who did not enter through the front door and past the main mourners. By entering from the rear, Sally and Nancy were able to view the mourners as they entered.

Sally's hand flew to her mouth as she witnessed pale, drawn and emotional David's entrance into the chapel. She was of a mind to fly down to him and assist him with his grief. Luckily a young woman, whom Sally judged to be one of his daughters, slipped her arm through his and he turned and acknowledged her kindness with a weak smile. The rest of the main party was made up of two weeping young women, who were supporting each other, and some elderly relatives.

The service went well but when David stood back to offer his hand to an elderly couple, the man just looked contemptuously at him. The old man then turned to the lady and he took her arm and tucked it into his. However, before they left the crematorium they spoke to the two weeping young women. All four then looked accusingly at David and all he appeared to be able to do was shrug his shoulders and raise his hands in a sign of hopelessness or was it surrender?

'What's all that about?' Nancy asked Sally.

'Don't know and here, look at the other aisle.' Nancy turned to look where Sally was indicating and was amazed to see Phil Watson and an older man and woman.

She became even more dumbfounded when the trio made their way over to the young woman who had comforted David and they began an earnest conversation with her.

'Here, Nancy,' Sally mumbled, 'is that lassie pregnant?'

'And how,' blurted Nancy.

Sally and Nancy stood waiting outside the crematorium to summon a taxi when they were approached by Phil Watson.

Without an introduction he announced, 'I was invited to the boiled ham tea but och, it's no my scene.' Sally and Nancy did not respond so Phil, who obviously wanted to impart something to them, continued. 'Says a lot for you, Sally. What I mean is, there's no many that would have pitched up here the day to pay their respects . . .'

Sally had made up her mind not to rise to his bait but Nancy replied, 'And why should Sally no turn up here? David and she have been more than pals for years.'

'Aye,' scoffed Phil, 'she got away with that with poor Elspeth but now that sneaky Davie has put our Barbara up the . . .'

'Your sister, Barbara,' Nancy gasped, grabbing hold of Phil's coat lapels, 'has been put in the family way by David Stock?'

Phil began to cackle. 'Oh my gawd, dinnae tell me you didnae ken?' He now put his arms about Sally who was gaping. 'Are you saying he never telt you?'

Sally slowly shook her head.

'But,' Phil stuttered and blustered, 'he said he was gonnae put you straight about Barbara when he called in to warn that loose cannon of a brother of yours not to start stirring the shite in that loser Irish's case.'

Sally had recovered somewhat and she burst out of Phil's hold to retaliate with, 'Well not only did he not tell me about his good news . . .'

'Which makes you wonder if at his age that somebody didnae have it in for him?' Nancy quipped and was surprised when she was withered by a glower from Sally.

'But,' Sally continued, returning her attention to Phil, 'he made no impression, and here I emphasise, no impression on my brother either. But then he couldn't because he'll never be the upstanding man my brother is. And as to you, sonny boy, I'd watch out because not only does my brother have you in his sights but so also does my son.' Sally paused to savour the minute before adding, 'And a formidable team they are so I hope your coat is not hanging on a shoogly nail!'

She said no more and was thankful that Nancy had got the attention of a passing taxi and it had just pulled up to take them on board when Sally jumped in.

'Where to, ladies?' the cab driver enquired.

Nancy and Sally answered in unison. Nancy suggested Seaview Terrace and Sally the Royal Stuart in Easter Road.

Rattling his knuckles on the glass divisional panel the driver asked, 'Will I guess which one or will one of you . . . ?'

'The Four Marys on the Shore,' Sally ordered.

'Is it a pub crawl or something you're going on?' the cabbie asked, scratching his head.

Sally and Nancy both ignored the man. However, Nancy did ask Sally, 'Are you sure you want to go to work today . . . after . . . ?'

'Look, Nancy,' Sally faltered, 'if you think I'm going to run and hide then you don't know me!' Nancy leaned back and nodded. 'Don't you realise,' Sally continued in a voice that grew stronger with each utterance, 'if I learned anything from Harry deserting me it is that you *face* your demons – no way will I hide. This isn't my embarrassment, it's David's.'

'So?' the impatient driver demanded.

'You heard the lady,' Nancy crooned, 'she's not for turning so it's all speed ahead towards the Four Marys on the Shore.'

The taxi had just departed with Nancy who had instructed the driver to take her to the Royal Stuart on Easter Road when Sally strutted into the Four Marys.

Rita was behind the bar having a verbal argument with a pint of McEwan's Best and Sally lifted the hatch and took the troublesome drink from her and poured off half of the offending froth.

'Know something?'

Sally sniggered. Rita always started off a conversation with 'Know something,' and Sally's habitual reply was, 'Not 'til you tell me, Rita.' Today was no different and Sally obliged with, 'Not 'til you tell me, Rita.'

'It's just that I don't think I'm ever going to get the hang of changing a barrel of beer.'

'Is this you telling me that I need to slip off my shoes and go down into the cellar and do just that?'

Rita nodded before turning to address the customers, 'You're in luck now. Sure, Sally will get down into the bowels of the earth and sort out the beer problem.'

Stepping back and opening up the trapdoor Sally was soon tripping down the wooden stairs into the cellar and, as was the correct safety procedure, Rita banged the cellar door shut again. Deftly, Sally changed the problem barrel for a new one. Having checked all the other barrels and counting the numbers that were still in stock, Sally felt an overwhelming sense of cold gloom engulf her. Sinking against the old, damp, musty stone wall she knew that here in this medieval, ghostly atmosphere, where plague victims had been housed, she would be able to allow herself the luxury of weeping out her disappointment and humiliation. Here she was all alone and only this cellar would be witness to how she really felt about David Stock's betrayal.

Tears cascading, body quivering, she stayed there until the sharp banging of Rita's heel on the trapdoor had her sniff, wipe her eyes and call out, 'Just give me another minute and I'll come up.'

Emerging from the dungeon, Sally was a bit breathless.

'Here,' remarked Rita, 'did you get a splash back . . . your mascara's fled from your eyes down to your cheeks.'

Sally managed a weak smile. 'No, it's just so damp down there that I hadn't realised that when I leant my face against the wall it would get soaked.'

Rita was about to ask why Sally required to rest her face on the wall to change a barrel of beer when she remembered the mess she had got into was all because Sally had arrived late. 'Here Sally,' she began, 'I'm sorry about the shambles but where have you been? You're an hour late.'

Taking out a handkerchief Sally began to wipe her face. 'If you must know I went to Elspeth Stock's funeral.'

'You what?' shrieked Rita, finishing with a splutter.

'I did because I wished to pay my respects. And before you go on I'm pleased I did because there was an old couple there, which I now know were her parents. Oh, Rita, they were gutted.'

'Well they would be and tell me, was Elspeth's replacement there?'

'Yes,' was Sally's curt reply before trying to push her brow up into her hairline.

'Well at least now you're not kidding on that the lassie and the predicament don't exist.'

A slow hissing sound escaped from Sally before she quietly said, 'I really was ignorant of the situation. You see, none of you, my supposed friends, told me.'

'What?' exploded Rita, 'Don't tell me the cowardly bastard never confessed to you?'

Sally, who was making her way to the ladies to clean herself up, just shook her head.

'Aw well,' responded Rita defiantly, 'I might as well tell you the rest that you seem not to know.' Sally turned to look directly at Rita who gleefully went on, 'Everybody's saying last man frees all.'

Sally full of sarcasm chuckled. 'Know what, Rita?'

'No 'til you tell me, Sally.'

'You and Nancy certainly have some wonderful turns of phrases.'

Before Rita could respond, the front door opened and in walked Luke.

'Morning, sorry, good afternoon, ladies,' he trilled.

Rita nodded but Sally disappeared into the toilet.

By the time Sally presented herself in the public bar again Luke had already put in his order for lunch and he was busy reading the morning paper.

'Slumming today are you?' Sally joked, pulling the paper away from Luke.

'Aye, you see I have this wee problem with a sister that I have to get sorted out.'

Guessing wrongly that Luke was going to go on about

David Stock, Sally hissed, 'Okay, so you were right about David Stock. But listen and listen good because I am up to here with it.' Sally's hand was now indicating above her head. 'So why don't you go and eat where you ate yesterday?'

This outburst wrong-footed Luke. 'Here, wait a minute, I came in here to speak about our Josie and you go into a tirade about something I know nothing about.'

'Luke, dinnae tell me,' Rita huffed, 'that you're like Sally and didnae ken 'til now that David Stock has put a lassie younger than his daughters in the family way?'

Obviously not knowing whether he should be looking to Sally or Rita for confirmation, Luke's head swung from side to side.

'You're not alone at being left in the dark, Luke. Didn't stupid me go to his wife's funeral to show him support and lo and behold it wasn't my arm he needed. No, idiot that he is, requires a refresher course on how to change shitty nappies!'

'Now Sally, be truthful, you know I always,' Luke began then stopped to give an exaggerated shudder, 'was wary of him. To me he came over as an unctuous, slimy sneak.'

Sally sighed before rolling her eyes and looking up to the ceiling for assistance.

On the other hand, Rita was relishing the assassination of David's character and she wanted to be in on it so she added, 'Snake in the grass is what I judged him to be.'

Before lowering her eyes Sally withered both Luke and Rita with a warning stare. Without saying a word Rita disappeared into the kitchen. Luke, who it would appear, did not know when to come in out of the rain, whispered discreetly to Sally. 'Now,' he began, taking a seat at the table in front of him, 'let's forget all about that apology of a man you were smitten with. We as a family have other important things to get sorted out. Now, why I called in here today is to . . .'

The loud banging open of the ranch-style door of the kitchen was followed by Rita calling out, 'Right, Luke, here's your lunch,' and a plate was flung down in front of him.

Looking down at the contents of the plate Luke became amused. 'Rita,' he chuckled, 'this is egg and chips and I ordered steak pie and two veg.'

'Ah well,' retorted Rita, 'if that was what you wanted you should have come in here yesterday – Friday. Today is Saturday and all the office and business workers either don't work on a Saturday or they skedaddle hame at lunchtime so there's nae use in doing lunches on a Saturday and that menu you ordered from was Friday's.'

Luke looked at Sally for confirmation. She just nodded.

Rita, of course, was not finished and flicking a tea towel over the bar she continued, 'And seeing you're the wee brother of the boss I especially made you some egg and chips. But if you dinnae want them pass them back.'

Lifting the salt cellar Luke sprinkled some salt on the chips before starting to devour them. Between mouthfuls he gabbled, 'Now, about Josie . . .'

'Luke, I've had enough of bampots for one day so if you don't mind, could the sorting out of our Josie wait?'

'But I was just thinking it would be best for both of you if Josie . . .'

'Look,' Sally interrupted, 'if you don't mind I'd like to go quietly insane on my own.'

Ignoring Sally's remark Luke went on, 'It would just

145

mean Josie coming back in here which would leave you to stay out of it all in your guest house.'

'That right? Well if you or anybody else thinks I'll not be in residence here all of next week then think again. One thing I intend is for everyone to think I am not bothered and that I am getting on with my life. And who knows, in time I could probably end up having bigger fish to fry than David Stock.'

When Sally arrived home at Seaview Terrace, Maggie was still on duty.

'Had a good day?' was Maggie's oily greeting.

'Aye,' replied Sally to gloating Maggie.

'Any shocks?'

'Aye, my brother Luke thinks we should do Saturday lunches in the Four Marys.'

'Oh. Well there have been three surprises in here.'

'Like what?'

'For a start your mother-in-law wants you to put her and her sister up next week. And that's probably why Harry's coming to see you tomorrow.'

'No way does he put a foot in that door.'

'Well you tell him that because I'm still not talking to him after what he did to me. Gutted I was when he left me for a warbling bimbo.'

Sally was about to remind Maggie that both she and Harry had subjected her to worse but she was too tired and considered it wasn't worth the effort. So, stifling a yawn she mumbled, 'And the third problem?'

'No exactly a problem, Sally. It was a telephone call from a Mrs Kelly in Donegal and she says that her son has told her you will put her up when she comes to visit him next week.'

A long sigh escaped Sally before she uttered, 'That will be just fine. I'm really looking forward to meeting Irish's mum and I'm even happier to put her up.'

Leith Links is like Portobello's promenade. No matter what time of day or night it is you will be sure to meet someone who will wish to pass the time of day with you.

Sitting on one of the benches that faced the bandstand, Nancy had been approached by two people. The first was a lady walking her dog: to be truthful she wasn't walking it but carrying it. 'Would you believe them up at the Dick Vet say I should just have him put doon,' the woman croaked as she massaged the dog's right ear.

Nancy smiled. To be truthful, from her first glance at the dog she had come to the same conclusion as the vets. The broken-hearted woman had then just wandered away. Two minutes later a small urchin-like boy approached, but before he sat down beside her he looked furtively about. Licking his lips he then started to beguile her. 'See that bus,' he began with a backward jerk of his thumb, 'it's going back up to Lochend where I bide and the snotty conductor won't let me on unless I have the whole fare.' Winking and looking into Nancy eyes he went on, 'So missus, could you lend me a bob?'

'A bob?' shrieked Nancy. 'But a bus fare doesn't cost anything like a whole shilling.'

'Aye, but I'm hungry tae and I'll need to get a bag of chips before I go hame,' the waif argued convincingly.

Nancy was about to refuse the boy when she noticed Benny racing over the links towards her. Fishing in her purse she took out a florin and thrust it into the astonished urchin's hand.

Benny arrived at her side in time to hear the laddie exclaim, 'Thanks a million, missus. I'll try and see you again next week. And dinnae bother gieing ony o' yer money to ony scrounging chancers until you've seen me all right?'

'What was all that about?' Benny enquired before sitting down on the bench beside her.

'Just a wee streetwise bairn that thinks my head buttons up the back. But never mind him, I'm so pleased to see you.' Nancy started wringing her hands together as she looked away into the distance. 'You see, I thought you wouldn't want to know me or ever speak to me again after I told you the truth about myself.'

Rocking uneasily on the bench, Benny allowed his fingers to drum over the wooden surface until he had taken Nancy's hand into his. 'No speak to you? But me saying nothing wasnae that I thought badly of you, oh no.' Benny paused. Nancy tried to look into his eyes but he kept his gaze averted. 'No. I was ashamed of myself. There was you who had suffered more than me being honest enough to tell me the truth about yourself and there was me . . .'

'You have a secret too?'

Benny nodded before releasing Nancy's hand so he could vigorously wipe his hands over his suit jacket. 'Nancy, when I was wee my mammy died. My daddy took tae the booze, got married again and I ended up in care.'

'Whereabouts?'

The stroking of his suit jacket gained momentum. He was also gasping and shaking but he managed to blurt, 'It doesnae matter where it was. But if you have to ken it was oot Lasswade way and that's aw I'm saying.'

'Oh, Benny,' Nancy sobbed. 'You don't have to tell me

what happened to you. See these bastards that masquerade as disciples of God and then they go on to prey on wee laddies put into their care. Know what I would do? Castrate the lot with a blunt knife and no anaesthetic.'

'But how do ye ken about what happened there?'

'You're no first and unfortunately you won't be the last either, to have a need to tell what happened. And you don't need to tell me either that when you were being raped and you cried out in agony the blasted Fathers enjoyed it all the more. And not one Christian soul in that godforsaken place came to your rescue.'

Benny was now crying profusely and Nancy put her arm around him. 'Cry all you want, love. I'm here and I'll help to heal you. You see, when I was on the streets there would be men, who because of what had happened to them, were unable to have a proper relationship with a woman. So the poor sods would pick up a . . .' she hesitated, '. . . seasoned whore like me to practise on. They would confess to me how they couldn't quite face having natural sex with a woman after years of being . . .' She stopped. She appeared to have run out of steam. But it wasn't that, it was the knowledge that the abuse that Benny had suffered was still being carried out on other vulnerable young boys that was causing her grief. Sensing her distress, Benny tentatively put a strong, protective arm about her. 'But Benny, at least at times like that,' she whimpered, 'I felt I had done something to help some helpless human being and had not just been used as an expendable commodity.'

'Know something, Nancy?'

Snuffling, Nancy replied, 'Well as I'm not a mind reader . . . not until you tell me.'

'I'm always amazed at the big words you use. You're no a

dope and you seemed to have helped these poor men that were probably schooled with me so why could you no have helped yourself?'

Raising her head Nancy gazed up into the sky. 'When my sister committed suicide I lost all heart,' she mumbled. 'That was until Sally Mack came into my life . . . and now you. So now, don't you know, it'll be easy for me to live a decent life.'

'Are you saying you still think we should get married even though you now know I might never be able to . . . that I'm full of disgust and loathing about that side of life.'

'Sssh,' Nancy replied, squeezing his hand hard to draw his attention to the fact that some people had stopped to watch and listen to them. 'Don't say anther word.' She moved closer into him before whispering, 'Pull yourself together love, and in a minute or two we'll just get up and walk away quietly.'

He nodded before fishing in his pocket for a handkerchief to wipe his streaming nose and eyes.

The audience didn't appear to wish to leave so Nancy said, 'You know, Benny, when I was a wee lassie I used to come here with my mammy on a Sunday afternoon just to listen to the Leith band. They had some wonderful trumpeters. Trained they were either in the Boys Brigade or the Industrial School. Oh, look at the time. Elio's will be open in ten minutes. Honestly Benny,' she chorused, patting his hand, 'you just will never ever have tasted such fish and chips as darling Elio dishes up.'

Nancy and Benny rose together and Nancy smiled at the crowd and said, 'Hope you enjoyed the peep show. We're away to eat now but if you like you could always come and watch us through Elio's window.'

Linking arms the two made their way over the links, up Morton Street and then into Duke Street. 'Did you mean it when you said we were going to get our tea in Elio's?' Benny enquired like a little boy asking for a treat.

'Of course. Mind you, you'll be paying. But if you're good I'll supply you with a nice cup of tea and some chocolate biscuits when we get home to my place.'

Looking about furtively Benny then whispered, 'Oh, Nancy, you'll never need to worry about money again. Sure I've been a long-distance lorry driver all of my working life and I always put a wee bit by.' He cocked his head and winked at her. 'Would you believe it's all safely stored in the co-op savings bank?'

Nancy laughed. 'Did you never go out and enjoy yourself with the boys or go on holiday?'

He shook his head. 'No. Never trusted anybody enough. Frightened I was that they would find out about me and be . . . och well.' He shrugged, sniffed, and sighed before his demeanour lightened. 'But,' he began, a wide grin now on his face, 'all that's going to change. I've now got you and, God willing, I'll never need anybody else.' Squeezing her arm tighter he added huskily, 'I just can't believe I'll never be lonely again.'

'Hmmmm,' was all she replied, but inwardly she thought, *And amen to that.*

It had been her intention to do some work on her books. She had sat down on the comfy settee with the cash book on her knee. She noted that the sun was shining brightly through the downstairs lounge window and it seemed only natural to turn her face towards its welcoming glow. Yesterday had been such an awful day – raining relentlessly both outside and in her heart. Closing her eyes she allowed the warmth of the rays to relax her.

The shrill ringing of the doorbell suddenly awakened her and as she jumped up the cash book dropped at her feet. Not waiting to pick up the ledger she ran into the hallway and pulled open the outside door.

Sally had been tutored by Flora, a highland lady, who never resorted to swearing no matter how sorely she was tried. Nonetheless, the gentleman standing on the doorstep had Sally forget herself. 'What the hell do you want?' she hissed through clenched teeth. 'If it's accommodation, as you can see I have no vacancies and furthermore you are no longer welcome in my home.'

'I know you're angry and disappointed in me,' David Stock burst out. 'But hear me out and not here on the doorstep where we may be overheard.'

Sally stood back to allow him to enter.

Once they were in her private lounge Sally seated herself down on an armchair. No way was she going to sit on the settee where David and she usually sat intimately together.

Pacing the room David began. 'I know I should have told you that I had become involved with Barbara. I want you to know that I'm sorry.'

Spluttering, Sally crowed, 'Involved! Sorry! Have you lost your senses? Your wife was dying. You took advantage of an impressionable lassie who is younger than your daughters. You were her Commanding Officer. You're supposed to set an example of decency.'

David stopped to look out of the window which meant he had his back to Sally. 'Look, I didn't need to come here today to explain myself. But,' he emphasised, half turning towards her, 'what I wished to say was that yes – I will do the decent thing and marry Barbara. I will be truthful with her and tell her about our arrangements. She will also require to be accepting that our relationship, which has always been platonic, will continue in that vein.'

Sinking back in her chair Sally looked dumbfounded. 'David,' she gasped, incredulity ringing in her voice, 'if the police force has a head shrinker on hand could I suggest you make an appointment? You've lost the place – that is if you ever had it. Surely you are aware of the hurt and humiliation you have caused.'

Before responding he took a few steps towards her but halted when she put up a restraining hand. 'And who exactly, other than yourself, have I hurt and humiliated?'

Her mouth gaped and her head rocked from side to side as his audacity shocked her. 'Didn't you see the effect your actions are having on Elspeth's parents?' she spat. 'How do you think your lassies feel? Their mother wasn't even dead and you were bedding someone younger than they are.' Her final taunt was to jeer, 'David, the humiliation is yours and yours alone. You were the most respected of police officers and now you are the laughing stock – an object of ridicule.'

He advanced towards the door, but before exiting he turned. 'I take it from what you have said that our relationship is at an end.'

Sally scrambled to her feet. 'David, why don't you grow up? Do you think that Barbara won't put the screws on you once the ring is on her finger?' She paused to reflect. 'She has already. After all, why did you come here to warn my brother off trying to get justice for Irish?' Sally gave a derisive titter before adding, 'And please note Irish is going to be the death of Phil Watson, your brother-in-law to be.'

'You think so?'

'I know so because there is evidence that things were not done by the rules. And David, you never would have wrongly used your position to assist him if Barbara hadn't wheedled.'

The kettle had just started to sing when the door bell rang again. *Surely*, Sally thought, *that David Stock has not come to my door again for round two.*

Opening the door she was again surprised. This time it was Margo accompanied by her father, Harry, carrying a large bouquet of red roses.

A long exhale hissed from Sally's lips. 'You know I must go and check the calendar.'

'Why would you do that, Mum?' Margo twittered as she proceeded into the house.

'Because with the goings-on of the morning I am beginning to think it must be April Fool's day instead of the end of blooming June.'

All three had just got themselves seated in the lounge when Margo pulled a grimace before blurting, 'Oh Mum, we found out by accident. Well to be truthful it's the talk of the place, about David Stock.'

'And?'

'Mum, Dad and I are here to support you. Both of us are heart sorry that you've had such a . . .'

'What?'

'Shock. I mean it was no secret that you cherished hopes that some day you and David Stock would . . .'

'That's very good of you but could I say I don't require any . . . anything from anybody, especially you two.'

Harry gave a few guttural coughs before he spoke. 'Sally,

don't be brave. Now that you and I are going to be grandparents, wouldn't it be nice to show the world we are one big happy family?'

'But, Harry, you hardly know our son, Bobby, and you have never met his wife, Lois, so why do you . . . ?'

'It's not Bobby's baby that's going to bring us all together but Margo's. See when she told me!' He turned to face Margo. 'It's over three weeks now since you announced your good news to the world.' Margo nodded and smiled.

'Not the world, Harry, just you. And thank you for telling me that I will soon be welcoming another grandchild.'

Sally got up on her feet, made a show of dusting herself down, before spitting, 'Now if that's all for today, could I bid you goodbye. I have a lot to tend to and don't forget to take your roses with you.'

Margo was astounded. 'Mum, have you nothing to say to me?' she cried.

'Not that I would wish a stranger to hear,' Sally emphasised before indicating with several jabs of her right thumb that Harry and Margo should leave. Flinging the door open wide she smiled sweetly at them as they passed by her.

'But, Mum,' pleaded Margo, 'surely you wish to congratulate me on becoming pregnant. I'm giving you your wish to become a granny.'

'Ah,' Sally replied, triumphantly, 'Bobby beat you to that. And now will you please leave my home and don't return as long as you think I am an afterthought.'

Harry snorted, 'Can't you see that if you take up my offer to come back into your life you will be able to hold your head up. Be respected.'

Sally's derisive laughter echoed through the house. 'Take

you back,' she hissed. 'Oh, Harry, I may be desperate but I'm certainly not suicidal!'

After making sure Margo and Harry had left, Sally sank down on to the settee. Scalding tears rushed to her eyes. *I know*, she thought, *that he is a bounder and no matter what, he will always be yesterday's man to me. But Margo, you were my first born. I loved and still love you so much, so why do you always have to slap me in the face?* She sighed. *But, Margo, do you realise that by telling your father first about your baby, the baby that wouldn't have been if I hadn't financed your Swiss treatment, may prove to be your long overdue undoing.*

She was still sitting quietly when she heard the door open and Luke call, 'Sally, it's me. Hope you're in residence, my lady. Because how about the two of us nipping over to the Rockville restaurant on the other side of the street for a bite to eat?'

'One good idea,' Sally answered, 'because no way am I in the mood for cooking. Besides there's nothing other than bacon, sausages and black pudding in the fridge.'

The Rockville hotel which housed the restaurant and three letting bedrooms was owned and run by an Italian family. Sally regularly took her family to dine there on a Sunday.

Sally chuckled when Sophia, the mother of the family, approached to pass the time of day with her. During the three, nearly four, years that Sally had owned the bed and breakfast on the other side of the street a genuine interest in each other's businesses and a friendliness had developed between the families.

'Busy?' Sophia asked, handing Luke and Sally a menu.

Sally nodded. 'Yes. I'm booked out for next week and already the festival is proving a draw for tourists. How about you?'

'Hmmm,' Sophia mumbled, taking out a chair and sitting down beside Sally. 'We've got the chance of a prime site in Musselburgh, opposite the race course, so . . .'

'Och, don't tell me you'll be selling up?'

'To be truthful I'm not so keen. But we only have the three letting bedrooms and one of them is a single.' She blew out her lips. 'Tried to persuade Dom to stay, especially as,' Sophia leaned in closer to Sally to whisper, 'I heard, and from a reliable source, that the rundown house three doors along from you is coming on to the market.'

'Is it?' Sally exclaimed, looking at Luke.

'Aye, and won't that be a good buy for someone who wants something cheap that they can upgrade.'

Sally nodded.

'You wouldn't think of taking on that house yourself?'

'No, Sophia. You see I've extended out the back and now have eight letting rooms with facilities and when you add on my private apartment, well that's more than enough for me.' Sophia looked despondent. 'But tell you what, if I think of someone I'll give them the nod. Mind you, that will only be if you can't persuade Dom to stay in good old Porty and take the ramshackle place on.'

'That was an excellent meal,' Luke remarked as he finished off his tiramisu.

'Always is. If Sophia and Dom do leave I hope this place will be taken over by someone who knows how to cook.'

Looking about, Luke said, 'They do have a lot of ground.' Sally nodded. 'Then why don't they extend here?'

'Don't know,' she replied but he felt her thoughts were elsewhere now.

Pouring himself another cup of coffee from the pot Sophia had left on the table, Luke started to make clucking sounds by clicking his tongue. 'You want to say something?' he asked.

She nodded her head and then shook it.

Not sure what she was trying to indicate he rested his elbows on the table before tentatively continuing with, 'Well I have something to say but I'm frightened to open my mouth because you said I was not to mention Josie until . . . whenever.'

She exhaled deeply before replying, 'Look, with the day I've just had with some that are supposed to be my nearest and dearest, speaking about Josie right now would be the final straw.'

Adding another spoonful of sugar into his coffee, Luke allowed his tongue to click several times before saying, 'Sally, I met our half-brother, John, in Taylor Gardens and he had a wee lassie with him. A lovely wee bright thing.'

Simpering, Sally chimed, 'Our Ellen. Great bairn. Mind you I'll soon be having two wee ones of my own.'

'Lois is having twins?'

'No, Luke, would you believe that my Margo just happened to forget to tell me she was pregnant? Mind you she did remember to tell her dad.' Sally sighed. 'You have to hand it to my Margo for having the highest polished brass neck going.'

Luke mused. 'See when I met Ellen I realised I was going to miss the bus.'

'The bus?'

'What I mean is if I don't get hitched soon I'll be too old to be a doting daddy.'

'Right enough, you're racing towards thirty-nine.'

Straightening himself up Luke blustered, 'Okay, so I am. But I'm wearing well and everybody says I could be taken for twenty-nine.'

'That right?'

'Aye, and before you go shooting me down in flames just remember you're pushing fifty-five.'

'So I am. But I'm the mother of three adult children and like you I could pass for being ten years younger.'

'Back to where we should be,' Luke chanted as he positioned the salt cellar nearer to himself. 'I was wondering, as I have only another seven weeks leave to go, if you'd like to chum me down to London for a few days?'

'What?' exclaimed Sally. 'Are you forgetting you have to get Irish sorted out? Which means you still have to get Jessie Scott by the throat and try and discover why she gave the testament she did.'

'I know that we have to work out why she did what she did. And the other things I have to find out are who put her up to it and what was her motive. Mind you, to do that I will have to get hold of her.'

'What's keeping you back, Luke?'

'Just that I think someone may have whispered in her shell-like ear that her testimony was going to be looked at again. And that the powers that be will not be pleased if it can be proved that she lied.'

'And you get a custodial sentence for trying to pervert the course of justice.'

'Precisely. So I think she's done a runner. But knowing Jessie it'll be just for a day or two then when she's worked out a plan of action to save herself she'll surface again. Mind you, the minute she hears that there may be a whole judicial enquiry then,' he chuckled, 'she'll dive right down her bolthole again.'

'But why would she do that?'

Luke pondered. 'Well someone killed Marie and I think that Jessie just might know who and that information could cost her dearly.'

Perplexed, Sally muttered, 'Leave it with me. I'll ask Nancy where she thinks Jessie might be.'

'Good. Now back to London. Sally, before I left Hong Kong I was getting real friendly with a lassie. Her father's been on the force for years. She stays London way with her mother but she comes out regularly to visit her dad.'

'How old is she?'

'That's what's been holding me back. She's fifteen years younger than I am.'

'Oh, cradle snatching, are you?'

'No quite as bad as your pal David. He's at least twenty-five years older than Phil Watson's sister.'

'Right enough but some people like old age creeping over them.'

'Behave yourself, Sally. What I want is for you to meet Spring . . .'

'Spring! Is that really her name?'

'Aye, and as far as I'm concerned she's well named.'

'Okay, but Luke I have to be running both the guest house, which I could leave in Maggie's hands, and also the Four Marys. Surely, Luke,' she pleaded, 'you can see that after the humiliation David Stock has subjected me to that I just have to be seen working away there next week as if his betrayal is of no consequence to me.'

'That takes us back to Josie . . .'

'No, it doesn't!' Sally accented with such force, other diners looked towards her. 'And,' she confided in a softer tone, 'you should go to London on your own. You're picking a life companion for yourself so what you would consider as an ideal mate, most certainly, would not rate with me.' She gave a mocking chuckle before adding, 'And with my track record you really should consider if I am a competent judge.'

'Hmm.'

Ever since they had taken their place at the table Sally had kept glancing over at her outside door in case anyone should call. 'Oh,' she squealed, gripping the table to rise, 'would you believe it? There's Nancy pulling at my doorbell and I think she's brought the boyfriend to meet us.'

'Just the person we need to assist us,' Luke chortled.

'Luke, you pay the bill.' Sally then hesitated before adding, 'And I think it would be best if you leave Nancy to me.'

When Sally shouted, 'Cooee, cooee,' Nancy was so startled that she jumped backwards and nearly fell off the top step.

Regaining her balance and half turning she grumped, 'Sally, I was expecting you to open the door. Not to come dancing over the street.'

'Sorry. Luke and I were just having a meal at the Rockville.' Sally said no more. She was eyeing up Benny. She liked what she saw. He was of average height for a man and she guessed he had said hello to his late fifties. Nonetheless he was wearing well and although he seemed a bit hesitant, there was a masculine attraction about him. She grinned when he smiled directly at her. Indeed from that moment she was completely captivated by him.

'Pleased to meet you,' Benny said, thrusting his shovel-like right hand towards Sally.

'And I have heard so many good things about you that I am delighted to meet you in the flesh.'

By now Luke had joined the party at the door. 'Look let's all of us get inside,' he said pushing past Sally so he could open up both the storm and inner doors.

'We just had our tea in Elio's,' Nancy joked. 'You see, we've no got your kind of money, Luke.'

'Or Sally's brass neck,' Luke added with a wicked grin.

'That's him telling you that I rushed over here to meet you and left him to pay the bill.'

Once inside the living room Nancy grabbed hold of Benny's hand and steered him over towards the couch where they could sit side by side.

'Were you out for a wee dander?'

'Aye, Sally, we were. Would you believe we walked all the way from Leith Links to here? But we're out of puff now,' laughed Nancy.

'Bet you could murder a pint, Benny.'

Benny looked at Luke somewhat puzzled.

'Nothing to worry about, Benny,' twittered Sally. 'He's just looking for a pal to go with him to the Ormelie.'

'Ormelie?' echoed Benny.

'Aye, see go over there to the window and look left and you'll see it.'

'Serves a good pint so that wee pub does,' Luke added, before indicating with a nod of his head that Benny and he should stroll along for a pint. 'Nae need to worry, Nancy. We will only have one, okay maybe two, before we meander back.'

Nancy and Sally watched from the window as Benny and

162

Luke started to make their way to the Ormelie Tavern. 'Looks to me as if everything has been sorted out between you and Benny,' mused Sally.

Nancy had set herself down on the couch again before she replied, 'More than sorted out. Oh, Sally, he . . .' Nancy inhaled deeply and exhaled slowly before carrying on haltingly, 'We're – getting – married.'

'Good, and you rushed straight along here to ask me to be your Matron of Honour,' teased Sally before going over to sit next to Nancy who shied away.

'I would love to have you with me on my big day but Sally . . . it's not all as simple as it appears.'

'It's not.'

'No and I can't tell you because I have promised Benny I won't tell anyone . . .'

'He has a past? Been married before?'

Shaking her head Nancy whispered, 'Nothing like that. His sister and himself were taken into care. His mother had died, his father married again, the new wife didn't want . . . well once the ring was on her finger the bairns she made out that she adored, became surplus to requirements.'

'So?'

'Sally, I am trying to be fair to Benny. You see if he thought you knew the truth about him he would have to put distance between you. He would think that you would shun him.'

'For being taken into care. Didn't you tell him my brother Peter and I would have been taken into care if Flora, my darling mother-in-law, hadn't given us house room?'

Nancy bowed her head. 'Sally,' she mumbled, 'it wasn't being sent into care that was the problem, it was where he was sent. And I mustn't tell you.'

'Oh, I bet I know what happened to him.'

'You do?'

'Aye, he was sent to a home run by supposedly caring house-parents and they abused him.'

Nancy's head jerked up and her hand flew to her mouth. 'I never told you that, but Benny won't believe that I didn't.'

'Och, Nancy,' Sally spat with disgust, 'sure we all have heard so many stories about these sadistic pigs that we knew some of them had to be true. Now look, you have my word that I'll never mention where Benny was brought up to a soul.' Sally fixed her gaze on the mirror above the fireplace and she allowed time to tick slowly by before she asked cautiously, 'And his sister – is she younger than him and what happened to her?'

Nancy shrugged. 'Yes, she was younger. Poor soul, he never knew where she was sent and he never tried to find her because he thought she would despise him.'

'Hmmm.'

'Anyway, Sally, you can see why we must get married in a registry office and just ask two strangers in from the street to be our witnesses.'

'Hmmm.'

'What do you mean by, hmmm?'

'Just that that will be blinking right. No way will you have a hole in the wall affair of a wedding.'

'Have you not heard a word I've said?'

'Aye, and I repeat, we're going to lay all your and Benny's ghosts to rest. So you will have a proper wedding. Luke and I will be the witnesses and see,' Sally jumped to her feet and dashed over to the window, 'there on the other side of the street, the Rockville, that's where you're going to have your wedding reception. And don't worry about the cost because that's what I'll be giving you as a wedding present.'

'Sally, have you lost your marbles?'

'No. But what last week has taught me is that you should be good to those that stand by and support you. And Nancy, you're my best pal who has stood by me through thick and thin, so you have.'

Nancy grew tearful. 'Okay, but if Benny does agree to a wedding, what registry will we marry in?'

'None. I've been good to that St Philip's church since I came to stay here and the minister, the Rev. John Weir Cook, he's what all Christians should be, so I know he will be just so pleased to marry you. I can see it all – the flowers, the red carpet and you and I floating down the aisle in a sea of gossamer tulle towards Benny in his clan tartan.'

'Sally, his surname is . . .' Nancy's uncontrollable laughter rang out before she spluttered, 'Oh good heavens, I'm just about to take his name and I haven't got a clue what it is.'

7

Sally had so much on her mind that she'd forgotten to be nervous about driving her brand-new replacement car up to the Waverley Station.

The bright red Ford had just been parked in the car park when she alighted and proceeded over the concourse. She couldn't believe her eyes. Flora and Shonag clutching their luggage and managing to look like two abandoned refugees were huddled together awaiting their pick up.

When Flora caught sight of Sally she waved her umbrella and hollered, 'It's us over here.'

So it is, Sally thought, as she skipped over towards the ladies.

'Was the train early?'

'No,' replied Flora, 'it's you that's late.'

'Oh,' Sally replied, relieving both women of their heaviest bags. 'I must confess I never checked the time since I left. Maggie was bending my ear and I'd just about lost the will to live . . .'

Flora, quickly interrupting, appeared to bristle. 'And I hope Maggie will not be in residence when Shonag and I are staying with you.'

The open hostility between Flora and Maggie was something that Sally was well aware of. Sally was also conscious of the fact that her guest house must appear, to her paying clients, to be a place of harmony and peace. She could just ignore Flora's remarks but she knew that Flora would go on and on about it.

'Flora,' Sally reproached, 'Maggie will not be a problem to you. She comes in early in the morning about seven o'clock and she leaves at noon. During her time in the house she clears up after breakfast and then she cleans all the bedrooms. In short she is a skivvy.'

Once the two women were safely on board Sally steered the car out of the station and headed it down Market Street. 'Sorry about you getting shoogled about because of these cobbles but once we're down on to Meadowbank things will calm down.'

'Don't you be worrying about Shonag and me getting a wee bit shook up, that won't cause us any bother. On the other hand, what will cause us grief is Maggie being around us. So Sally, just you tell her that Shonag and I will clean up after ourselves and that will include making our beds and washing our dishes.'

Sally felt the desire to retort to Flora. But getting involved in a controversy with her would distract her concentration. Grudgingly she admitted that ever since the car accident on the Forth Bridge she was ultra cautious. Oh yes, in no way did she wish another collision so she conceded to Flora's outrageous demands with a curt nod.

After installing Flora and Shonag in, what to them was the last word in luxury, a twin-bedded, sea-facing room with en suite facilities, and deflating Maggie's ego by issuing Flora's ultimatum, Sally then drove herself to the Four Marys.

'Nice of you to come in when the hurly-burly's all over,' Rita huffed while dragging a mop over the floor.

Glancing about the bar Sally could see by the number of glasses that were drying on the bar that Rita had been busy, very busy. 'Sorry, Rita,' she managed to mumble, 'I knew you were in on your own but I just had to pick up Flora and Shonag from the station.'

'Look Sally, you and I chasing our tails has got to come to an end. You know you have too many irons in the fire so why don't you just . . .'

'Don't dare say – get Josie in.'

'Any why for no? After all if anyone can keep this place going it's her. And before you say another word, do you know some of your staunch regulars went elsewhere for their dinner, sorry lunch, because I couldnae keep up with everything.'

Glancing around the salon Sally could see that even although Rita was trying her best, things were beginning to slide. She had put an advert in the *Edinburgh Evening News* situations vacant column for a replacement for Josie but so far there wasn't one applicant that she considered worthy of an interview. Another solution that occurred to her was that she should transfer Duncan, Nancy's very capable barman in the Royal Stuart, down to take over in the Four Marys. However, with Nancy going to tie the knot there was a distinct possibility that she may not wish to continue working after she was married.

She was still considering her options when the outside door slowly opened and in slunk Josie.

'Now,' Rita chanted, 'before the two of you start to knock hell oot o each other would it no make mair sense if I just knocked yer heids thegither?'

Both Sally and Josie were about to respond when the outside door opened again and a stranger came in. The newcomer's entrance not only stupefied Sally and Josie but the ever verbose Rita was rendered speechless.

The lassie, who Sally judged to be just in her late teens,

was a vision to behold. She was above average height for a woman and her nylon-stocking-clad legs seemed to go on forever. Another striking feature about her was her light auburn hair which had obviously been recently dressed to make it look like it naturally tumbled about her shoulders. The picture was completed with green cat-like eyes and drooling lips that were so sensuous that Sally, Josie and even Rita knew every male that came into contact with her would find her hard to resist.

'Can I help you?' Sally managed to croak.

'Y-e-e-e-s. My name is Dove.' She gave an exaggerated flutter of her eyelashes before adding, 'Bird and I have an interview with a Mr Stan Roper for a position within his organisation.'

Josie, Sally and Rita all checked out each other's astonished reactions before Sally responded, 'And just exactly what kind of position are you hoping to fill?'

Preening, Dove cooed, 'To take charge of the organisation's headquarters and supervise and motivate the other members of the team and by example demonstrate how they can reach their full earning capacity, but I'm not sure where his office is.'

'Eh?' exclaimed Rita.

'Is this a wind up?' spluttered Josie.

'You're joking,' Sally gasped.

Dove shook her head. 'No. I met him in the George Hotel on George Street and I told him I had just completed a hostess course and was looking for a suitable position.'

'Look, my dear,' Sally cautioned, 'Stan is a weasel and a pimp who's taking you for a hurl. What I'm saying is, he does run a stable – but just for naive, brainless fillies.'

'I know that,' Dove giggled. 'He explained that I would

be filling the position just recently vacated by his,' she gave a shrug before adding, 'the devil that he is – he called her his blue-eyed manageress and without giving him any notice hasn't she just . . . disappeared.'

'She's what?'

'You heard her Sally, Jessie Scott has vanished.'

'I know that, Rita. Luke already told me that but he thought she was just away to work things out. But . . . oh my goodness, this lassie turning up here looking for Stan Roper means she's really gone for good.' Sally swallowed hard before whispering, 'And I'm terrified to think what all this will mean for Irish's case. Everything was resting on Jessie retracting her statement.'

'Where's Luke? We need to tell him.'

'Luke's in London, billing and cooing, Josie.' Sally huffed before spitting, 'No doubt after getting lessons from you.'

The information Dove gathered from the conversations seemed to unsettle her and she whimpered, 'What exactly is Stan Roper's line of business?'

'To be truthful, anything that's illegal,' was Sally's blunt reply.

'And by that she means selling bonnie lassies like you, drugs, smuggling tobacco . . .'

'Okay, Dove's got the message, Rita,' Sally said, breaking into Rita's tirade and turning to face Dove. 'And now my dear, could I just suggest that you hightail it out of here before you end up being done for soliciting.'

Dove's mouth fell open. 'Are you saying you think it would be best if I got myself home to Blackhall.'

'Yes,' Sally, Josie and Rita chorused.

The door had just closed on Dove when Sally turned her attention to Josie. 'And why are you here?'

Josie looked to Rita for support. Rita discreetly waved her hands in a gesture which said get on with it yourself.

'Sally, I'm in a bit of bother. I need you to help me.'

'In what way?'

'Please, I don't like it when you clip your words.' Sally shrugged. 'It's just that I got a letter this morning from Angela and she's coming over to visit next week and she's bringing my grandson, Roy, with her.'

'So?'

'Sally, I've no job. Luke made me put my notice in everywhere before I could find a decent job. I can't pay the mortgage so I could get evicted. I have two lodgers and their rental helps to keep me afloat. So my house is full and all I want to know is, will you put Angela and Roy up?'

'No I won't. In case any of you don't know it I'm trying to run a paying guest house. But at this moment all I seem to be doing is running a charitable dosshouse for an army of misfits. So here is my proposal to you.'

Josie, lips quivering, looked contrite.

'None of my business, Sally, but do be careful here,' Rita warned, 'for the last thing you want to do is burn *all* of your boats.'

Sally tried to put Rita down with a warning glare but Rita retaliated with a loud snort. 'Starting this very minute,' Sally began while continually indicating by jabbing her right index finger towards Josie, 'you get your coat off and get dug in immediately to cleaning up and sorting this bar out.'

Josie, tears streaming, sniffed, 'Oh Sally, are you saying I'm in charge again?'

'Must be mad, but aye.'

'Josie, now's your chance, ask for a raise,' goaded Rita.
'Oh aye, with the mess you're going to have to clean up you'll deserve one.'

'Rita, are you bonkers? Give her a rise?'

'Aye, and Sally, while you're at it I think you should consider keeping me sweet and slip another couple of pounds into my pay packet an aw.'

Chuckling, Sally replied, 'Pay you more than I'm doing? Huh. Maybe I should just let you go.'

'Aye, you could do that but who'll be helping Josie in here while you're away playing Miss Marple with Poirot when he gets back from London?'

'Are you saying that you think that Luke and I should be going out to look for Jessie?'

'Beats goin hame to Maggie, does it no?'

Flora was so pleased when Sally arrived home early. 'Was the pub not busy?'

'Aye, but Josie's back in charge.'

'Good. Now let's you and I have a wee chat while we're on our own.'

Sally looked about the living room. 'Where's Shonag?'

Flora looked unseeingly ahead. 'Sally,' she drawled, 'I just don't know. What I'm saying is that I just cannae put my finger on it but Shonag . . . well it's as if the light inside her is beginning to dim.' She gave a nervous chuckle before adding, 'I suppose my own zest for living isn't exactly on the ascendancy.' She chuckled again. 'But then what can you expect at our age?'

Deciding it would not be politic to agree with her, that with the both of them now being on the wrong side of eighty she was right, Sally just smiled.

'Anyway, what I want to ask you is, seeing Lois has everything sorted out, better than we could ever have imagined, I was wondering how much of a backhander I should give her?'

'Eh,' was all Sally could utter.

'Well as you know we've signed all the papers. Work has started on the new boundaries . . .' Flora stopped, sniffed and tittered. 'I just can't believe it. Sally, it's the best thing that could have happened. We're in the money and still able to bide in our own homes and also sort out . . .' She sighed. 'How on earth did we manage to have two laddies, both in their sixties that still bring us home all their dirty . . . washing?'

It was difficult for Sally to suppress her laughter. In all the years she had known Flora she hadn't changed. She was a devoted family person who called a spade a spade. Harry, her only son, had been a disappointment to her. Sally remembered when he had left her and her three bairns, Flora's beloved grandchildren, she had shunned Harry. If anyone knew how difficult that was to do then it was Sally – how often did she wish herself that she could brush off Margo?

'Sally,' Flora's shrill voice echoed, 'pay attention. Now Lois didn't charge a fee. She did pay all the rest of them professional-like folk their dues but she said her work was a present for us.'

'So?' mumbled Sally who thought, *A 'present', eh? Little do you know I had already said I would pay! Mmm. That lassie is learning.*

Tutting and trying to rock her head off her shoulders, Flora spluttered, 'There is more than enough left after I buy a house for Harry to see the lassie right.'

'Know something, Flora? Sometimes the right thing to do is to accept a present graciously. What I'm saying is the lassie has put forward a hand in friendship – grasp it firmly.'

When Sally's car slowly crept past the taxi rank in the Waverley station a cabby enjoying a cigarette outside his cab shouted, 'Here, Sally, no content are you with running your pubs that you've had to get yourself into the car hire business an all?'

Waving her right hand out of her open window Sally replied, 'Nice to see you, Willie, and aye, with the number of times I've been up here lately, I think I am a taxi driver.'

She had just parked the car when she was startled by the back door suddenly flying open followed by a loud thud. Before she knew what was going on her driver's door was thrown wide and Luke growled, 'Right, move over.'

'Move over? This is my car. And why you decided to hand back your hired one in London and come back by train is a mystery to me.'

'Oh, Sally, stop carping. You know I had to get back quick and that hired car – do you know where I really should have driven it?'

'No.'

'Johansson junk yard on Salamander Street.' Rattling his fingers off the car roof he chirped, 'So shift your backside because I have no desire to be put in a state of fear and alarm by your driving.'

Without another word of protest Sally got out of the driver's seat and, adopting a sullen air, strode around the car and got into the passenger's seat.

For a full ten minutes not a word passed between them.

They were approaching the traffic lights at Meadowbank before Luke broke the silence. 'Penny for them, Sally,' he cackled.

'Oh, I was just thinking back to that day in the Four Marys when old Jock told us that he had fathered us both. Overjoyed I was . . .'

'So was I,' he replied, patting her knee.

'That right?' she hissed before adopting an insincere melodic tone to simper, 'Yes, fool that I am I was just so delighted to discover that you were my wonderful full brother!'

'Is this all because I, a police advanced driver, thought I should take the stress off you and drive home?'

'Advanced pompous police idiot is what you are! Don't you understand that I'm trying to get my confidence back since I was involved in that blooming accident?'

He lightly tapped her knee again. 'Please,' he implored, 'no tears.' He then took time to deliberate before softly saying, 'Now, be truthful . . . it's not so much me taking over the driving today because I know you like me being your chauffeur . . . admit it, you were looking for an excuse to hit out at someone.'

She turned her head away from him. No way did she wish him to see that he was right and that her heart was broken. Tired she was of her life being like the bible; so many fat times followed so quickly by another dose of the lean.

'Here,' Luke jovially chorused, as her knee got another slap, 'do you know what? She said . . . yes!'

Rubbing under her nose Sally speered, 'Are you saying that you and Spring are going to be . . . ?'

'Uh huh,' he chorused, 'next summer in Hong Kong. Now is that not something for you to look forward to?'

Sally chuckled. 'Hong Kong next summer! Now I just have to start saving for that.'

It seemed only sensible to Sally that Luke, after seeing Flora and Shonag safely on to the early-afternoon Inverness train, should just go and have a coffee and wait for Irish's mother whose train was due to arrive an hour later.

He'd left the car in the station car park and then run up the Waverley Steps and on to Princes Street. He had turned towards the North British Hotel where he wished to make tentative enquiries about how much a double room would cost for three nights. This information was being sought because he had toyed with the idea of inviting Spring to come up to Edinburgh for three days before the end of his leave. He was so in love with her that he wished his nearest and dearest to meet her. It was only proper, he argued, that Sally and Josie should get acquainted with Spring before next year's wedding. Under normal circumstances she could have just bunked in with him but . . . well . . . Sally just hadn't moved with the times and she'd be expecting Spring, like she had done herself when she moved in with Flora, to share Sally's sleeping accommodation or have a single room to herself. He grimaced. No way would Sally accept that Spring was getting married in white if she was still not a virgin! Luke chuckled as he thought that with the way things were going, white weddings would soon be a thing of the past.

He was just about to mount the steps of the hotel when his attention was drawn to the paper vendor on the other side of Princes Street. The man was shouting, 'Read all about it. Young lassie hauled out of Newhaven Harbour.'

Traffic lights had been installed on this General Post

Office junction since 1971 which included a pedestrian phase. Nonetheless, Luke was in such haste that he could not or would not wait for the signal that he could cross in safety. To the amazement of the foot-travellers he dashed out into the street and began dodging through cars, buses and lorries. Once he arrived on the north pavement the paper seller remarked, 'Tired of living, son?'

Shaking his head Luke pressed some coins into the man's outstretched hand and grabbed an *Edinburgh Evening News* from him.

So engrossed did he become in the lead story that he had to be restrained by the vendor when he unconsciously started to step back out into the traffic again. 'Look, son,' the vender shouted, 'you might be suicidal but see they bus drivers, they dinnae want to get catapulted through their windscreen because they had to brake to miss you.'

'Look. Look. It's another one,' Luke mumbled while drawing the man's attention to the fate of the young woman.

'I've read the story,' the man huffed. 'She's probably just a whore. Naebudy will miss her, no even her customers. Ten a penny lassies like her are.'

The pedestrian signal had now turned to green and as if in a trance Luke made his way back over Princes Street and then down into the station again.

Sally had the right personality to be a guest house owner. She had that special knack of making everybody feel as if they were the most important person to her and that they were doing her a favour by staying in her house. Where Mrs Kelly was concerned, the foregoing was true.

'Did you have a good journey?'

'Aye, I did that. Do you know it seems such a long time

since I've seen my boy. The last time was in the holding cell of your High Court. Been through the wringer he has since then.' Sally nodded. Luke brought in a teapot which Sally took from him so she could play mother.

'Back in a minute,' Luke called back to them as he dashed out of the room.

Sally immediately poured a cup of tea for Mrs Kelly. No sooner had Sally handed the steaming beverage to her guest than she began to sip from it. While savouring the tea she began tentatively, 'Do you think there really is a chance he'll get out?' Sally encouraged Mrs Kelly's enthusiasm with a smile. 'You see, I just want people to know the truth – see my boy as I see him – know that he's no killer.'

'I don't often make prophesies Mrs Kelly, and I don't know why but for weeks now I have had this feeling that everything will work out for your son.'

A comfortable silence fell between the two women. Nothing was heard except the ticking of the clock until Luke burst into the room brandishing the newspaper.

'Is the house on fire or something?' shrieked Sally, jumping to her feet.

'No. No. Read this. I've just spoken to our brother John, and he says that all he knows at the moment is that all leave is cancelled for all Edinburgh detectives.'

Grabbing the paper from him Sally questioned, 'But why?'

'Well, even Holmes and Watson will be asking themselves if this is a copycat killing like Marie or . . .'

'Another of the same,' Sally whispered, 'and carried out by the person or persons who did for . . . Marie.'

Mrs Kelly, whose eyes had bulged with fear when Luke had thundered in, quietly got up and stood alongside Sally so she too could read from the newspaper. 'What does this mean?' she beseeched.

Turning her face fully to look directly at Mrs Kelly, Sally mumbled, 'It may mean nothing. But one thing for sure is that one way or another it is good news.'

Mrs Kelly shied away from Sally. 'Good news! What kind of a person are you that you would think that a young woman being murdered and dumped in a harbour is good news?'

Putting out her hand to calm Mrs Kelly, Sally stuttered, 'No. No. You haven't quite grasped what I was implying. It's not good news that the lassie met such an awful end, of course it's not, and I'm not suggesting that. The good news is that because there is another death similar to Marie's it means that it will strengthen Irish's miscarriage of justice case.' Mrs Kelly was still quite uptight and agitated so Sally added, 'My son, Bobby, said to Luke, only last week, that he was sure he was going to win Joe's case for you but to be doubly certain he could do with something else that would cause the judges to really doubt.'

Mrs Kelly began to rub her hands together. 'I see. You are a good woman and a true friend to my boy.' Sally nodded. Both women were awash with emotion. 'My name,' Mrs Kelly said, taking Sally's hand in hers, 'is Kathleen, please call me that.'

Sally returned to the living room having shown Kathleen, who was not only exhausted from her journey but from the emotions that had been stirred up in her by the article in the evening paper, to her room.

Luke, telephone against his ear, put up a hand to silence Sally when she tried to speak to him. 'Okay, John,' she heard him say, 'I know they will be playing their cards close to their chest but if you hear anything, even a squeak, then ring me.'

'What was all that about?'

'Just that I thought I would ring John again as there may have been developments.'

'In fifteen minutes?' huffed Sally.

'Okay,' Luke sniped. 'But you never can tell. They could have got a name for the woman in that time.'

'Is it Jessie Scott?'

'Could be,' Luke mumbled, 'but unfortunately no positive identification yet.'

'What do you think?'

'Well they can hardly blame Irish this time. Surely being locked up in a secure penitentiary can be nothing other than a cast-iron alibi.'

'You think that there are similarities between Marie's death and this one?'

Luke was now staring out of the window. He lifted his hand and waved at a small boat that was sailing down the Forth. A man on board then waved back frantically. 'Sally,' he said, squinting, 'do you think that man is waving to me or has his boat lost power and it's now drifting out of control?'

Looking at the boat, and in particular to the man who had now removed his shirt and was waving it frantically to attract their attention, Sally gasped, 'Oh, Luke, the poor soul is being swept along by the current. Quick, phone the police and coastguard.'

Without a doubt the emergency services in Scotland are second to none. Sally had just watched the poor man and his boat disappear from sight as the undertow sucked them towards Musselburgh and beyond when the coastguard rescue launch came into sight.

She was about to turn around to tell Luke about the salvage vessel when a police car, siren blaring and warning light flashing, drew up just before the Rockville restaurant. The two officers had just jumped out from their vehicle when they were approached by a sprinting Luke.

Still looking out from a window but now from the upstairs lounge, Sally thought how typical it was of Luke to shake hands with the officer who was not receiving messages through his radio. Sally noted that once the radio was switched off both constables then engaged in an animated conversation with Luke. If Sally hadn't known otherwise she would have judged the trio were friends enjoying a prearranged meeting.

Nonetheless, the congregation was called to an abrupt end when one of the constables lifted his radio to his ear again. While still conversing on the phone the officer signalled urgently to his colleague and the duo jumped into the police car and it sped off.

Patience was not one of Sally's strong points and by the time Luke was re-entering the house Sally, tapping her foot impatiently, had taken up a stance in the hallway. 'What a time you've been and what were you and those officers talking about?'

Luke grabbed her by the arm and steered her towards the back kitchen. 'Ssssh,' he said, putting a finger over his lips, 'I don't wish anyone to hear what I have to say. At first, and by the way I'd worked with the older of the two guys when we were both stationed at Leith, we spoke about the man in the boat. Here I'm pleased to say that all is under control. According to the messages they received, the boat is securely under tow and will be arriving at Musselburgh harbour as we speak. Then I pretended I was a bit naive and I asked if they knew if there was any identification yet on the body fished out of Newhaven Harbour.'

'But you had just asked John.'

'Yes, but John is not really in the know. And I have this feeling that . . .'

'Like me that you know that the dead woman is Jessie Scott and that she's probably committed suicide because she was the one who murdered . . .' Sally knew from the look of abject horror that was now on Luke's face that she had got it wrong. 'Oh no, you think the poor soul herself was murdered,' she whimpered.

Luke now appeared to be going to bang his head off the wall. 'Look, Sally, the woman who was dumped in the harbour is not and I repeat *not* Jessie Scott.'

'Then who is she?'

'These officers I just spoke to don't know. All they are sure of is that the poor victim was not a known pro – you know, not a local whore. And as we all know, Jessie Scott is.'

'What does this mean?'

'I don't know and I don't want you to discuss anything I have just told you with anyone – and anyone includes Nancy.' Luke switched on the kettle. 'You are so bright, Sally, that I have always stood in awe of you. But just recently you seem never to put your analytical brain into gear. Always your fertile imagination is allowed to run away with itself.'

'Sorry. I just so want Irish to be free and yes, because I want the culprit to be someone I don't admire . . . Jessie Scott would fit the bill.'

* * *

The visiting halls of any prison are, or appear to the visitors to be, cold, soulless echoing tombs. Any time Luke had to visit any of the prisons his free spirit felt trapped and he always wondered how such environments could inspire anybody to rehabilitate. Today he was accompanying Kathleen Kelly. She was a woman whose beliefs had been sorely tried since her son was convicted of the most heinous of crimes – murder.

As they walked towards the prison visiting hall Luke wondered how this small, dainty, devout woman was going to cope in this environment. It was a desolate and soulless place where she would not be allowed to cradle her son to her breast and whisper to him that she loved him – that she believed in him – that she knew, had always known, that he was innocent.

Luke need not have concerned himself about Kathleen. On entering the hall she sat herself down at a table and, placing her hands in her lap, she waited patiently for her son to join her.

No one could have foretold the difference that there would be in Irish since Luke had last seen him in Peterhead Prison.

'Saughton suit you better?' an impressed Luke asked as he offered Irish his hand.

'Aye. And I don't know why but these last few days I am not only treated well but with respect.'

'Ah,' was all Luke replied.

'Son,' Kathleen began as she slipped her hands over the table towards him. 'Luke here, his sister and her son are working very hard to get you released.' She hesitated to purse her lips. 'Don't want to build your hopes up but they say, and I don't think they would try to fool us, that it's looking promising.'

Irish was now gently stroking his mother's work-worn hands but his eyes challenged Luke when he uttered, 'No one had better try to fool us again.' Kathleen frowned. Irish massaged her hands. 'No need to worry, Mother. As I said, I'm being treated with respect now so I know that things will probably work out for us.' Closing his eyes he appeared to be dreaming. Time stood still. Silence was golden. Healing had arrived at the threshold.

It had been difficult for Sally to stand at the gate of her guest house and watch Luke drive off in her car. *Why*, she wondered, *did I not summon him a taxi?* True he was taking Kathleen to visit her son in Saughton Prison but Sally required to be getting herself over to the Royal Stuart pub in Easter Road for a meeting with Nancy.

The thought that Nancy was going to be married – have someone to care for her, to provide for her – was a dream come true for Sally.

She had rung for a taxi and was waiting on the top step when a voice behind her said, 'You going to the Four Marys?'

Sally shrugged. 'No, Maggie, I'm not. Josie is back there in charge and it is up to her whether she makes a kirk or a mill of it.'

'Oh, so where are you off to?'

'I am going over to the Royal Stuart,' was Sally's terse reply through gritted teeth.

'That right and here is me needing to talk to you.'

'About what?'

'Just that I will be sixty next week and so I'll be getting my old-age pension from the state. That has set me thinking of leaving here and just getting a wee part-time job – maybe packing shelves in ASDA.'

Sally was caught wrong-footed. 'But you only work here part-time.'

'Aye,' sniffed Maggie as she wiped her nose on her fingers, 'but I'm no appreciated. Well I'm no given the same time of day as . . . let's say . . . a whore.'

Sally bristled. Incensed she was but she thought before she replied, 'You're quite right, Maggie. Everyone should broaden their horizons and ASDA will open up a whole new world for you. Now do you wish to work your week's notice or do you wish to leave today?'

'Em. Em. Em,' Maggie stuttered, 'I havenae applied to ASDA yet so I suppose I'll work the week's notice.'

Pulling on her leather gloves Sally smiled. 'Good. That will give me time to find a replacement. Oh look, here's my cab.' Running down the stairs Sally chirped back, 'See you, Maggie, and believe me, I think that you going to work elsewhere will work out to all our advantages.'

Why is it, Sally thought when she looked at Nancy, *that a woman who knows she's loved takes on such a beautiful glow?* She further acknowledged that Nancy just seemed like a spring day and nowadays a smile was never far from her face.

'It's yourself, Sally.'

'Aye, Nancy, it is none other than me so pour me a coffee and let us have a powwow.'

Sally and Nancy were soon sitting opposite each other at a small table. 'Did you manage to speak to Benny about having a church wedding with a reception?'

Nancy nodded. 'He wasn't very keen when I first broached it but later on he said, if it was what I wanted then okay. But he's no wearing a kilt.'

Sally laughed. 'That's a pity for I'm sure he would have the legs . . .'

'And behind,' interrupted Nancy.

'. . . for it.'

Both women's laugher echoed around the room. Nancy was first to gain her composure and her demeanour changed. 'Here, Sally,' she whispered, 'is there any word on who the poor woman was that was fished out of Newhaven?'

'No.'

'I'm just so feared that it's going to end up being Jessie Scott or worse still her halfwit pal, Jenny Geddes.'

Forgetting that Luke had asked her not to discuss the case with anyone, especially Nancy, Sally blurted, 'No, it's neither of them. Whoever she is she is no a local . . . well you know, Nancy.'

Nancy looked perplexed. 'Neither of them?' she murmured. Sally shook her head. 'But, Sally, both of them have gone missing.'

'I know. Here, Nancy, you don't know where they might be holed up, that is if they are in hiding?'

Nancy at first shrugged then a peculiar look came to her face but it was a full two minutes before she said, 'Jessie had a mother once. And before you say it I know we all had a mother once but Jessie's mother stayed in Royston Mains Gardens – pillar of the church she was there.' Nancy tutted. 'But when Jessie went on the game her mother disowned her and she moved back down to the fishing port in East Lothian that she had come from – fisher folk are usually family minded and as far as I know she was welcomed back.'

'So what are you saying?'

'Just that with Jessie's mother being all holy and . . .

possibly forgiving . . . well she just might . . . sort of harbour them.'

Sally sat quietly mulling over what Nancy had told her and she was just about to ask Nancy which port in East Lothian Jessie's mother came from when Nancy said, 'I remember now where Jessie's mother hailed from – Port Seton. And before you ask, Jessie's mother's name is Martha Liston.'

'Not Scott?'

'Naw. Scott was the name of the man she was married to but he got blind drunk one night and that was the end of him.'

Sally looked bemused and giving a little titter she suggested, 'But getting blind drunk doesn't usually lead to your demise.'

Nancy huffed and sniffed before quipping, 'Does if you fa' under a number six bus.'

Solicitors make appointments to see their clients in prison which saves them having to cope with the relatives who are always badgering to know why their beloved, always innocent and misjudged, are not being released.

On the day Bobby had arranged to meet with Irish in Saughton Prison he was apprehensive. Luke, who was usually cautious, had built up Irish's expectations. Bobby knew that Luke had a guilt complex about Irish – but he also knew guilt complexes never swayed the argument with the Law Lords.

Bobby was sure that he had built a watertight case but the senior of the three judges, who would be assessing the appeal, was the Lord Justice Clerk – the aptly named Lord Granite – a hardliner who very few could persuade, no matter how long they chipped away at him, to change the original verdict.

Today Bobby was going to have to tell Irish that yes he had built up the strongest of cases. And yes another body being found in similar circumstances and killed in a similar way added weight to their submission, but they had drawn the short straw with Lord Granite.

When Irish was shown into the small interview room Bobby's jaw dropped. The last time he had seen Irish he had been a wreck of a man who had been crushed by the system. Today he walked into the room with an air of hope and jubilation. Immediately, he offered his hand to Bobby and when he accepted it Bobby noted that even Irish's handshake was strong and reassuring. Hope had been reborn in the man.

Swallowing hard, Bobby began, 'Just here today to let you know we have a date for a full hearing.' He stalled before slowly appending, 'Lord Granite will be in the chair.' He grimaced. 'I know that will worry you but I still think we may win.'

Irish offered a shrug of his shoulders and smirked, 'Aye, but the other two who will be sitting with him are Lord Grey and Lord Semple – and they're known for their leniency?'

Bobby leaned back in his chair. He couldn't help but laugh uproariously. Shouldn't he have known that the secret information about the judges he had received only that morning would have already been filtered into this secure-walled penal institution yesterday?

The old man, wiping some froth from his whiskers after taking a slurp from his pint, looked adoringly at Josie. 'Ken hen,' he began, giving her a lecherous wink, 'this place wasnae the same without you. Without a doubt you are a ray of sunshine.'

Knowing the man was only speaking the truth, Josie beamed. 'Aye, away on a management training course I was.'

'You were?'

Josie nodded her agreement. 'Well, nowadays you have to update your skills, and the other folk on the course – boy did they learn from me.'

Before the old man could reply to her, two men, quite evidently plain-clothed police officers, entered. 'The manager in?' the older of the two men asked with a cold edge to his voice.

'Aye,' replied Josie who was immediately aware that the officers were not from Leith 'D' Division.

'Tell him we wish to speak to him.'

'That'll be difficult,' the old man said taking another slurp from his beer.

'Why's that?'

'Because there's nae a *he* in charge here.' He cackled. 'Do you no ken this is Sally Mack's pub and she only employs women.'

The men exchanged exasperated glances with each other before the younger of the two sneered, 'So can we speak to this suffragette landlady, this Sally Mack?'

'No,' was Josie's terse reply, 'but you can speak to me, Josie Mack, because I'm the manageress in here.'

Immediately, the shorter of the men took out a rolled-up paper which he then straightened out. 'See this photograph,' he began, while thrusting the paper in front of Josie's eyes. 'Have you ever seen her around here?'

Josie peered at the likeness and she had to stop herself from blurting, 'Yes'. Something was telling her to deny having met the woman. Especially as it was evident that the photograph had been taken after the poor soul was dead. 'Is this the woman that was found in Newhaven?' she gulped.

Both men nodded. 'Anyone else here that might have seen her?'

'No,' Josie lied.

'Aye, Josie, you ken fine Rita might hae.' The old man turned to the detectives. 'See Rita, she kens mair about everybody's business than her ain.'

'Oh yes,' Josie chuckled nervously, 'Rita, she's our cook and . . .'

'Underpaid dogsbody,' Rita announced as she emerged from the kitchen.

Squinting at the photograph, Rita wondered why Josie had denied ever seeing the victim. There was no way that Sally, Josie or herself could forget this lassie. Nonetheless, Rita decided to take her cue from Josie and, nonchalantly passing the photograph back to the detective, she confirmed, 'No she's never been in here.'

The detectives had just left when Josie and Rita huddled themselves into the kitchen. 'Did you lie because you didn't want the pub involved in this murder?'

'No, Rita. It's . . . oh . . . I just feel it in my bones that it has something to do with Irish, and poor Marie's murder.'

'Right enough the whole thing has just too many coincidences for there no to be a link.' Rita's tongue began to circle her mouth before she tentatively croaked, 'But what are you going to do?'

'The only thing I can do – get hold of Luke or Sally and warn them.' Lifting her coat off the hanger she picked up from where she had finished. 'Can you hold on here, Rita, 'til I come back?'

Rita had just taken up her position behind the bar when she heard Josie herald a taxi.

8

Luke and Sally were staring at Josie who was confused because the two of them looked completely confounded.

'Did we do wrong?'

After a few gulps followed by a deep inhale Sally managed to mumble, 'Josie, what we are finding difficult to take in is . . .'

'That the woman was in Newhaven harbour and . . .'

'No,' expounded Sally, 'not that she was in the harbour, but why you told the police you didn't know who she was.'

'Oh.'

Luke coughed. 'Now the two of you can skip around this all day if you like but what I want to know is who the hell this woman is.'

Waving her hands wildly to indicate the complexity of it all Sally replied, 'Of course you don't know. Well, Luke, her name is Dove Bird and she came into the Four Marys the night before . . .' She halted and Luke could see that she was going over every detail in her mind before she stressed, 'Yes, it was definitely the night before she was found dead! And she said she was trying to find Stan Roper because she had an appointment with him.'

Butting into the conversation Josie quickly spluttered, 'And we told her he was a wrong one and to hightail it back to where she came from.'

Luke found himself looking from Josie to Sally and back to Josie again before uttering, 'But what I need to know,

Josie, is *why* did you say to the police then that you didn't know who the dead woman was?'

Becoming agitated, Josie spluttered, 'To help you of course.'

'Me?'

'Aye, I was frightened that somehow this lassie getting herself killed might muck up the case you had built up for Irish.'

'In what way?'

'Just that if we said we knew her they might think that one of us did it to make sure Irish got out.'

Sally and Luke looked at the ceiling, out of the window, down at the carpet, anywhere but at each other or Josie.

After a while Luke went over and took Josie by the hand and sat her down on the settee. 'Josie, I know you were trying to help but . . . och, lassie . . .' He paused. 'Police work is not like it is in the pictures where weird and wonderful things happen.' Stopping to gaze up at the ceiling for guidance he forcefully added, 'Believe me it is only in Hollywood that all crimes are solved and the baddies end up swinging on a rope. In reality when a crime is solved it has been brought about by the police putting in some traditional hard slogging, following up the clues.' He stopped to look at crestfallen Josie and grudgingly added, 'And okay, they are sometimes helped by a big dollop of good luck dropping into their laps but that does not happen very often. In short what I'm saying is we'll have to tell the police who this young woman is and how you came to meet her.'

'I'm sorry. I've caused trouble again,' she whimpered.

Shaking his head, Luke smiled. 'No. We can put it right and I know you were just trying to help. And you have.' He rubbed his hands together and grinned. 'Oh aye, what's good about all this is that I now have something to work on.'

When Luke came into the room Sally looked up. 'Did you get her back to the Four Marys?'

'Aye, and I also told Rita that the police were to be told the truth.' Luke then whistled a merry little tune before drawling, 'I think I should go looking for Jessie Scott. You wouldn't like to come with me, Sally?'

'I could do but I was going to go looking for someone myself.'

'And who in the name of heavens would that be?'

'Benny's sister.'

'Benny has a sister? And when did he last see her?'

'About fifty years ago.'

'Sally,' Luke faltered through his laughter, 'is it not bad enough our Josie being unhinged without you . . . thinking that you can find someone after fifty years.'

Sally ignored Luke's sarcasm. 'Tell you what, Charlie Chan, I'll help you to find Jessie on condition that you assist me to trace Benny's sister. And to make it easy for you I'll not only find out what her full name is but how old she is.' She looked quizzically at him before suggesting, 'Deal?'

Sally and Luke knew before embarking on their trip to Port Seton that it was just a hop, skip and a jump of eight miles from Portobello. They also were aware that it was once a flourishing fishing port but today it had just a few small boats operating from it. What Sally found most surprising about this small town was that although it was just fifteen miles from the centre of Edinburgh, the magnificent ancient capital of Scotland, it still retained its individuality and old-world charm.

When starting out on their journey they were glad that the spectacular thunderstorm of half an hour ago had rumbled on to the west and the sun had felt safe to re-emerge.

Sally, content to be in the passenger's seat, wound down the window so that she could feel the dazzling solar rays on her face.

As the car sped on its way she lazily admired the race course. Musselburgh was so proud of this course and today after the rains the grass looked lush. Turning her head towards Luke and pointing backwards to the track, she said, 'Do you know that old Jock loved to come here and have a flutter on the ponies?'

Luke laughed and banged the steering wheel. 'And here was me,' he chortled, 'thinking the only filly in his life was our mum.'

Sally gave him a playful nudge. 'Don't suppose you believe me but sometimes I think I would like to have known him a bit better.'

'Sally, do you think that it's true that men grow to be like their fathers?'

'God forbid. Please don't say you're trying to tell me that you've fathered a multitude in Hong Kong.'

'No. But I did date quite a few nubile maidens when I was trying to learn to speak Cantonese.'

Sally poked him again. 'Luke, you don't need to know the lingo to father a . . .'

'Look, Sally, that sign says we're there.'

'So we are. Now go to the end of the High Street. We'll park there and walk back.'

* * *

Life is funny in that whenever you have to ask for directions or if somebody knows a person you happen to be looking for, you always seem to ask a stranger.

Luke and Sally had just come unstuck for the third time when Sally stopped and sniffed. 'Smell that. That tempting smell is coming from down there.'

'The harbour?'

'Yes, you get to it just down this street here on the right.'

'So?'

'Let's go and get a couple of fish suppers and we can devour them while sitting on the sea wall.' Luke was hesitant so Sally added, 'It will be like going down memory lane for me. Lost count of the times I took my kids on a day treat down here and always we ended up getting stuffed with fresh-caught Port Seton fish and chips made with East Lothian tatties.'

Sally, swinging her legs backwards and forwards, had herself seated on the harbour wall when Luke returned with the newspaper-wrapped feast.

'There's only one way to eat this,' Sally informed, unwrapping the parcel, 'and that is with your fingers. So brother dear, get stuck in.'

Luke grinned. He felt that there was something so vulnerable about Sally as she sat there in the sunshine gorging herself. She had come a long, difficult way in her lifetime. He smiled as he noted that when in Leith she dressed, acted and behaved like the lady she had grown into. Today in Port Seton, time had been rolled back and she had become a carefree young mother again. Regularly stopping to suck the muck sauce from her fingers, he conceded she did look much younger than her years. He noted that her hair still had its red highlights and the sun appeared to be picking out every red strand.

Sally sighed as she finished her supper and when she had rolled up the paper and was about to throw it into the waste-paper basket she became aware of a woman, she judged to be about the same age as herself, staring at her.

'Do I know you?' Sally sweetly enquired.

'No, I don't think so. It was just so good to see you enjoying your meal. Reminded me, it did, of when I was growing up here. Often at the weekend we would come down here just to see the townies eating. Like going to the zoo it was.' The woman chuckled.

'So you were brought up here?'

'Yes,' was her reply to Sally, 'but I left here when I was fourteen. You see, my mum was born and bred in Aberlady, the next village down, and she always felt she had married beneath herself by marring a fisherman from Port Seton.' The woman chortled. 'So when her mother died and left her a house in Aberlady she immediately moved us all over there. Disappointed she was when I married, like herself, beneath myself, a Polish refugee and settled over there in Fife.'

The woman pointed over her shoulder and sure enough from the harbour you could see across the Firth of Forth and beyond to green fertile Fife.

Moving closer to the woman, Sally simpered, 'Here, I don't suppose you ever came across a family in Port Seton called Liston?' Sally's eyes popped when a nod of the head confirmed that the lady had. Trying to control her excitement she then asked in a devil-may-care way, 'Martha Liston?'

'Aye, now let me see, the Listons' house was halfway up Gosford Road. That's the street just behind here. Don't know the number.' The woman became animated before confiding, 'But you can't miss it. Sitting in their front window are two ornaments. Honestly I saw them just a few minutes ago and I still thought that these two Siamese cats were the weirdest, ugliest and eeriest falderals I have ever seen.'

Luke, who hadn't gorged his meal but had eaten it slowly as it should be, was screwing up the paper wrapping when Sally jumped down from the wall. 'Luke, I think I know where Martha Liston might be.'

'You do?'

Sally turned to point at the woman but it was as if she had been a ghost because she had simply vanished.

Holding on to Luke to steady herself, Sally acknowledged that the pavements in the small port did not lend themselves to being tottered on by ladies in high-heeled shoes – especially when they were in danger of being pushed off the narrow pavement by a lassie pushing a pram.

Halfway up the street Sally and Luke began to peer into all the windows. Suddenly they were looking into the cold, lifeless eyes of two horrible cat ornaments. To add to their excitement Sally pointed to the nameplate on the door. It was marked 'Liston'.

After that had knocked only once an elderly lady who looked so wretched that she could have taken, without make-up, the part of Mary Magdalene in a passion play, opened up the door to them.

'Sorry to bother you,' Luke began.

The woman opened the door wider and with a sweep of her hand she bade them enter.

'Are you Martha Liston?'

She nodded.

'This is my sister, Sally Mack, and I'm Luke Doyle, a . . .'

'No need to tell me. I know who you are. I have been expecting you.'

Sally gave an involuntary shudder as her blood ran cold. She didn't believe in the psychic world. Fisher folk she knew were supposed to have the second sight but common sense told her that that was just a myth. Nonetheless, she was unnerved firstly by the woman at the harbour who knew the person Luke and she sought. And now this other woman was telling them that their arrival was anticipated.

Martha Liston indicated to Sally and Luke that they should take a seat. An eerie silence, only broken by the sound of the incoming tide, then descended upon the room.

Sally took this enforced silence to appraise Martha Liston. She noted that the woman sighed a lot and that the look in her eyes was that of utter despair. Sally identified with this woman's dilemma. She had once been where Martha Liston was now. Life has become so intolerable that you are weighed down by the heaviest weight you will ever carry in your life – a deep depression that is blacker than black.

'Mrs Liston,' Luke kicked off, 'I am taking it that Jessie Scott is your daughter?'

Martha nodded.

'Do you know where she is?'

Her head bobbed again.

'Is she here in Port Seton?'

A cry like that of a wounded animal escaped Martha and she turned from Luke to face Sally. 'You try your best to steer them well,' she sobbed, 'but sometimes your seed is rotten and no matter what you try to do to save them, redeem them, have them repent, the evil one's hold over them is too great.'

'Your daughter has done something awful?' Sally whispered.

Martha nodded. 'She met a man, Satan in disguise he is, and he corrupted her. She became a whore to keep him. And now he has brought in younger women for his vile trade, she has . . .' she hesitated.

'Lost heart?' suggested Sally.

Martha let out a loud cry. 'Sweet Lord, if that was the half of it.'

'Jenny Geddes. Do you know if she is with Jessie?' Sally pleaded.

Martha nodded. 'That lassie is through by.' She now pointed back with her thumb towards another door. 'She's completely dominated by my Jessie.'

Luke got up and went over into the other room. Quietly opening up the door, he entered and called out, 'Okay, Jenny, come on out. Nobody's going to harm you.'

Jenny took her time to emerge from the room. Sally had forgotten how utterly washed out Jenny looked when she hadn't had time to plaster on make-up. Her hair, which a decade ago had been her crowning glory, now hung like a dank, dirty, listless mop. Sally thought if any lassie required a salutary lesson on why she should not seek a career on the street then a good look at Jenny Geddes right now was all she would need.

Sally now turned to assess Martha Liston. She noted that Martha's frozen face, cold snake-like eyes and pursed lips belied that there was any Christian charity in the woman.

'Jenny,' Martha's voice echoed around the room like a

sacred mantra, 'as we decided when we prayed together, the time has come for you to own up to your sins. The police are now here so put your trust in the lord Jesus Christ and he will help you to unburden your soul.'

Sally and Luke exchanged astonished, secretive glances.

Jenny began by adopting a cowed, sorrowful look. Sally knew this was an insincere trick. She knew that anyone who had made their living on the streets ended up as hard as nails. No way could they be easily cowed or bullied.

'Well,' Jenny wailed, 'I only helped because I was scared stiff of Jessie. I didnae . . . kill anybody, honestly I didnae. I only helped with the tidying up.'

This confession completely rocked Luke. He had hoped that the two women would know something about the killing of Marie and Dove but here, if he was reading between the lines correctly, was Jenny Geddes saying that she and Jessie were *directly* involved. Scratching his ear before gnawing on his thumb, Sally could see that his mind was racing on wheels. 'Now,' he said slowly and deliberately, 'let me get this straight. You and Jessie were present when Marie was killed?'

'I was present,' Jenny stuttered, 'but it was Jessie who . . . put an end to her. And it wasn't her fault. You have to understand that if Stan Roper hadn't brought Marie in to be number one then Jessie wouldn't have needed to have sorted her out.'

'But just a minute,' interrupted Sally, 'if you are also saying that Dove was got rid of by Jessie for the same reason, how can that be? It's common knowledge that Jessie had disappeared before Dove arrived.'

'Aye,' sneered Jenny, forgetting she had now to appear a victim here, 'we did come down here and asked her mother to take us in and we were going to go straight. Isn't that right, Mrs Liston?'

Martha nodded.

'But Jessie said we should go up and get our things and then come back and . . . repent . . . but as we arrived at the flat we met the lassie who was going to replace Jessie at the foot of the stairs and she asked us for directions to Stan Roper's flat.' Jenny laughed. 'We never told her it was just one flat up and then not only did we direct her to Newhaven but we chummed her there.' Jenny sighed before adding quietly, 'And I thought we were just going to leave her there but Jessie lost it again and jumped on the lassie's back and well . . . she did her in.'

'Told you my seed was evil,' sniffed Martha who had adopted a pained look similar to that of Mary as she witnessed the crucifixion of Christ.

Luke began to get a feeling of dread and quietly he asked, 'And where is Jessie now?'

'Just before you arrived she left to go down to the harbour. She always goes to sit there ever since . . . Well, that's all past and in the past it should remain.'

Sally jumped so abruptly from her chair that it toppled over. Yanking open the outside door she began to run for the harbour. 'Please God,' she pleaded, 'don't let it be that the lassie . . .' Fortunately when the harbour wall came into view, delief washed over Sally. There sitting with her legs dangling over the side sat Jessie.

Howerver, before Sally approached Jessie she thought back to her own childhood and how her mother's behaviour had been such a blight on her life. How, she wondered, would she have coped with Martha Liston, the exact opposite to her mother? She further considered what effect this over-zealous Christian woman had had on her daughter and she conceded that Jessie, like herself but differently, had decided to survive one way or another.

Jumping up on the wall, Sally sat alongside Jessie and like Jessie she stared unseeingly out to the horizon. 'Are you scared, Jessie?' she whispered.

Sally just sat quietly until Jessie uttered, 'Scared? No, when the scariest, saddest thing has already happened to you – dehumanised you – what is there to be frightened of?'

This answer unnerved Sally. What was it that had happened to Jessie to turn her into the uncaring wretch that she now was?

'You know that your mum has talked Jenny into giving herself up but what are you going to do?'

Jessie laughed coarsely. 'My mum didn't talk Jenny into giving herself up . . . I did!'

'You did!'

'Of course. I'm not exactly a dummy. As soon as I dumped that lassie in Newhaven harbour I hightailed it back here. Knew I did that Stan Roper might have had his doubts about who killed Marie but when I convinced the polis, and they were happy to be persuaded, that I had seen Irish arguing with her he gave me the benefit of the doubt. But I should never have touched that other lassie.' She turned to face Sally full on. 'You see, I was so full of spite about being thrown out of the flat and having to punt for business on the street along with the others on the slide, I couldn't see straight. And that coupled with that smart-arsed lawyer that's going to get Irish's conviction quashed . . . well . . . Stan will come after Jenny and me, he would have to, can't you see that?'

'So you'll be safer in prison?'

'Aye and that won't worry me. I have been doing time since I was fifteen.'

'But surely Stan wouldn't . . .'

'Oh no, he wouldn't kill us. No, no. He's too wily for that but he would make sure we weren't . . . how can I put it . . . anybody's first choice.'

'Okay. So come on. We'll give you a lift back into the police station.'

'Aye, but just let me enjoy the sunset for another five minutes.'

Looking at the blood-red rays of the sun dipping into the crystal-blue ocean, Sally wondered how someone like Jessie could wish to hold this picture in her mind, yet that same human being had so callously ended the lives of two young women.

Without really speaking to Sally and more to herself Jessie whispered, 'It was on a night like this that I sat here on this wall. I didn't really see the sunset because my eyes were awash with tears. I'd escaped from my mother's house as I couldn't bear to see my baby being taken away by my cousin. It was for the best, my mother said. Whose best? Not mine and maybe not my baby's. She'll be a young woman now. Brought up in Australia. My barren cousin wanted a bairn and as she was emigrating on a ten-pound passage . . . well.' Jessie bowed her head and a long moan escaped from her.

'Do you ever hear about her?'

'No. After they took her, my life with my draconian mother was even more . . . Well at fifteen I thought I've had enough of being constantly shackled and a life selling myself to the highest bidder seemed preferable.'

* * *

It was a taciturn journey back from Port Seton. The car, driven by Luke, was leaving Musselburgh and heading for Portobello when Luke said, 'I think it would be best if we made for the guest house and we can summon the police to come there to pick the women up.'

'What?' exclaimed Sally who was sitting in the back with Jessie. 'No way will we do that. Go straight to Portobello Police Station.'

'Why?'

'Because, Luke, I do not wish my house to be associated with . . . well you know and more importantly Irish's mother is my guest there.'

'Oh,' was all Luke replied.

'Yes, oh. There is no way I would wish her to come face to face with Jessie and Jenny.'

'What like is Irish's mother?' Jessie asked.

'She is everything a mother should be. She has believed in her son's innocence and she is all keyed up about him getting out . . . and after what you have told me today . . . it could be as soon as next week.'

When they arrived at the police station Sally took control. 'Right,' she said to the women, 'out you get and you are on your own now.' Luke made to move. 'No, Luke,' Sally ordered. 'This is their problem and we stay out of it.'

The women were on the pavement when Sally came forward to grasp Jessie's hand. 'I wish you well. Albeit it, you should never have laid the blame on Irish but . . .'

'Of course you're right. Could you tell him and his mother that I am sorry, very sorry?'

'I'm afraid not. You see, you destroyed his life and that of his mother, so you being sorry . . . well . . . will it give either of them back these stolen years that have changed them forever? Will it breathe life back into Marie?'

Jessie looked skywards before letting go of Sally's hand. Turning to Jenny she said, 'Okay. There's nothing else for it, pal. Let's go and face the music.'

Sally was just about to get back into the car when someone called her name. Turning, she was surprised to be faced with recently promoted Superintendent David Stock.

'Hello Sally,' he said in such a friendly manner anyone listening would have thought they were bosom friends, 'were you in at the station?'

'No. I was just dropping two people off.'

'Police officers?'

'No. Just two persons that will be welcomed by some police officers right enough, especially the CID. Mind you,' Sally continued with a sweet smile, 'your intended brother-in-law ... well ... he will wish that they'd continued running.'

The sun was still setting when Luke and Sally arrived home. So spectacular and soothing were the dying rays on the tranquil sea that they both stood on the doorstep to marvel at the sight.

'Sally, will we tell Irish's mother about what Jessie and Jenny ... ?'

'No,' Sally curtly interrupted. 'Sorry to be so abrupt, Luke, but it's just in case anything goes wrong, I don't wish her hopes built up.'

Luke nodded. 'Now as far as we are concerned it's finished. All I ever wanted was to see Irish released and Jessie and Jenny well ... they have to sink or swim now on their own.'

'Hmmm,' Sally mused, linking her arm through Luke's, 'but brother, we're not finished. We still have to find Benny's sister.'

On entering the house Sally exchanged a quizzical look with Luke. Voices were coming from the downstairs lounge. Advancing into the room, Sally firstly saw Kathleen and she was entertaining a woman that Sally had never met before.

'Ah,' exclaimed Kathleen, turning to the woman, 'didn't I tell you they would not be long?'

The woman smiled and, rising, she advanced towards Sally with an outstretched hand. When Sally shook the woman's work-worn calloused hand she knew that this woman was a hard worker.

'My name is Jean MacDonald and I've come about the job. Saw your advert in the newsagent's shop at the top of Bellfield Street, so I did.'

Sally was impressed. She had only put the advert in that shop window yesterday and here was a woman she thought could more than fill Maggie's shoes asking to be considered for the post.

A quick ten-minute interview and Jean MacDonald, a mother of nine from Magdalene, was appointed to Maggie's post.

Jean had just left when Kathleen tentatively asked, 'Did you have any luck down at Port Seton?'

'Possibly, but you see . . .'

The ringing door bell saved Sally from having to lie to Kathleen. She was just about to answer the fortuitous summons when Josie, followed by Angela and little Roy, entered.

Motherhood had been good for Angela. She had matured and there was a radiance about her now. Sally had just taken her into an embrace when she started taking the mickey out of her mother, Josie. 'Aunt Sally,' she began, 'you won't believe this but my mother is refusing to put Roy and me up. No room at the inn for poor little us.'

'What?' was Sally's reaction as she turned to look accusingly at Josie.

'Look. Of course I want her and darling wee Roy,' Josie defended, 'it's just that I had to give my lodgers notice and they won't move out for another four days.'

Sally immediately blurted, 'There's room here for you.'

Having heard the commotion, Luke, recently showered, put in an appearance. 'Oh my darling niece,' he expounded, grabbing hold of Angela and twirling her around. 'The beautiful Angela and her offspring. Hello young master, I'm your great Uncle Luke.' Turning back to Angela he asked, 'Hope I will see some of you while you're here.'

'You will,' interrupted Sally, 'because she'll be staying here.'

'Good. Oh, by the way, that will be great because I have just invited Spring up next week to meet the family. And as she will need somewhere to stay . . .'

Sally's face fell. The only vacant room she had was now to be occupied by Angela. 'Luke,' she quickly interjected, 'I'm afraid I have to put you into an invidious position in that . . . I know you are an honourable man but if Spring is coming she will need to share your room. I will put in a put-you-up. Will that be okay?'

Not wishing to let Sally know that the situation she had just proposed would be more than 'okay' to him he pretended to be slightly put out and he just slowly nodded his acceptance but he also gave a sly wink to Josie.

* * *

The wedding plans were going better than expected. The date that was agreed was the Saturday that Luke would be leaving to return to Hong Kong. Nancy and Sally, who were having a meeting in Sally's house, had just decided against tulle and lace. 'I think ladies of our mature years . . .'

'Here, Sally, is that you saying diplomatically that we're over the hill?'

Sally ignored Nancy's observation and went on, 'Always look best if dressed by Alexon or Lerose. Jenners have a good selection of both labels. So that's where we'll go this week for our outfits.'

Nancy nodded. 'Benny's excited. Poor lamb.'

'Here,' wheedled Sally, 'remember you said he had a sister. Any idea how old she is?' Sally started to cackle. 'And by the way what is his surname? I need it for the invitations.'

'Turnbull, and his sister is three years younger than him so that would put her at about fifty-five right now.' Nancy pondered before divulging, 'And I think her name was Yvonne – I'm right she was an Yvonne Turnbull.'

Nancy got up and looked out of the window and up to her right. 'Here Sally, is that house three doors up really for sale?'

'Aye, it's a tip. But know something, it would be well worth buying because it will go cheap and it could be made into something like this.'

'You think so?'

'Nancy, I know so.'

One of the first priorities for Sally was that the house must always appear to be a harmonious, welcoming place to the guest. With this in mind she waited until Maggie had done all her chores before she advised her that she had engaged her replacement.

'You rotten bitch,' Maggie spat. 'You just couldnae wait to pull the rug from under my feet, could you?' Sally just smiled. 'Know something?'

'Not 'til you tell me, Maggie,' Sally sang.

'I just ken you have waited all these years to get even with me.'

'That's where you're wrong. Have you forgotten that I was the only one to offer you a hand up when you were in the gutter? And it was you who gave me the ultimatum last week. And see when it comes to ultimatums, Maggie, always take into consideration that the person will go a different way from what you think. Then ask yourself if they do just that – will you be able to live with it?'

'Right,' Maggie huffed. 'I'm leaving today.'

'So be it,' replied Sally, who had reckoned that Maggie would walk out today and she had therefore engaged Jean as from tomorrow.

The delicious smell of frying bacon and sausages permeated through the ground floor of the house. Sally was feeling pleased with herself in that she was up and the breakfast for eighteen, with the exception of the eggs, was all ready.

Prompt on seven o'clock the doorbell rang and Jean, laden with the morning newspapers, entered.

'Havenae read the full story,' she announced, passing the bundle to Sally, 'but the headlines are saying that they've got two women, would you believe women, for the murder of the lassie in Newhaven.'

'Hmmm,' was all Sally replied as she lifted the top newspaper and began reading the story.

As was to be expected from the tabloids the capture was headline news and an exclusive. According to the top crime reporter of the local daily, two women suspects, already known to the murder squad detectives, were chased along Portobello promenade and apprehended after a struggle. There were further stories about the incident and subsequent arrests from spectators who did not wish to be named. A derisive laugh escaped from Sally when she read the final paragraph where it stated that there were similarities to the recent murder of Dove Bird to that of Marie Kelly. However, it was too early to draw comparisons or conclusions. The article went on to point out that it was unfortunate but the chief investigating officer on the Marie Kelly case, if you took into consideration annual leave due to him, had reached his thirty years service yesterday and had therefore retired. A senior officer, Superintendent David Stock, stated that the officer's retiring was purely coincidental. He went on to say that the junior officer on the case was no longer in the CID as he had been transferred back to uniform to serve in 'B' Division's Drylaw Unit.

Sally had just reached the end of the article when Luke came into the kitchen. Imitating the 'Ah Bisto' boy he sniffed loudly. 'Oh, I'm so pleased you have my breakfast ready. I have to be away early,' he chanted.

'Here,' Sally said, pushing the newspaper into his hand. 'Read that while I fry you an egg.'

The egg had just been broken into the pan and was sizzling and spitting when Luke announced, 'Bloody hell. How do they get away with printing this garbage? I mean, what chase along the prom?'

Flipping the egg over, Sally chuckled. 'Makes you

wonder if the last paragraph is based on fact or just another fairy story.'

Musing, Luke read the last section again. 'Well,' he began, much to Jean's amusement, 'I'll tell you what happened. Just as soon as the two women coughed, warning bells began to peel. Holmes and Watson were summoned to force headquarters and they were grilled. And I can tell you when the powers that be worked out what a mess they had on their hands, Drew Washington alias Holmes was offered, no told, to put his ticket in and retire and Phil Watson alias Watson was directed to the clothing store where he was fitted up just like he had fitted Irish up.'

'How do you ken aw that?' Jean asked.

'Because he, and by the way Jean, he is my brother Luke, is a Detective Inspector in the Colonial Service attached to Hong Kong. And I'm not saying this just because he is my kith and kin but he knows how many beans make five and why the senior officers at Fettes headquarters will now be in free fall – especially as they will have worked out that there is the probability of a large compensation claim winging its way towards them.'

'Aw,' Jean, who would turn out to be an excellent worker but was a person who liked to take her time to get things right before commenting, slowly uttered, 'but Hong Kong is a long way from here. Did the Edinburgh Polis ask him to come ower here to help them solve the case?'

Sally and Luke both started to giggle. 'No Jean, they are just so . . .'

'Pissed off with me . . .'

'That they're having a whip round to buy him a ticket on the next Hong Kong-bound flight.'

No more was said on the newspaper's headlines because

the telephone began to ring sharply. Both Luke and Sally raced into the hall but it was Luke who lifted the receiver. All Sally could do was look at him quizzically when she heard him say, 'Good morning, Bobby. Yes, son, we've just read the story and okay it has a thread of truth but.' Luke grew silent. 'That's great news. Yes, I'll tell your mum but not Kathleen Kelly.'

Replacing the phone in its cradle Luke turned to address Sally. 'That was Bobby and he says he's going to petition for the quashing of the guilty verdict against Irish. In the meantime, he's asked for interim liberation until the final verdict is issued. And okay they may ask for bail.'

Sally screamed, 'That's wonderful!' Luke then grabbed her around the waist and the two of them danced and jigged up the hall.

9

They say that the wheels of justice grind slowly but, probably because the appeal was well on its way, the quashing of Irish's conviction was speedy.

On the morning of his release his mother had risen early and, still fasting, she'd gone to St John's Chapel on Brighton Place to thank Jesus personally for answering her prayers. As she sat in the cool, quiet and comforting church she felt more than ever that the spirit of Jesus was with her. Wiping tears from her eyes she not only thanked him for getting her son back but for also guiding her feet towards Sally and Luke.

Two hours later she was patiently standing at the lower lounge window. Sally had said to her that she should sit down because it could be up to two hours before all the administration was sorted out and her Joseph was returned to her as a free man.

Bobby's car had drawn up on the front street before Kathleen realised that this was the vehicle that was bringing her son back to her. She could have gone to the prison and waited there but she knew that his walking towards her as a declared innocent man would be too emotional for her and she didn't wish to embarrass her Joe by weeping in public.

Kathleen knew she should run out to greet Joe but her legs seemed rooted to the spot. She didn't even see him run into the room because tears were blinding her but she did feel her son wrap his arms about her while he whispered,

'We'll soon be going home, Mum. Back to Donegal, and I think I never, ever will leave it again.'

'That's right,' Kathleen sobbed as she put her hand up to brush Joe's tears off his cheek. 'You know fine that I carry no passengers so as soon as you can you will be out earning your living just like your other five brothers.'

Irish rocked her as he held her ever closer. Here she was, his mother, who in a few words had given him back some normality.

Sally and Luke had stayed out of the room to allow Irish and Kathleen the privacy that they needed. After half an hour Sally knocked on the door and she entered followed by Luke carrying the tea tray.

'Thought you would need a cuppa,' Sally said, observing that Kathleen and Joe were still holding on to each other.

Breaking away from her Joe, everybody else's Irish, Kathleen blew into a handkerchief before saying, 'You're right. It's time for tea.'

Once everyone was seated Sally turned to Irish. 'Is there anything you would like to do? I know your mum has arranged for you both to leave for Ireland tomorrow but we have the rest of the day and the whole of the night.'

'Yeah, how about we have a party to celebrate?' said Luke.

Kathleen shook her head. 'Joe's not into parties.' Joe nodded in agreement. 'And it is wrong to force parties on to those of us who don't like them.'

Irish was now on his feet and looking from the window at the long promenade. 'Where does that go?' he asked, pointing out to the walkway.

Sally got up and joined him at the window. Linking her arm through his she said, 'See at the far end there, Irish, that's where Leith begins. Takes forty minutes so it does, or to be correct, for an old crock like me, to walk from Joppa here to Seafield over there. When I get the time I often do that walk. Like to know I do that I am in walking distance of the place where I grew up – the wonderful place that has always provided for me.'

She was surprised when Irish replied, 'Would you like to walk there today? I would like to. I think the sea air blowing in my face will really bring it home to me that I am free. And I would . . .' He didn't finish what he was about to say. He didn't need to tell Sally. She knew he needed for one last time to go back to Leith. He needed to visit the place he first met Marie and relive the happy times he had had with her there. For all that had happened to him Sally instinctively knew that Irish still loved Marie. He would probably go on and marry again but Marie would always be the love of his life.

The day before had been such an exhausting day, especially when Sally, Luke and Irish had walked all the way into Leith and had then eaten fish and chips in the Four Marys cooked by Rita who had fussed over Irish.

During their visit to the pub Sally had started to think about not only her future but that of Josie's. Nonetheless, she decided to sleep on what she knew she had to do and the first thing was to talk it all over with Josie, but today was not the time to do that so it would have to wait until at least tomorrow.

Sally yawned as she looked at her bedside clock. It was gone seven thirty. Within five minutes she was not only up but showered, dressed and standing in the kitchen.

'Heavy night?' Jean asked.

Sally looked about the kitchen. Everything was in order. The breakfast was cooking away. The urn was boiling. Toast was popping. 'Have you been here all night?' she chortled.

'Naw. I was five minutes early but as you weren't up I thought I would just get started.'

'And you've done better than I could have,' Sally remarked.

Smiling, Sally conceded Jean was a worthy. Probably because she was the mother of nine she had to be organised and these skills were what was needed in the guest house. *Funny*, she thought, *I haven't missed Maggie. In fact, I can't remember giving her a thought until now. Hope*, she further mused, *that she somehow finds happiness and a special someone to hold on to. Everybody deserves that.*

'Sally, see there.' Jean was now pointing to the morning papers she had brought in. Lifting up the top one, Sally beamed. This morning's leader was a scoop and a photograph of a brilliant young lawyer, her Bobby, standing with the recently released innocent Joseph Kelly.

Kathleen and Irish were being taken to the train station by Luke. They had insisted on taking a taxi but Luke said he was going to the station anyway so he would give them a lift.

Sally was shaking hands with Irish when he said, 'I hope these two murdering, lying monsters rot in prison, especially that evil bitch Jessie.'

Taken somewhat aback by the venom in his voice Sally held on to his hand and muttered, 'Yes, I acknowledge that she is an evil monster but, Irish, she was not born evil. Unfortunately life turned her into what she is.'

Snatching his hand from Sally's grasp, Irish replied, 'I

know you are like my mother – you see something good in the worst of us – but I hope every day for the rest of her miserable life that Jessie feels hell's fires roasting her.'

Sally accepted there was no use in trying to moderate Irish's view. No, it was time to say goodbye. She turned to nod to Kathleen and all the time she was wondering, *If Jessie had had a mother like Kathleen, how would she have turned out?* Turning back to Irish she thought but never said, *Oh Irish, when my brother first befriended you, you were one of nature's gentle creatures. You fell in love with a lassie most people would have shunned, but look what life in prison has done to you. I do so earnestly pray that your experiences in the years to follow restore your faith in your brother man or, more importantly, your sister woman.*

Having Angela and Roy staying at the guest house meant that Sally didn't have time to dwell on the emotional goodbye to Kathleen and Irish.

Roy was such a lively wee boy and he obviously had inherited from someone a bubbly, infectious personality, his grandfather, Roy, according to Josie and his father according to Angela.

The wee boy had just burst into the lounge followed by his mother at a more sedate pace when the doorbell rang. Without a word to anyone, Roy sped back out of the room and raced towards the front door.

'Uncle Luke, Uncle Luke,' he shrieked when he saw that Luke, followed by a young woman, had just come into the house. 'Aunty Sally, it's Uncle Luke and he's brought a friend with him.'

Angela and Sally both shrugged as they exchanged expectant glances when they heard the thud of a suitcase being dumped down in the hall. Luke, with a cat-that-got-the-cream look on his face, stepped into the room. 'Sally,' he trumpeted, 'let me introduce you to Spring – my darling fiancée.'

It is true that some babies grow into the name that has been chosen for them. In Spring's case it was most certainly true. Sally immediately saw in the young woman what had attracted Luke. She was fair of face and hair. Her twinkling blue eyes mesmerised you and when she began to smile it was like an April sunrise. Instinctively Sally stood up and offered the young woman her hand. Mixed emotions were battling within her. She did wish to see Luke happily married – he deserved that and she could see that Spring would meet all of his needs. But since he had come home on leave these four, nearly five, hectic months ago he had filled a void in her life. They had achieved so much together because they had worked like a team. Now she must step back and allow him to fly free.

Jean's voice saying, 'Heard the bell. And here Sally, would you like me to make tea for your guests?' had Sally come back out of her dream world.

'Yes, Jean, I would. And this here is Luke's intended and I will just show her up to a room so she can freshen up.'

Luke sprang towards the door and grabbing the suitcase up from the floor, he called back, 'No need for you to give Spring a room, she's sharing with me.'

Jean and Angela didn't comment but their mischievous chuckles conveyed so much. Sally, on the other hand, had been going to say to Luke that she did have a spare room that Spring could occupy. Nonetheless, when she gazed at the two of them mounting the stairs so eagerly she somehow knew that even if all of her letting bedrooms had been available Luke and Spring would rather have slept in the cupboard under the stairs so long as they were together.

Half an hour later Nancy and Benny arrived. Sally, although not expecting them, was delighted to see them. Like Luke and Spring there was the magic about them. That is the magic when two people are hopelessly in love and everybody else in their lives are just necessary hangers on.

'Have you been out walking?'

'Well, yes and no,' Benny replied, taking Nancy's hand and squeezing it. 'We came to ask your advice.'

'About what?'

'The ramshackle house three up from you.'

Sally, who wasn't sitting down, advanced over to the window and she looked towards the house in question. The 'For Sale' notice was still in evidence.

Turning back to face Benny she remarked, 'Can't tell you much about it except it requires a lot of attention. Mind you, it could be changed into a beautiful home or guest house. Plenty of business around here except in November and early December. But why do you ask?'

Looking at Nancy and Benny, anyone could see that they were like two children on Christmas Eve waiting expectantly for Santa Claus. *Oh no*, thought Sally, *please don't tell me they think they could afford that house. Yes it is broken down but property in this part of Joppa was always sought after.* She grimaced when she remembered that the price paid for the last house for sale had resembled Monopoly money.

Benny went over to the window before answering. 'Sally, we're going to put in an offer.'

'Eh?'

'Yeah.'

'But would you get a mortgage for the amount you'll have to pay?'

Nancy preened. 'We don't need to borrow money. All his life Benny has saved. Never squandered a penny he hasn't.'

'You really have enough to buy it?' Sally gasped.

Nancy and Benny nodded in unison to her.

'The only thing that's stopping us is . . . Sally, you have been so good to me. If it wasn't for you I wouldn't be marrying my Benny and getting a home of my own and a wee business. Having said that it means, and Benny and I have talked it over and he wants me to,' she paused before murmuring, 'give up working in the pub. Let you down.'

'Oh, Nancy, my dear, I'm delighted for you. And just think, we will still be able to be working together. I can see it all, there will be us sending each other paying guests that we cannot put up. Doing holiday switches.' Sally was elated. This was more than she had hoped for Nancy. And sure was it not what Nancy deserved, to be loved and cared for by Benny who would also be providing her with a grand house of her own?

Taking centre stage in the middle of the lounge, Sally, gesturing with open hands, looked directly at Nancy and stated, 'Go for it, Nancy. They say things go in threes and they have this day. Irish is free and on his way back to Ireland. Luke is holed upstairs in his room with the love of his life, Spring. And now you and Benny are going to own a guest house. Isn't life just so wonderful?'

Angela, who was looking out of the window, let out a whoop. 'Aw well, Aunty Sally,' she chuckled, 'your run of good luck may be coming to an end, for a taxi has just dropped off my mother.'

Sally's facial expression quickly changed from delight to concern.

It was true that Sally had made up her mind about some changes that she wished to make to her life. These changes would have a profound effect upon Josie and it had been Sally's intention to speak to Josie in a day or two but she had the feeling that Josie had something that she wished to impart to her that may change everything.

Josie waited until she had Sally to herself in the kitchen before she haltingly said, 'Sally, I know I gave you a promise not to get mixed up with a man again until . . .'

'Not another half-baked gigolo?'

'No. No. You remember that liquor traveller from Melrose Drover that you liked.'

'Colin Jackson. But is he not retired now?'

'Oh,' blustered Josie, 'he's not that old. He doesn't retire until next week.'

'So he is sixty-five.' Josie nodded. 'And you're forty five. Oh no, don't tell me he wants to adopt you.'

'What makes you say that?'

'Because when his wife died five years ago he confided to me that they had both regretted not being able to have had children. He also said that he would have adopted but his wife wasn't up for that.'

Josie, crestfallen, retorted, 'No, he doesn't want to adopt me. What he said was he was tired of trying to catch me between love affairs . . .'

'How astute of him,' chortled Sally.

Josie continued as if Sally had not interrupted, 'And as time is marching on for both of us he'd like to put our relationship on a permanent footing.'

Sally would like to have commented on what Josie had just imparted to her but she was completely dumbfounded.

'So, Sally, I'm afraid I have to break my promise. You have to accept that I'm going to allow him to court me and we will be married by Christmas. This means that I have to make changes . . .'

Collapsing down on a chair, Sally mumbled, 'Are you saying that he wants you to stop working in the Four Marys?'

Tutting, Josie scoffed, 'Of course not. The Four Marys is my life and I'm just too young to give up working.' Josie preened. 'I know people will think that I'm marrying Colin because he's well heeled, as any sugar daddy should be. But, Sally, imagine it – after I sell my little house in Ryehill I'll be moving into his five-roomed luxury,' and she emphasised and lingered on the 'l' of luxury, 'bungalow in Duddingston View no less.'

Thinking back to when Colin Jackson came into the Four Marys for his monthly order, Sally remembered how he always looked like a lovesick puppy when Josie was around. Wasn't an older, mature man, a father figure, what Josie really required? She readily acknowledged that it was. At last she would have genuine love and security. Could Sally wish for anything else for her? No. It would work. It would need to work, she argued with herself, because she was getting too old to be forever sorting out Josie's lost love affairs.

'Sally, I'm waiting,' Josie sharply butted in to Sally's thoughts, 'on what you have to say about Colin and me?'

'Well, I'm so pleased. I'm bowled over. I'm sure I'm dreaming. And you won't believe this but I have made up my mind about changes I wish to make to my life. The most important thing is I am going to give up the tenancies of The Royal Stuart and The Four Marys. With regard to the Four Marys I will suggest to the brewers that they transfer the tenancy to you. I was a bit wary but now with you having Colin to support you I am convinced that I am making the right decision.'

'You're giving up your pubs?'

'Yes. Oh, I have loved them. They put me where I am today. I'll miss Leith but it is just ten minutes away by car. And to be truthful, Portobello is worming its way into my heart. I love this guest house.' Sally stopped to indicate with her outstretched hands how she felt about the house. 'The mortgage is paid off,' she jubilantly continued, 'and the revenue this house brings in will more than keep me in comfort. Most importantly, Josie, it will give me time to be a good granny. You see I really objected to having to work so hard that I missed so much of my children's growing up – I won't make the same mistake with my grandchildren.'

Josie exhaled. 'You know you were so lucky with Flora that the kids missed out on nothing.' She sighed again. 'And not only was she a good grandmother but she was the best mother-in-law you could have had.'

'Yes, I know you're right about that. And recently I've taken to wondering if I married Harry not because I was so much in love with him but that I needed a mother figure for Peter and me, and Flora . . . well . . . she was the epitome of a mother and nobody can deny that.'

'Sally, Sally, where are you?' Luke shouted.

'In here with Josie,' Sally replied.

When he came into the room Sally thought how much younger he looked since he had got engaged to Spring. She certainly was keeping him sprightly.

'By the look of you two, you look as if you have just won the football pools,' he remarked merrily.

'Better than that. Our Josie has just decided to settle down and be a one-man woman.'

'That'll be the day,' was Luke's cheeky response. 'Now, I just popped in to say Spring and I are just going up to Register House to see if we can track down Benny's sister.'

'You think you might be able to trace her there?'

'Yes, Sally, they have records on us all. You can't get born, marry or die without it being recorded there. And you never know, she just might have got hitched and it will be documented there.'

It was late in the evening before Luke and Spring returned. 'Sorry we're late back,' Luke said to Sally.

'I wondered where you'd got to. I knew for certain that the registry office closed around five at night.'

'It does,' exclaimed Spring, sinking down on an easy chair. 'But you are never going to believe this. I had just said to Luke that my visit to Edinburgh would be complete if I could see a showing of the tattoo, when we bumped into your brother John.'

'What has he to do with the tattoo? Besides, it doesn't start until tomorrow.'

'True he has nothing to do with putting on the tattoo but . . .' Luke said, before he was interrupted by Spring.

Waggling her shoulders in delight she butted in with, 'But he told us he is in the know with one of the officers down at Earl Haig House and hadn't they just by chance given him some complimentary tickets for tonight's dress rehearsal.' Spring exhaled and simpered, 'It was such a fabulous show. Honestly I was so taken with the march of the massed bands that I was up jigging in time to their music.'

'Mmmm. Glad you enjoyed it, Spring.' Turning to Luke she simpered, 'And what about the investigation you were carrying out?' Luke looked perplexed. 'Surely you remember you left here to try and find Benny's sister.'

'Oh yeah, yeah,' he replied, fishing in his pocket and bringing out a piece of paper. 'Would you believe there are three Yvonne Turnbulls on this list? So I will try and follow them up tomorrow.'

Sally scanned the list. One which was listed illegitimate as the father was unknown, she dismissed immediately. That left two. Immediately she vowed to follow them up tomorrow if Luke was otherwise engaged. Looking at Spring, somehow she accepted that he would be.

It was midday when Sally found herself parked outside the small castle-like ancestral structure that stood within its own miniature estate on Duddingston Crescent, just a short five minutes drive from where she lived. In her bones she thought that this was very unlikely to be the place where she would discover Benny's sister, Yvonne. She was tempted to drive off towards Clermiston, the other address on the list. However, she knew that if she drew a blank at Clermiston then there was no way she would ever find out what happened to Benny's sister.

The traffic on Duddingston Crescent is always heavy, so to ensure she was not knocked down she decided to drive her car into the driveway.

She had just alighted when a young man came out of the front door. 'Hope you're on business here because my mum gets so pissed off when people use our driveway as a parking lot.'

Pissed off, thought Sally. *Now is that really the kind of language that a young man sporting a prestigious Edinburgh University scarf should use?*

Before she could engage the young lad in conversation he jumped on to a moped and sped off. Nothing else for it she thought and she rang the front doorbell.

When the door was opened and Sally was faced by a mature matron-like lady she swallowed hard. She did not require to be asking this woman if she was Yvonne Turnbull, the younger sister of one Benjamin Turnbull. Anyone could see that she and Benny were siblings.

'I'm sorry, but if you're selling anything I don't buy on the doorstep.'

Sally shook her head. 'No. No. I'm not selling. Look, could I come in because what I have to ask, or to be correct have to tell you, may be upsetting.'

The woman frowned but opening up the door a bit wider she indicated that Sally should enter.

Fifteen minutes later Sally had imparted to the woman most of Benny's heart-rending story. She did not of course tell her about the sexual abuse he had suffered; only he had the right to divulge that secret.

Yvonne Turnbull or, to be correct, Marshall, as she had been known since she married Fraser Marshall, sat pensively. Her rosy cheeks had lost their pallor and she somehow looked bewildered and lost.

'You do remember that you had a brother?'

Her lip trembled. She nodded.

'He would have looked for you but he thought you wouldn't wish to be reminded of . . . well you know . . .

your early childhood. But I know he would like to meet up with you now.'

Yvonne breathed in deeply. 'It's not that easy. I was adopted and my new parents discouraged me from talking about my earlier years. In time I forgot. My husband and my children know nothing of my background. Don't you see, I could hardly present a long-lost brother now? I just couldn't. And you haven't said, but I feel there is more to his story. Was he ever a convicted criminal?'

'No. He was sinned against but that is his story to tell. He has now found happiness for the first time in his life with a woman . . . and I won't lie to you here . . . who had a past – a past that has now been past tense for years.' Sally could sense that instead of pacifying Yvonne her news was making her decidedly more uneasy. 'Look, Yvonne, I may call you Yvonne?' Yvonne nodded. 'I just want to say that they're getting married on Saturday. You would be very welcome to come and I do hope you can make it on his special day.' Sally could see that Yvonne was wavering so she added, 'You being there could make it even more than special. It's being held at two o'clock down the road in the Rockville.' Sally gave a nervous little laugh. 'Would you believe it was to be a church service in St Philip's, but Benny thought he would rather just be married in front of his guests at the restaurant. The minister, of course, will still be conducting the necessary rituals.'

An uneasy pause was broken when Yvonne said, 'No. It's too late.' She stood to indicate to Sally that their meeting was definitely over.

Sally was just about to hear the outside door close behind her when Yvonne mumbled, 'Thank you for coming. I did need to know that somehow he survived. Let's face it, he's in the last quarter of his life and he has managed to get there without knowing me so I just feel he will more than cope now he has . . . what is her name . . . ?'

'Nancy.'

The door clicked shut.

10

The sun streaming through a gap in Sally's bedroom curtains awakened her. A lovely sunny day, she said to herself as she stretched herself out on the bed, just what I prayed for. Oh yes, today we require brilliance all the way. She turned her head to look at the clock. Six thirty it registered. *Time I was up and about*, she told herself.

The fine spray from the shower was gradually awakening the remainder of Sally's senses that had been reluctant to leave their dreamlike sleep. As she became fully aware, Sally conceded that today would be a day of mixed emotions.

She knew that no matter how hard they worked, there wouldn't be enough time in the morning to deal with all the final preparations for Nancy's wedding. Busy, busy in a good way they were all going to be. Turning her face up to allow the jets of warm water to massage her nose, cheeks and chin, her thoughts turned from Nancy to her immediate family.

Her niece Angela and her little boy Roy had spent the last few days at Ryehill with Josie. That was only right. After all, Josie was Angela's mother and she had spent a lot of time trying to make up to Angela for the mistakes she had made in the past. Sally smiled when she acknowledged that in the last five years Angela had wormed her way into her heart. Indeed, Sally wished that she would stay longer but there were London relatives of her grandmother's that she wished to visit before going home to America.

By the time Sally was dressed and brushing her hair, her thoughts had flown to Luke. She knew that one day he would complete his thirty years in the police and on retirement he would settle, she hoped, in Scotland or nearby England. Tears began to well in her eyes when she thought about how she was going to miss him.

Sitting on the edge of her bed she allowed herself the luxury of reminiscing. Her thoughts flew back to five years ago when Luke and herself at best tolerated each other but really most of the time hated each other.

Sally could still feel the warm glow that had engulfed her when old Jock had confessed he had fathered them both. That warmth had riveted them so tightly together that the last eighteen weeks had been one of the best times in her life. She sniffed and visibly relaxed as she marvelled at how they had bonded into the completely dependent, strong and loving unit they now were.

Nonetheless, some tension did return to her body when she accepted that, as the foregoing was more than true, tonight would be so difficult for her. Tonight, accompanied by Spring, Angela and wee Roy, Luke would board the overnight sleeper train to London, leaving her with just her enduring memories of him.

Normally when she was down she would have Nancy's shoulder to cry on, but Nancy and Benny would also be journeying off tonight. In their case they would be honeymooning in her flat in Menorca. This was possible because Helen, Sally's youngest, had now taken up a permanent teaching post in Barcelona and Sally's flat in Santa Tomas was back to being what it was intended for: a holiday, or honeymoon, home to escape to.

* * *

Anyone who did not know the relationship between Nancy and Sally could think, because of the fuss Sally was making, that she was a doting sister who was deputising for the deceased mother of the bride.

Sally had ensured that Nancy was looking her best. Her outfit, an azure blue dress with matching jacket, had been selected from the designer range in Jenners and Nancy had spent the morning there having her hair dressed and face made up.

'Will I do?' Nancy asked Sally as she did a pirouette when she entered the lounge.

It was difficult for Sally to respond. Emotion was bubbling over. Why, she wondered, had no one ever seen the beautiful, flawless pearl that Nancy was? Never did Sally regret giving Nancy a chance. She knew in the years ahead, Nancy and she would become even stronger friends than they were today.

'Right, madam,' she manage to croak, 'Let's you I and pick up our bouquets from the table in the hall and get ourselves over to the Rockville.'

Nancy was hesitant. 'But should we not wait to make sure that Benny has turned up?'

Throwing back her head Sally laughed uproariously. 'Look Nancy, while you were taking your time to look fabulous I was down here making sure that you were not going to end up a Mary-Ellen.'

Nancy had no nerves about the ceremony but Benny shifted from foot to foot and instead of being emphatic about taking Nancy for better or for worse he said, 'She kens I dae!'

The minister laughed, so did the guests, and the service was over. Nancy and Benny who both had endured such awful starts in life didn't kiss in front of their guests. Benny just sought for her right hand and squeezed it; nonetheless, everybody knew they were beginning a good chapter in their lives. It was true they were approaching their twilight years but at least these precious years promised to be the best they had ever lived.

Before going through to the dining area the guests lined up to congratulate the newly-weds. Most of the people were unknown to Benny but the last lady in the queue was an acquaintance of neither of them. Benny smiled at the lady and then looked at Nancy to tell him who she was. Nancy shrugged. But Sally jumped forward and laid a steadying hand on Benny's arm before gently uttering in an emotionally charged voice, 'Benny, this lady is Yvonne Marshall.' Benny smiled and shook Yvonne's hand. 'But when you last saw her,' Sally continued, 'you knew her as Yvonne Turnbull.'

Benny was still holding on to Yvonne's hand but now he was gripping it tightly while his breath started to come in short pants. Eyes brimming over with hot salty tears, he could only mumble, 'Are you really my sister – my very own wee sister?'

To Sally's amazement, Yvonne raised up her hand to stroke his cheek before whispering, 'I never forgot you, Benjamin.' She could say no more as the enormity of the occasion became too much for her and when their out of control emotions swamped both of them all she could do was pull him into a strong comforting embrace.

They were not the only ones to be affected by the occasion. Nancy and Sally were both finding it difficult not to weep.

Sally was the first to recover and she began ushering the guests through to the dining area. Looking back to the trio she felt somehow they all deserved to have their transgressors say sorry to them. Sally grunted as she conceded that when sorry is not enough, as it was in each of their cases, and it would never be, all you can do is treat that impostor with the contempt that it deserves.

The reception and party were all that Sally had hoped they would be. Everyone joined in the celebrations and Nancy and Benny for the first time in their lives were the centre of attention. All too soon it was time for the bride and groom to leave on their honeymoon.

Everybody was out on the pavement and grassy area at the side to wave them goodbye. Even the incoming tide noisily rushed in to kiss the shore as a salute to them.

Sally was still waving her silk scarf when Nancy and Benny's taxi disappeared along Seaview Terrace.

'You did well,' her brother's familiar voice stated. 'And I meant to say how beautiful and well dressed the bridesmaid was.' Sally turned and quickly brushed her hand over Luke's arm. 'You looked quite stunning today.' Sally huffed. 'Honestly, Sally,' he continued, locking his arm though hers, 'I'm always amazed at how well you scrub up.'

She was about to respond when she saw another taxi had drawn up at her guest house.

A look of horror crossed Luke's face and quickly he glanced at his watch. 'Oh good lord,' he exclaimed, 'that's probably the cab that's going to take Angela, wee Roy, Spring and myself to the station.' He stopped to grip her by the shoulders. 'I want you to know I'm just going to hate not seeing you for a year.'

'Oh,' she protested, 'but that's not a long time. Have we not just survived being apart for three plus years?'

'Yes. But I didn't love you as much as I do now.' He stopped to tweak her nose before saying, 'Because really I never truly knew you until I came home five months ago.'

She nodded and patted his shoulder. 'You're right,' she blurted, 'and know something else, I'm glad you're not the pain in the backside to me that you used to be.'

Before releasing her he rocked her backwards and forwards. 'Look, Sally,' he began, 'you go and round them all up and I'll go over and get the luggage on board. Then I'll get the cabbie to circle about and pick them up here.'

She should have gone back then into the Rockville hotel to tell them their taxi had arrived but she felt a need to watch him sprint lightly towards her home. The image of him being young, strong and vibrant was the one that she wished to carry for the rest of her life.

Luke had got them all safely on board and he turned to say one last farewell to Sally. Not wishing to have her weep, he joked, 'Know, Sally, the best of this holiday has been you and I being sleuths together. Look at what we achieved.' He clucked before adding, 'Straight up, in my opinion, you really did miss your vocation.'

Sally didn't know why but as the taxi disappeared from view she felt a cold shroud of loneliness engulf her. She thought this feeling would stay with her until Nancy returned but she turned when she heard a chorus of 'For She's a Jolly Good Fellow' ring out and she was encircled by the remaining guests, led of course by Bobby and Lois.

'Well done, Mum,' he said. 'I'm so proud of you.'

Sally laughed and replied, 'And me of you and Lois.' Patting Lois' swollen abdomen she added, 'And may I also say that you're looking swell, Lois.'

'Mum,' a voice that was not Bobby's said, 'how about you and I going for a drive tomorrow and me treating you to a coffee down in the Mallard at Gullane?'

Turning to face pregnant Margo who now had a need to build bridges between them, Sally smiled. 'Yes, Margo, I think you and I having coffee together is long overdue. And,' she continued more to herself, 'if we are both prepared to make compromises then before you know it we could be considering sitting down to lunch or even dinner together.'

Unconsciously her gaze then wandered beyond Margo to focus on the long, sea-kissed promenade that was her favourite link route back to Leith. Chuckling to herself she reflected that it had been a long, long, up-and-down journey from there to here and what changes there had been along the way. But hadn't her life always been like the tide? One day it was rushing into the shore ready to embrace and carry all the challenges that were thrown at it. Then slowly it would start to ebb as all of its vigour and energies were ruthlessly sucked from it. A moment passed before Sally's shoulders began to hunch with delight. Her face then relaxed into a broad grin as she recalled that always on the morrow the tide, her faithful tide, would trickle back and before she was aware of it she would be riding on the crest of a wave again.